DARK CRIES OF GRAY OAKS

LEE KARR

ZEBRA BOOKS
KENSINGTON PUBLISHING CORP.

ZEBRA BOOKS

are published by

Kensington Publishing Corp.
475 Park Avenue South
New York, NY 10016

First printing: August, 1989

Printed in the United States of America

To my Family Fan Club: Aunt Alice and Pat, Aunt Martha and Cathy, and Dora Dillon and her wonderful gals.

Chapter One

Rain beat against the windows of the fashionable train which the millionaire, Henry Flagler, had recently purchased to bring visitors from New York to his elegant resort hotel in St. Augustine, Florida. Wealthy guests at the Ponce de Leon Hotel would soon be calling it the "Newport of the South."

Seated inside a private car of the new Eastern Pacific Railroad, I turned my anxious gaze away from the rain-washed Florida landscape sweeping past the window and studied the sleeping young woman I had been hired to accompany to St. Augustine. Cassie Danzel lay on her side, her black hair spread loosely upon the pillow and her slight figure rounded in a hunched position. As I looked upon her thin and pale face, I thought she looked more like a girl of ten or twelve than a young woman of seventeen.

I took a deep breath and tried to relax. There was no hint of madness in Cassie's narrow face now touched with deep sleep. With her eyes closed, Cassie's heavy-lidded, half-squinting look was gone. Most of the time she never looked directly at anyone, but on rare occasions those dark eyes would fly wide open. The action was so unexpected that the young woman's raw, piercing stare would make me catch my breath. It was then that I wondered why I thought myself capable of being a companion to such a tormented person. Of course, I had had little choice but to accept the assignment. Things would have been different if I hadn't just come through a long nightmare that left me without funds.

Three years ago, my father, who was a history professor at the University of Pennsylvania, began slowly to lose his mental faculties. Almost imperceptibly, he became unable to function on campus or at home. He couldn't remember what he was doing from one moment to the next. He lost all sense of self-direction and his behavior became erratic. Even now I couldn't believe that it had really happened. My mother had died when I was only a child and I had shared a comfortable Philadelphia brick home on the Schuylkill River with my widowed father. As the debilitating disease descended upon him, our family savings went to pay for hospitals and medical treatment, and when he died our home was gone. At the age of twenty-three I was left without any financial resources.

I became acquainted with Vance Danzel when he visited his sister, Cassie, at Gray Oaks, the sanitarium where my father had spent the last year of his life. The day of the funeral, Vance Danzel told me that Cassie was to be released. He offered me the position of companion to her while the Danzel family spent three months in St. Augustine. I gratefully accepted. However, the few days I spent with the family in New York before our departure had fueled my anxiety and my sense of inadequacy. Cassie's mental disorder was nothing like my father's slow deterioration. I should have backed out, but I had no other options open to me at the moment. "You will do fine, Brianna," Vance had reassured me. So here I was, a few miles out of St. Augustine, nurse-companion to a heavily sedated, young mad woman.

Well, it did no good to think about the whys and wherefores now, I thought with an impatient, silent scolding and a pugnacious lift of my chin. I had given my word and I would do whatever was necessary to carry out my duties. Because of strong medication, Cassie had been sleeping peacefully ever since we left New York. When the young woman awoke, she might want some refreshment, I thought, needing a cup of tea myself.

I stood up and smoothed my traveling dress of soft twilled wool in a midnight blue as dark as my eyes. A simple straw bonnet with ecru ruching framed my face and dark brown hair. I had tied the cream-colored streamers in a bow under my chin. On occasion, I had been told that mine was a classic beauty of finely molded bone structure but I found my face uninteresting and lacking the plump prettiness that was the current definition of feminine beauty. My slender, tall stature was like my mother's, so my father had said, and I would have preferred to be rounded and petite and fair-haired.

Once more, I looked down at the sleeping Cassie to assure myself that the young woman was sound asleep. Then, quietly closing the door of the compartment, I started down the train to the dining car. I had covered a short distance in the narrow passageway when a compartment door just ahead of me opened and a gentleman started to emerge. Seeing my approach, he stepped back to let me go by. I glimpsed dark hair, bold grayish eyes, and a well-formed mouth and chin before I demurely lowered my eyes and started past him.

At that moment a train whistle sounded. Frantic, short blasts cut the air. A sharp squeal of hot braked wheels caused the car to give a violent jolt.

"What—!" I gasped as I lost my balance and was thrown against the male passenger standing in the open doorway. The lurch sent us back into his compartment and, as the stranger took the brunt of my weight, he lost his balance and we went down. I cried out as my head hit the edge of a cabinet, and pain like a bright fire ball sucked me downward into swirling gray darkness.

When my eyelids fluttered open, I was lying on a berth and the stranger's face was inches from mine. A gray-green softness in his eyes hypnotized me. I could feel his warm breath upon my face as his face poised tantalizingly near my own. For a long, long moment I thought his mouth was lowering to kiss my parted lips. In my befuddled state, I waited for the pressure of his mouth upon mine. The expectation was a pleasant one. If my arms had not been so detached and weightless, I might have raised them and slipped them around his neck to draw him closer. I felt his fingers fumble with the fastenings of my bodice and his touch upon my bare skin suddenly dispelled my lethargy.

"Lie still." He held my head firmly in position between his two hands. Once more I thought he was going to lower his mouth to mine as his face came closer. I tried to turn my head away but his grasp was firm.

"Let me go," I gasped, realizing I had lost my bonnet and my thick brown hair had slipped its pins and lay in a tangled mass upon the pillow. For a moment I couldn't tell whether the roar filling my ears was inside my head or out. What was this stranger doing to me?

"Please, let me go."

"Don't be frightened. You've had a bump on the head but your pulse and breathing are steady. I need to check your eyes. Please lie still. It's all right. I'm a doctor. Your virtue is not in peril." A smile was reflected in curved lines at the edges of his mouth and in his gray-green agate eyes.

He gently pulled back an eyelid and flashed a small light into each eye. He grunted in satisfaction. "Everything's normal. Just a nasty bump on the head. The blow knocked you out for a few minutes.

I'm sorry I wasn't a better cushion in the fall." His tone was lightly teasing. He deftly fastened my bodice up again and I realized he had listened to my heartbeat with his stethoscope.

"A doctor?" I echoed.

"Yes." He stood up and put his stethoscope and small light back into a kit bag. "Gavin Rodene. Pleased to make your acquaintance, Miss . . . ?

"Anderson. . . . Brianna Anderson."

"Well, Miss Anderson. No sign of a concussion on your head. Just a bump that may be tender for a while. Your heart and breathing are back to normal. I pronounce you hale and hearty." At that moment, the train gave a laboring grunt and started moving forward again.

I tried to remember the events leading up to the moment when I was mesmerized by this stranger's nearness. Even now, I was mortified that I had reacted in such a wanton manner to his professional administrations. No man had ever had that effect on me before. I looked away from the sensuous mouth and fixed my gaze somewhere beyond his square chin. "What happened?"

"From what I could tell from the shouting I heard, there must have been some livestock on the track. The engineer hit the brakes and sent us tumbling. But we're moving again, so I guess they've cleared the track. You must have been on your way to the dining car . . ."

"Oh, my goodness," I gasped, widening my eyes in horror. *What had happened to Cassie?* "How long have I been gone?" My voice rose in a panic. I stood up but wavered with the onslaught of vertigo.

"Here, now! Take it easy." He steadied me with firm hands and eased me back down on the edge of the berth, keeping his hands on my shoulders to steady me.

"I've got to get back. I shouldn't have left her

alone. What if she's hurt . . . ?"

"Who?" he prodded gently.

"Cassie Danzel . . . the young woman in my charge. She's my responsibility . . . and I left her alone . . ."

He looked as if I had struck him across the face. *"Cassie Danzel!"* A muscle flickered in his lean cheek. "What in God's name is she doing in your custody?"

"You know her?"

"I know the family. My father was a good friend of the late Tony Danzel. I haven't seen any of the family for years but I used to play with Cassie's older brother Vance when we were little. Cassie was a disturbed little thing, even then. The family wouldn't admit it, but my father suspected she was as dangerous as they come. Are you a trained nurse?"

"No. I was hired to be a companion to her while her brother and sister vacation in St. Augustine. I met the Danzel family when my father was at Gray Oaks Manor. It's in Philadelphia, a sanitarium for—"

"I know what it is," he cut me off. "What were you doing there?"

"My father was mentally ill for some time. He was a patient there. He died just about the time Cassie was released," I said, with a catch in my throat, and then firmed my chin. "Mr. Vance Danzel offered me the position as companion to his sister because he liked the way I cared for my father. He was confident that I would be capable of looking after her, and now . . . now she may be hurt because I left her. Please, I must hurry. I'll never forgive myself if something's happened to her."

"Just a minute. I'll go with you." He picked up my squashed straw bonnet. The crown was flat and the brim broken. "I'm afraid we landed on it," he said apologetically as he took my arm and guided me down the moving car to my compartment.

I let out a sigh of relief. Cassie was still peacefully

sleeping. Her small figure was motionless and her head turned to one side in the same position I had left her. I couldn't believe she had slept through the upheaval of noise and movement. Suddenly I was frightened. "She's all right, isn't she?"

Gavin sat on the edge of the berth and felt the young woman's pulse, noted her regular but heavy breathing. "What have you been giving her?"

I handed him a bottle of medicine.

He looked at the color and then smelled it. "Laudanum." He read the label. "Pretty strong dosage. Why did the family take her away from Gray Oaks? She should be under constant medical care." His gray-green eyes were accusing and there was an expression in them that I could not read. Anger and fright mingled as I became aware of his critical attitude and resented it. He was going to interfere! I stiffened my chin pugnaciously. Now that I had a good look at him, I saw that he was not handsome in the current vogue of debonair masculinity, even though he probably could not enter a room without causing several coquettish eyes to travel over his manly, graceful frame. His black coat fashioned of imported, expensive serge was tailored to fit smoothly over a silk brocade vest and striped gray trousers. His starched white linen shirt and the small diamond stickpin in his silk cravat blended to make his appearance a quiet declaration of wealth. Even a casual observer would have judged him to be a man of decision and determination, certainly not given to wild, impulsive action. Now he was glaring at me as if I were responsible for his displeasure.

"Those in charge of her welfare decided that a change of scenery would be good for her," I told him. "Mr. Danzel wanted Cassie to accompany him and their older sister, Lady Edwina, and her husband, Sir Wilfred, to St. Augustine this year. Their parents were killed in a tragic accident two years ago while touring

Italy."

"Yes, I remember. Left their fortune to their three children. Of course, Cassie's is in trust. She's been in and out of institutions since she was ten."

"No wonder her brother thought it important for the three of them to be together," I said crisply. "I assure you, Dr. Rodene, that I take my responsibilities seriously. Only an unexpected mishap like this would have kept me from Cassie's side. I appreciate your concern," I finished, in a tone of dismissal. This haughty physician needn't think that I was going to bow and scrape before his holier-than-thou attitude.

"Where is Vance Danzel?" He frowned. "I think I should have a talk with him."

The heat of rising anger flooded my cheeks. Why was this man intruding into something that was none of his affair? I couldn't forbid him to seek out my employer, but neither would I suffer silence at this blatant interference. A few words to Vance Danzel and I might be dismissed with a return ticket to New York on the next train, I thought with sudden despair.

"They're in a car just beyond this one," I told him. "I'll show you." Since Cassie was still sound asleep, I wanted to be present if Dr. Rodene recommended to the Danzels that I be replaced with someone more qualified.

I quickly repinned my dark hair into its modest coil on the nape of my neck. I felt his eyes upon me as I rather haughtily preceded him out of the compartment and through the doors to an adjoining car.

We entered a fashionable parlor car furnished with deep wine-colored upholstered chairs and settees set around small polished cherry wood tables. Floral gold-fringed draperies framed the windows. Vance Danzel turned his tawny head in our direction. Instantly charm spilled from his broad smile, deep eyes, and bubbling vitality. "What is it, Brianna?" he asked me. "Is Cassie—?" A worried frown chased across his handsome face.

"Your sister is fine. Still sleeping," I assured him quickly. Dr. Rodene says that—"

"Gavin Rodene! Well, well, it's been a long time." Vance came forward extending his hand but I thought the enthusiasm in his voice was slightly forced. It was as if he had been braced for such a meeting and now that it was here, he couldn't quite summon a ring of sincerity in his greeting.

"Yes, quite a while. The last time I saw you was at your father's funeral, I believe," responded Gavin, a smile on his face that indicated he had intended to keep his distance from the Danzel family and found it ironic that he was now seeking out their company.

This was the first time I had seen any cracks in Vance's smooth, outgoing, charming manner. Everyone seemed to like the tawny-haired young man and I had heard the servants whispering about "his way with the ladies." I knew that the Danzels were third generation Irish whiskey barons who had made a fortune in grain monopolies. The grandfather, Danny Danzel, had been hand-in-glove with Henry Flagler since that tycoon made his first $50,000. It was no surprise to me that the Danzel family was going to spend the season at the millionaire's elegant resort on the Florida coast. From what I knew about them, they represented the idle rich who wintered at luxurious resorts in warm climates, or traveled on the continent, enjoying social seasons in Paris, Venice, and London.

Vance Danzel seemed to have trouble keeping his affable manner at surface level as he chatted. "That was quite a jolt we had. Edwina was thrown to the floor in that confounded stop. And Miss Dorcas was shaken up considerably." He motioned toward two women sitting at one end of the car. "Edwina, you remember Gavin Rodene?"

Was there a warning in his tone, I wondered?

Lady Edwina had long since passed the point of "pleasingly plump." She was undisputably fat. Her dark green traveling dress, which encompassed yards and yards of beaded brocade and satin, overflowed and filled up the wide upholstered settee on which she sat. She listlessly moved a fan in front of her face as if all her strength was being used up by such laborious activity. The family fortune had acquired a husband for Edwina Danzel, a titled but impoverished Baronet, Sir William Wilfred. Gossip had it that the marriage was a rocky one. Spending money seemed to be one thing they had in common. Sir Wilfred's title gained Edwina an entrance into elite circles and her father's money provided the wherewithal to pay for their fashionable way of life.

"Gavin Rodene? Old Dr. William Rodene's son? Yes, I guess I do remember," she said a little ungraciously.

"Gavin is a doctor now," said Vance. "Following in his father's footsteps."

"Really?" Once Lady Edwina realized that she was in the presence of a physician, her attitude completely changed. She unleashed a flow of physical complaints that quickly rose to flood level. When the obese woman finally paused for breath, she smiled in a coy fashion. "It's such a relief to talk to someone who understands. I'm afraid my back was wrenched when the train stopped so suddenly."

"Cassie wasn't disturbed?" Vance asked me quietly.

"No. She's been asleep the whole trip. I've been giving her the medication as directed. She seems deeply sedated."

"Good. You look tired, Brianna. Sit down and have a cup of tea with us. You, too, Dr. Rodene. Have you met our dear friend, Amelia Dorcas?"

"No, I haven't had the pleasure," said Gavin smoothly but his polite smile did not reach his wintry gray eyes.

The older woman was well-groomed, her gray hair tucked under a stylish bonnet, ropes of pearls accenting a lavender velvet traveling suit. Her elongated, unattractive face remained harsh despite elaborate lace ruching at her neck and the ribbons and flowers on her wide-brimmed hat. Sharp, black eyes dominated her coarse features.

I had decided that Amelia Dorcas had only one purpose in life—to know everything about everybody else and send it around the gossip circles as expediently as possible. Miss Dorcas seemed to have the nose of a bloodhound when it came to ferreting out marital rifts and clandestine relationships. I had overheard enough of her conversations to know that she was vicious and cruel.

"Do join us, Dr. Rodene," Amelia said in a throaty voice that scraped like sandpaper. Her black eyes gleamed. "I understand you returned from studies in Vienna as recently as two months ago." Her black sharp eyes bit into his with satisfaction. "And here you are, heading for St. Augustine alone . . . ?"

Gavin did not answer. Instead he took a cup from a tray offered by a white-coated servant who had solicitously appeared at his elbow. The black man turned and offered me a fragrant, steaming cup which I took gratefully.

Amelia leaned toward the doctor. "I understand that St. Augustine offers some very nice vacation facilities."

"I'm going there for the baths," interrupted Lady Edwina as if she refused to allow the conversation to veer too far away from her own interests. "I've been suffering from excruciating pain in all my joints. Terrible, terrible! Why I can scarcely walk sometimes. Just being on my feet wears me out. I understand the sulphur treatments do wonders for some people. What do you think, Doctor? Should I expose myself to the cold plunge baths?"

"I'm sure there will be a physician there to advise you, Lady Edwina." Gavin answered smoothly.

"And you, Dr. Rodene?" asked Amelia, grabbing the conversation away from Lady Edwina. "Are you going to St. Augustine for enjoyment or for the therapeutic baths . . . ?"

"Neither."

"Business then . . . ?"

"Yes. I've been asked to render some professional services at the St. Augustine School for Deaf and Blind Children."

"What a disappointment for Lynette Talbot. We'd all been expecting an exciting announcement of your wedding date the minute you returned from your studies in Europe." Her thin lips curved in a tight smile. "My seamstress tells me Lynette had been buying a very elaborate trousseau . . . and here you are, you naughty boy, looking after business when that dear girl had been waiting so devotedly for your return. You two haven't had a lover's tiff, have you?"

"Now Amelia," chided Lady Edwina. "You're embarrassing the Doctor. You must forgive Amelia. She can't resist prying into other people's affairs." Ignoring her friend's dagger-sharp glare, Lady Edwina deftly turned the conversation back to herself and a discussion of upcoming social activities which she might condescend to attend while in St. Augustine.

I let the fashionable chitchat wash over me. *He was going to marry someone named Lynette Talbot.* I didn't know why the knowledge should surprise or disturb me. I resented Dr. Rodene's intrusion into my affairs and I waited for him to bring up the subject of Cassie so I could tell him so.

Polite conversation came to an end when Lady Edwina's husband entered the car. Sir William Wilfred's navigation was wobbly, a combination of drink and poor balance. A tall, stately man in his sixties, the Baronet wore a jaunty soft tie at his throat to cover his withered neck. Gold cuff links harmonized with the fasionable cut of his coat and trousers and he carried a gold-headed cane. His expression was a gentle one, almost apologetic, as if his presence were somehow an intrusion. His fat wife gave him a scathing look and then dismissed him. I instantly felt sorry for him because of the rude way Vance and Lady Edwina ignored him. It was Gavin who offered Sir Wilfred a seat and introduced himself.

The older gentleman looked askance at the tea tray and ordered a scotch and water from the hovering waiter. He sent his wife a wistful smile, like a child reaching for an extra cookie, and he acted as if he half-expected her to countermand the order. He touched his small, gray mustache with a nervous gesture.

I was ill at ease in the gathering. How long would it be before the interfering Dr. Rodene brought up his concern about my lack of professional training? I wondered how firmly Vance would stand against Dr. Rodene's objections to my employment.

In the middle of chitchat about the social season, Amelia Dorcas leaned forward and fixed her preying eyes on Gavin's face. "I was never quite sure exactly what happened that day, when little Teddy Danzel fell out of that fourth-story window to his death. Your father said he might have been pushed, as I recall."

There was a suspended moment of dead silence.

A muscle bulged in Gavin Rodene's neck and a flush of anger crept up into his cheeks. "My father suggested the possibility that it wasn't an accident."

"You were there that day weren't you, Dr. Rodene? In fact, you and Vance and Lynette had been all over the house that day, the servants said. It's strange that none of you saw anything. That poor little boy falling out the window, his body broken on the flagstones below."

Vance glared at her. "That is all in the past now, Amelia. The authorities were satisfied that Teddy fell."

"Didn't they think Cassie might have been responsible?" The gossipmonger smiled her vicious smile. "In fact, Gavin, I believe your father said he thought Cassie was more disturbed than people had been led to believe. It's possible that she could have pushed her baby brother out the window." Amelia Dorcas gave a malicious laugh. "Or seen the one who did it!"

Chapter Two

As if an ugly specter had suddenly arisen in their midst, color bleached from Vance's face, anger flashed from Gavin Rodene's eyes, Lady Edwina pursed her lips in an ugly line. Sir Wilfred ordered another scotch and drank it thirstily. My heart caught in my throat. *Cassie's little brother had fallen to his death seven years ago and Amelia Dorcas was insinuating that one of these people had been responsible for it!* The malicious gossipmonger was the only one who seemed perfectly at ease, as if we had been discussing the weather or some other innocuous subject.

"We have put all that behind us, Amelia," snapped Lady Edwina. "After all, the unfortunate accident happened over seven years ago."

"Of course, of course. And we all know that dear Cassie is not to be held accountable for any of her actions."

Vance frowned. Then he turned and smiled apologetically at me. "Perhaps you'd best get back to my sister. Her behavior is . . . unpredictable."

I knew that Dr. Rodene was going to voice his objections to Cassie being under my care; there was nothing I could do but obey my employer and gracefully make my exit.

I found Cassie beginning to rouse from her drugged sleep. As I bathed the young girl's face and made preparations for us to leave the train, I wondered what Dr. Rodene was saying about me and my lack of training. Perhaps when we reached St. Augustine, I would find myself discharged.

Anger made me tug nervously at my lower lip. I bristled with indignation. How dare he interfere in something that was none of his business? I couldn't identify the undercurrents surging between him and the Danzels, but I had felt them. The Danzels weren't all that happy to see Dr. Gavin Rodene, that much I knew. In fact, they seemed a little frightened of him, unsure of what he might do or say. Would they let him change their minds about my remaining as a companion to Cassie? By the time the train whistle warned that we were approaching St. Augustine, my stomach was in a tight little knot.

A blue mist which had gathered sparkles of sunlight softened the southern sky and earth like the watery sweep of an artist's brush. As the train eased its way into the station, I caught my first glimpse of the old city of St. Augustine, founded in 1565 by Don Pedro Menendez de Aviles. Its Spanish beginnings were evident in walled houses, inner courtyards, its cobbled streets and red tiled roofs, newly washed by rain and freshly glistening. Palm trees, rampant vines and tropical plants shone green-gold everywhere and fragrant hibiscus bushes, oleanders, and trumpet vines climbed over walls and fences with carefree abandon. Rain droplets still sparkled on colorful flowers that overflowed baskets and pots set on wrought iron balconies and filled riotous window boxes.

As I stepped down from the train, I could not keep from scanning the bustling crowd for Dr. Rodene's dark head and hard, firm shoulders. A mixture of disappointment and relief flooded me. He was not in sight. In my mind I had been forming all kinds of conversations with him. This imaginary dialogue was caught between a desire to tell him to mind his own business, and a need to verify the peculiar feelings I had experienced as he bent over me to look into my eyes.

I walked on one side, and Vance on the other, as we supported a groggy Cassie down the platform and into the station. In appearance Cassie resembled a small, undeveloped girl, only reaching up to my shoulders in height. Her head lolled as she squinted through half-closed eyes. More than one person quickly averted their eyes, and I heard a rumble of whispers as we passed through the crowded depot. Even though I had followed doctor's orders in administering the medicine, I worried that the dosage of laudanum had been too potent. Cassie had been difficult to rouse, and even now she was almost out on her feet.

Coaches, buggies, and carriages lined up outside the station, waiting to take arriving visitors down King Street to three major resort hotels, the Ponce de Leon, the Cordova, and the Alcazar. Vendors of all kinds hawked their wares and carriage drivers pushed and shoved to get to the arriving tourists first.

In a loud voice, Lady Edwina sent Sir Wilfred ahead to secure a carriage for them, and then she emitted groans and complaints as she entered a well-sprung carriage which dipped with her bulk. Amelia Dorcas took a seat opposite Edwina and thin, self-effacing Sir William, whose eyes were quite glassy from the number of drinks he had enjoyed on the train.

Vance was left to assume all responsibility for me and Cassie. He engaged another carriage and helped us into it. Then he told the driver to wait while he checked on the luggage.

As Vance walked away to speak with the driver of a dray wagon, I saw Gavin Rodene come out of the station. My heartbeat quickened as he headed my way. For an insane moment, I thought he might join us in our carriage. Maybe he would ride to the Hotel with us! A unbidden spiral of excitement tingled in my chest. Then disappointment was immediate. From the depths of a small lady's buggy waiting nearby, I heard a sweet feminine voice call his name. "Gavin! Gavin! Over here!"

I swiveled around to find out who was sitting in the buggy but I couldn't see inside it. Gavin Rodene waved and smiled broadly at the occupant as he handed his belongings to the driver and then swung himself up into the buggy and disappeared from view. A high stepping sorrel horse pulled away from the depot in a quick trot, sending red buggy wheels rumbling on the cobbled street.

Vance followed my gaze. "So now we know why Dr. Rodene left Miss Lynette cooling her heels in New York. I bet Amelia Dorcas's nose is twitching already." He sat down in a spacious, leather-tufted seat opposite Cassie and me, and gave the driver a signal.

"Do you know who it was?" I asked, inwardly aghast at myself for prying.

"No. But it shouldn't be too hard to find out. Since the good doctor has seen fit to poke his nose into our affairs, we'd be amiss not to keep abreast of his, don't you agree?"

My chest instantly tightened. Gavin Rodene must have expressed his reservations about my ability to be in charge of Cassie. Had he convinced Vance and Lady Edwina that they had made a mistake? Was I going to be politely dismissed as soon as someone else was secured? Anxiety, anger, and resentment at his interference made my hands tighten upon the chain of my reticule. "What did Dr. Rodene have to say about me?"

"Well, he asked a good many questions, about Cassie . . . and about you. Frankly, I thought his interest went beyond the bounds of polite conversation. Do you know what was on his mind?"

"No," I lied. I wasn't about to admit that he had seemed ready to ask Vance to dismiss me.

Vance sighed. "His father was a close friend of my parents. As children, Gavin, Lynette, and I were together quite a bit, not really the best of friends, but we belonged to the same summer crowds at Newport and Cape Cod. I always found Gavin to be a dark, brooding sort of fellow but the girls seem to go for that strong, silent aura of his. Ever since she could walk, Lynette Talbot followed him around like he was some god from Mount Olympus. No one was surprised when they became engaged just before his recent trip to Europe. No wedding date set, though. Ah well," he sighed again. "For some reason, even though the elder Rodene wasn't our family physician, my father called him when my baby brother fell to his death from an attic window. It's this past connection with the family which Gavin Rodene assumes gives him the right to offer his unsolicited opinion."

"What did you tell him about me?"

"Very little. I really don't know much about you, I'm afraid. Of course, Brianna, I hope to remedy that while we're vacationing here." His warm glance touched on the flirtatious. "You need a change of scenery after your ordeal, and I'm pleased that you accepted my offer. I told Dr. Rodene exactly that."

"Thank you."

"I explained that I met you while your father was at Gray Oaks and that I was impressed by your conduct. Very impressed. It must have been excruciating to watch your father deteriorate like that." Vance's frown was sympathetic. "An intelligent, professional man turned into a vacuous, empty shell. You were wonderful with him, Brianna. I used to see you sitting on the grass beside his chair, talking and smiling at him even though there wasn't a flicker of recognition in his expression."

These word pictures brought back the years of emotional strain, and the emptiness that my father's illness and, finally, his death had brought. As long as I could remember my life had been organized around my father. Without him, my days stretched emptily in front of me. What would I do, where would I go if Vance decided to dismiss me? I stiffened against a trembling that threatened to enfold me. Vance reached over and patted my gloved hand.

"Don't frown like that, it spoils your lovely face. You needn't worry, Brianna. I told the good doctor that his professional advice was not needed. There's no doubt in my mind that my sister is in the best possible hands." Vance's warm gaze bathed my face.

I let out the breath I had been holding. "I promise that I will do my utmost to care for your sister in the best way possible."

"Good. I know you're a little uneasy. That's to be expected. You really don't know Cassie, nor do you know what to expect from her behavior."

That was true. I had only seen his sister in the protected environment of the sanitarium, and there the girl had always been withdrawn and passive. There had been nothing of the good Samaritan in my decision to take the position as companion; it had been pure financial necessity that had made me consider the offer and accept the very generous wages Vance Danzel would pay me. Now that the responsibility had begun, I was suddenly apprehensive. Maybe Gavin Rodene was right. Maybe I had no business thinking I could handle Cassie Danzel.

I had come to New York only a week ago to join the Danzel family. During that time, a registered nurse had been in charge of the disturbed Cassie, but once the train pulled out of Grand Central Station, Cassie had become my responsibility. Surely the doctors at Gray Oaks would not have released her if there had been any doubts about her adjustment outside the sanitarium, I reasoned. But what would happen when the mentally disturbed young woman was no longer heavily sedated?

Anxious thoughts darted about in my head like a swarm of locusts. I shot a glance at Cassie's relaxed mouth and half-lidded eyes and a swell of compassion overcame my fear. The seventeen-year-old girl was so small, so vulnerable that a protective instinct helped me regain confidence in my ability to handle the situation. I smiled back at my employer.

"That's better. Well, we're almost there. Behold Henry Flagler's magnificent pleasure palace. The Ponce de Leon Hotel!"

Our carriage turned into a cobbled courtyard on the west side of a mammoth structure which resembled a Spanish Renaissance castle. My gaze feasted on the sunny courts, lush tropical gardens, numerous fountains shaped like dolphins, and four floors of vine-covered loggias stretching along several wings of the hotel. Built of oyster-white coquina, a solidified rock made from shells and mixed with cement, the white pebbled exterior contrasted dramatically with the red Spanish tile roof and brick arches. Turrets, frescoes, and carvings decorated the structure which sprawled over a five-acre lot. Adjacent to the grounds were a large orange grove and a wooded area which offered a cool, dark green retreat from the bright Florida sun.

I had never seen anything like it! My stomach churned with excitement. I couldn't believe that I was going to stay there! Under the excitement, there was a quiver of apprehension. It was the first time I had been anywhere without my father. He would have loved the beauty of the Spanish Renaissance architecture, I thought with a deep sense of loss. It seemed bitter irony that his death had made it possible for me to enjoy this visit to St. Augustine. For the first time in my life I was on my own.

My amazement did not lessen as we entered the hotel through a grand archway and passed through a forest of oak and marble columns into a magnificent rotunda inlaid with richly colored mosaic work. This was the center of the hotel and balconies on every floor opened onto it. My head went back as I raised my eyes upward to the dome, four stories above, decorated with paintings—which seemed to be an allegorical representation of the history of Spain and Florida—blended with figures carved in high relief upon the dome. The impact of the bright color and light was blinding.

I tried to take in everything as my senses were bombarded with unbelievable splendor. To the right of the rotunda were offices, small parlors, and an arcade of shops, and on the left, a magnificent grand parlor.

The lobby was crowded with fashionably dressed guests and new arrivals. I had never seen so many silk and satin gowns, sparkling jewels and feathered hats. I would have panicked if I had been on my own.

Amelia Dorcas was at the desk demanding a room, and I heard Lady Edwina's querulous tones ordering Sir Wilfred to secure their registration immediately so she could retire to their suite.

Vance went to a different desk clerk, and in a moment he had secured the help of a young hotel attendant and ushered Cassie and me into a wide elevator with wrought iron sides, operated with precision by an officious gray-haired man in hotel uniform. I was grateful that Cassie remained passive as we were lifted silently upward. The young hotel steward kept his stony gaze away from Cassie but I could tell that curiosity about the drugged girl was taxing all his self-will and training.

"There are some four hundred and fifty sleeping accommodations for guests on the second, third, and fourth floors," Vance explained with a reassuring smile, sensing my trepidation. "And there is a small private suite in a fifth-floor tower which will be suitable for you and Cassie. Not that you are confined to these quarters," he assured me in that affable way of his.

I realized when I tried to smile back at him that my lips were stiff with nervousness.

"I've arranged for someone to relieve you a few hours each day. I want you to enjoy your stay here."

"Thank you. I know I shall."

"And I hope that my sister will be well enough for you to take her for walks in the gardens. I'm hopeful that she is going to benefit from the health treatments provided here. You will take her across the street every day to an establishment called the Casino." He looked down at his sister. "I know we're going to see a big improvement in her."

The young woman still had her head lowered in a listless fashion but it was not lolling to one side any more. The drug must be wearing off, I thought. I had the impression that at any moment Cassie might look up with that dark, intense stare of hers.

The hall was short and dim, with only one door opening onto it. The isolation of these fifth-story tower accommodations was suddenly brought home to me. All sounds had been left below. It was difficult to believe that this dark hall was in the same building as the glittering rotunda downstairs. There was no life here, no color, no sense of human inhabitants.

As I stood there in that windowless corridor waiting for one of the hotel stewards to open the door, rising panic made my breathing rapid. Even the corridors at Gray Oaks had been wide and polished, reflecting light through mullioned windows. Was I about to be forced into an isolation worse than that imposed upon the inmates of an asylum? Or locked away in prison quarters like those for the nobility in the history books my father had read so ardently? *Confined in luxury . . . until a dire sentence was carried out.*

The attendant unlocked the door and the dark miasma of the hall was left behind. I almost laughed with relief as we entered a sitting room with several windows and a small balcony which gave onto a view of the front courtyard. As if someone had decided to make up for the shadows lurking in the hall, the suite was boldly decorated. Its walls were papered with gaudy red cabbage roses that shrank the dimensions of the room and even dwarfed the high ceiling. A settee, several parlor chairs, and footstools were upholstered in a bold print of trailing green vines, or covered in bright raspberry velvet. The carpet was an expensive Aubusson in a floral pattern, the same persimmon color as the draperies' tasseled valances. Lamps flaunting bright shades and dangling crystal prisms stood on marble tables, and above them, gilded frames suspended on thick gold cords held bright oil paintings that might have been pleasant had they not been overshadowed by the vivid wallpaper. Everything clashed. The decor was like a scraping sound upon raw nerves.

It seemed to me that a child could have done better in picking out colors and patterns that didn't fight with each other. And, in spite of the rampant Victorian decor, an oppressive miasma seeped from the walls and a deathly stillness hovered in the isolated suite.

Two bedrooms opened off the small hall and were as overpowering as the sitting room in their decor: floral coverlets, paisley print wallpaper, and brightly upholstered stools and chairs. What kind of environment is this for an emotionally distraught young girl, I asked myself as Vance eased Cassie down on a bilious green velvet chaise longue.

"Do you find everything to your satisfaction?" asked Vance quickly, as if responding to my shadowed expression.

I hesitated and then nodded. I mustn't let some insidious apprehension color my response. "Yes. Fine."

"They told me that this suite had been decorated by an eccentric old lady who took these rooms when the hotel first opened," explained Vance. "As a favor to her, Henry Flagler allowed her to decorate it the way she wanted. When I inquired about the best facilities for my sister, the manager, Mr. Markham, said the tower suite would be available but that there wouldn't be time to redecorate it. I didn't realize the decor was so awful. I'm wondering if the dear lady could have been blind."

His quip brought a faint smile to my lips. "At least color-blind." Making a joke out of the awful decor helped, but I wondered how I could stand remaining more than a few minutes in these rooms.

"Sorry. I don't know what I can do about it now. Apparently these are the only accommodations in the hotel with this kind of privacy. I felt fortunate that this suite became vacant when—" He swallowed the rest of the sentence and I was sure he was about to say . . . *when the woman died.*

I had never been one to give much credence to ghosts and spirits, but I felt like an intruder in these rooms, as if the old woman were lurking about, intent upon making any new resident unwelcome in every way possible.

"Well, I guess I'd best leave you and see that Edwina and Sir Wilfred are settled in. If there's anything not to your satisfaction, please let me know. Meals will be brought up to you . . . although occasionally you may want to take some of your meals in a dining room. I understand that there are several provided for those who are . . . in employment here." His manner and instructions deftly delineated the social status which would govern my stay at the hotel. The main dining hall was not for me. I was hired help

. . . not a guest.

"See you tomorrow, Cassie." Vance touched his sister's shoulder with an affectionate squeeze as she reclined listlessly on the chaise longue. She gave no response. Vance gave his practiced smile to me again. "Bye for now." I swallowed against a dry, tight constriction in my throat. I didn't want him to leave! I didn't want to be left alone. For a moment I almost voiced my panic and then some stern, inner strength took control. My father would have chided me for having such nervous vapors.

I accompanied Vance to the door.

"Be sure to keep the doors locked," he said. "A precaution. I'm sure no one is going to bother you. I doubt that many people even know that these accommodations exist. You'll have this tower all to yourself."

The statement was supposed to be reassuring—but it only emphasized my isolation!

Chapter Three

A strange bed and unfamiliar surroundings, combined with an uneasy wariness, kept me mentally and physically tense for most of the night. I stared at shadows flickering upon the high ceiling, shaped and reshaped with the passage of clouds across the moon, and waited for morning. My bedroom door was directly across the hall from Cassie's, and every low moan or movement of the heavily drugged girl seemed close enough to be in the same room.

Several times I got out of bed and checked on Cassie, reassuring myself that her moaning and whimpering were part of a drugged sleep. You're going to be no good to yourself or her if you don't get some rest, I lectured myself, and tried to put everything out of my mind as I consciously courted sleep. When slumber finally came, it was fitful, and when I awoke, I felt less refreshed than when I'd gone to bed.

Morning broke, and in sharp contrast to my dour mood, the bright saffron sun shone down upon the magnificent hotel and its gardens. I had never been one to despond, and my spirits rose with the bright new day. Optimistically I began the ritual of dressing myself and Cassie and ordering breakfast for both of us. The morning passed quickly as I unpacked while Cassie lay passively on the green chaise longue.

The luncheon cart had just been removed by an efficient young hotel maid when a knock sounded loudly on the door. It was so demanding and purposeful that I expected to see a man when I opened it.

In fact my heart fluttered foolishly for a few seconds, wondering if it might be Dr. Rodene checking up on me. After all, I had received a bump on the head, I reasoned, taking a deep breath as I opened the door.

My welcoming smile wavered momentarily when I saw a large, muscular woman, in a black dress and white pinafore, whose bulk filled the doorway.

"I Domincea Oliveros," she said with a heavy accent. "I come every day to relieve you . . . two hours." Her graying black hair was parted in the middle and pulled tightly back in a coiled braid at the nape of her head. Her accent was foreign, her complexion olive, and she had strong features which I thought might be Italian.

"Yes, good morning. I'm Brianna Anderson. Please come in, Miss Oliveros." I could not still a prickling of disappointment. I had hoped that Vance had hired someone young and companionable to help with Cassie. Sharing duties with someone I could have talked with would have eased my sense of isolation from the rest of the hotel. I knew that one of my failings was to make snap judgments about people, so I tried not to dislike Domincea Oliveros, but I was unable to initiate any conversation between the two of us. This formidable-looking woman did not invite confidences.

The exchange of information between us was brief. Domincea was an attendant working at the health facilities across the street, where the baths and swimming pool were located in a building attached to the Alcazar Hotel. Vance had arranged for Domincea to be relieved of her usual duties there for a few hours each day so she could give me some time away from Cassie.

The woman sat down in a chair near Cassie's bed and stared at the girl like a trained dog taking up a guard position. Her arms and shoulders were as muscular as any man's, I thought; she probably could have picked up both Cassie and me in one swoop. I showed her the medicine that Cassie was to be given in another hour. Domincea nodded, looked at her lapel watch, and folded her arms in a waiting gesture.

Grateful for a chance to escape the oppressive rooms, I grabbed a soft yellow scarf to tie around my head since my bonnet, crushed on the train yesterday, was beyond repair. I pulled on a pair of light green gloves that matched the sprigged print of my soft afternoon dress modestly trimmed with a lace chemisette and long sleeves which ended in ruffles at the wrist. I looped the chain of my reticule over my arm and gratefully left the fifth-floor apartment.

Bless Vance Danzel! I could not suppress a spiraling tingle of excitement as I waited in the shadowy hall for the elevator. When the door flew open, I smiled warmly at the waiting attendant, feeling that I had made contact with the world again. But the man didn't smile back. The elderly, white-haired operator moved to block my passage into the elevator.

"Servants' stairs that way." His thin, age-spotted hand stabbed the air as he pointed toward the end of the hall. His hotel name tag read "Ira Deitz." He had all the softness of a general rebuking a new recruit for inappropriate behavior. As he looked down his thin nose at me, I saw his hairy nostrils flare.

I couldn't believe that the hotel grapevine had already been alerted as to whom I was and what my position—hired help! I had never been on the receiving end of such discrimination. My first reaction was to laugh at his pompous protocol and tell him in ringing tones that I would either ride down in the elevator or call the manager. But even as the impulse to defy him was there, an inner voice cautioned me not to make a scene.

I gave him my sweetest smile. "Thank you, very much. I wouldn't have wanted to make such a mistake my first day. You will make sure that I don't overstep my position, won't you, Mr. Deitz?"

The sarcasm washed over him without making any visible impression. "Yes, ma'am," he responded officiously. "Servants use the backstairs; they reach every floor. The Ponce prides itself on no help being visible to the guests," he informed me as if he were responsible for such an achievement. "Three dining rooms, two set up for white employees and one for colored. Service doors on the ground level lead to the outside—at the back of the hotel."

"Oh, my goodness, and I might have gone right out the front door!" I said with mock horror, deciding at that instant that I would do exactly that!

"Don't seem right anybody being up here in Liz Chantilly's rooms," he mused. "She won't like it. She never caused no trouble. No trouble at all." He glared at me as if I were somehow responsible for the situation. "Don't know why they had to take her away like that."

"She didn't die?" I asked, surprised.

He shook his head.

"What happened to her?"

Ira Deitz's smile was suddenly malicious. "Went plum batty, she did. They took her away screaming and yelling, swearing at the top of her lungs that she'd be back. Maybe she will, too. I'd keep my door locked if I was you." He chuckled as if he couldn't wait to see the crazy woman evicting a young upstart who thought she could use the elevator.

His dry laugh followed me to the stairwell at the end of the hall. As I leaned over the railing a moment of vertigo overtook me. A steep, narrow staircase circled downward for six floors to the basement. I drew back quickly and took several deep breaths before I started down the twisting, narrow steps, clinging tightly to the railing.

When I reached the lower floors, I had to squeeze to one side as uniformed maids hurriedly mounted or descended the steep steps, their arms filled with bedding, linens, or trays. I smiled at them but the women ignored my presence as if I were just another wooden baluster on the staircase. It seemed impossible to me that anyone could keep up that taxing pace as they climbed up and down stairs and hurried to carry out their duties on each level. By the time I had reached the main floor, I had decided that I had used the servants' staircase for the last time.

As I emerged on the main floor, I was about to follow through on my intention of going out the front door when my determination wavered. A bevy of ladies wearing large hats decorated with feathers and flowers promenaded across the marble floor laughing and chattering. Their elaborate taffeta and silk gowns and hidden petticoats rustled as they mounted steps to the dining room or exited through arched doorways onto the vine-covered loggias. Gentlemen guests were equally elegant in morning coats, striped trousers, soft cravats, and fancy vests, as they strolled about tipping high-brimmed hats. Alone or in groups, affluent male guests sauntered in and out of smoking rooms or escorted ladies into the magnificent main parlor which had been tastefully divided by screens and greenery into intimate areas for personal conversations.

Conscious of the plain scarf on my head and my simple summer frock, my courage deserted me. Even as I chided myself for being a coward, I turned away from the lobby and followed a hall leading to the back of the hotel. I exited through a rear door which opened onto an arched passageway that ran under the hotel. Carriages and huge drays rumbled through the passage, forcing me to skirt the edge of the building to keep from being run down.

My spirits lifted as I made my way to a flagged path which wound its way through landscaped tropical gardens. Fountains sprayed the air with droplets that looked like strings of jewels sparkling in the sun. I drew in deep breaths of redolent perfume as I passed mass plantings of roses, every hue and shade, and felt transported into another world. Towering palm trees, gardenia and camellia bushes, and huge tropical plants with scalloped green leaves were alien to the gardens of Philadelphia. It was like a fairyland, I thought, and was so intent upon seeing everything that I nearly bumped into a man sitting on a camp stool in front of an easel.

"Oh, I'm sorry," I gasped, catching my balance.

A pair of light brown eyes looked at me from under bushy red eyebrows. The young artist, somewhere in his early thirties, took his brush from the canvas and let it rest on his knee, an obviously habitual act, for his pants were stained with all colors of the spectrum. Shocks of unruly cinnamon hair stood out all around his rather craggy face, and a lop-sided grin harmonized with friendly freckles on his nose. He wore a blue work shirt, open at the neck, and his pants seemed short for his long legs.

"I almost ran into you," I said with an embarrassed laugh.

"Best piece of luck I could have had all day."

"I didn't mean to disturb you. I was just taking a walk, enjoying the gardens. We don't have anything like this in Pennsylvania . . ."

"In New Hampshire, either," he said getting to his feet in an unfolding procedure that was almost comical. "Jack Harvey. I'd shake hands but . . ." he held out fingers mottled with paint splotches.

"Brianna Anderson . . . glad to meet you. Are you staying in the hotel?"

"Well, not in the hotel, exactly. I have quarters there." He indicated a two-storied rectangular building that bordered a street at the far end of the grounds. "I was lucky enough to be accepted as a resident artist. Brought here by the management to hold shows for the guests Wednesday afternoons and Friday nights. Art patrons wander through our rooms, look at our paintings and enjoy a touch of Bohemia. Funny how rich people delight in—" Then he flushed. "Oh, I'm sorry . . .are you . . . ?"

I laughed at him. "Rich? No. and I'm not a guest. Just a few minutes ago I was reminded that I'm only hired help." I told him then about Ira Deitz. "I'm a paid companion to an ill young woman, and everyone in the hotel seems to know it."

"Sounds like quite a job . . . for someone as young and pretty as you."

I flushed at the compliment. To cover up my embarrassment, I looked at the painting he was working on and was surprised to see he was filling in the background behind two children and a woman who had the same facial characteristics as Domincea. I mentioned the resemblance. "I thought she might be Italian."

"Probably of Minorcan descent. Thousands of immigrants came here from Minorca in the mid-seventeen hundreds," he explained. "They landed in a settlement just down the coast. New Smyrna, it's called. The work conditions were appalling there in those days. Unbelievable. Hands cut off, men whipped, whole families starved to death. The Minorcans finally revolted against an overseer named Turnball and migrated here to St. Augustine. They're a strong people, sometimes as hard and cruel as their past, but they're survivors. I'm trying to get some of that into my paintings. They don't sell very well, though," he confessed. "The Hotel's rich clientele prefer water lilies and romantic sunsets."

"Well, I think you're very good," I said honestly. "You've captured the strength in those faces."

"Thanks." He gave me a hesitant, questioning look. "I was about to take a break. There's a nice dining room set up for—" he paused.

"Hired help?" I chuckled.

"And struggling artists," he added with a grin. "Would you like to join a paint-splattered Yankee for a mug of coffee?"

"I would indeed!"

He escorted me into a building attached at the back of the main building. I learned that most of the servants had quarters there. The addition was as large as a wing of the hotel itself and it housed kitchens, workshops, living quarters, and dining rooms for the white workers, chefs, musicians, engineers, plumbers, carpenters, and gardeners. The staff dining room was unadorned, filled with long tables crowded with people in hotel uniforms or work clothes. The bustle was reassuring and I decided that I would have my meals here as often as I could. Jack's unpretentious manner and easy laugh were therapeutic. Learning more about the hotel and its people made me feel a part of the bustling establishment, not cut off from it.

I chatted with Jack Harvey as if we were old friends and found we had several things in common. His father was also a professor, teaching fine arts at a small New England university, and was responsible for encouraging his son to pursue his talent.

"How would you like a little sight-seeing tour of St. Augustine? It has a charm all its own and I've painted nearly every blasted inch of it."

"Thank you. I'd like that."

"Shall we say tomorrow then . . . same time . . . same place?"

"Thank you. I'll look forward to it."

I left Jack at his easel and had just reached the back hotel entrance when I saw Sir William Wilfred. Somehow he had knocked off his tall silk hat, and it was about to be run over by a produce wagon lumbering under the archway. He was looking at it helplessly when I darted forward and retrieved it with the ease of a youngster diving after a ball.

"Oh, my dear, you shouldn't have! Risking your safety like that. Very kind. Very kind. Oh, thank you . . ."

"You're very welcome, Sir Wilfred."

He peered at me with his rheumy eyes as if searching for recognition, then smiled broadly. "Miss Anderson, isn't it? Yes, I thought so. Well, well. And how are you settling in at this magnificent establishment?"

"Just fine."

"Good. Good." He stroked his precise mustache. "I'm finding the accommodations equal to any of those on the continent. I was telling Lady Edwina that it wouldn't be amiss to spend a season here each year. She prefers going abroad, of course, but that is a good deal more expensive." His brow furrowed, and I knew that Lady Edwina had hammered away at him about how much of *her* money they were spending.

"It's very nice here," I said politely, once more feeling sorry for him. I was reminded of a quotation from Sir Walter Scott. "Wilfred, docile, soft, and mild, was fancy's spoiled and wayward child." That seemed to fit Sir William Wilfred, all right, I thought. I wished he'd found a pleasant, affectionate, rich wife to spoil him. He must pay dearly for the title he had bestowed upon Edwina Danzel.

"You must have tea with us again sometime," he said, remembering that I had been drinking tea with them on the train.

"Thank you. I really must hurry now . . . I've overstayed my time." I bid him goodbye and hurried back into the hotel, humming to myself because I felt capable of handling whatever awaited me in Liz Chantilly's rooms.

The thought of climbing those narrow steps to the tower suite dismayed me, so when I reached the main corridor, I went directly to the elevator and joined several people who were waiting for it. When it arrived, I slipped in before Ira Deitz spotted me. When he did, his beady eyes glowed hotly at me, but I knew that he was too well-trained to make a scene in front of the guests. I was certain he wouldn't make any effort to evict me as long as there were other people in the elevator. However, when the last one left at the fourth floor, I was not surprised when he turned his venomous glare upon me.

Before he could say anything, I gave him a bright smile. "Thank you. I'll walk up from here," and brushed past him. "There's only one floor to go."

"You forget yourself, Miss." He wagged a bony finger at me. "Them that aim too high have far to fall!"

I knew then that I had made an enemy. Ira Deitz would never forgive me for such defiance of my position, and on top of that, he seemed to resent my presence on the fifth floor. He must have liked Liz Chantilly.

Domincea stood up when I entered the sitting room, looking at her lapel watch.

"Am I late? The time went so fast . . ."

"Doctor's here," she said with a jerk of her head toward Cassie's bedroom.

Doctor! I couldn't keep a wild rush of excitement from leaping into my chest. Dr. Rodene! He had come! My pulse quickened and I realized with a start that he had never been far from my thoughts. Just his name made me feel giddy and breathless. Then my joy was tempered by a multitude of questions. What was he doing here examining Cassie? Vance Danzel had led me to believe that he had rejected the physician's interest in the matter. Had Vance changed his mind and engaged Dr. Rodene to look after his sister? If so, I might be immediately dismissed.

At that moment, the bedroom door opened and ended my speculation. It was not Dr. Rodene but a well-built man in his fifties who took obvious pride in his erect carriage. "I'm Dr. Conrad Vonfeldt. . . and you must be Miss Anderson." His smile was white-toothed, and his black hair, oiled and glossy, thickly framed broad German features. His jet eyes slid over my face and figure with a deliberateness that brought warmth into my neck.

"How do you do," I said formally.

"Mr. Vance asked me to see his sister. I'm in charge of all the health facilities at the Casino," he advised me, with an air of proprietorship. "However, I do accept some private patients and Mr. Vance has arranged for me to tend his sister while they are here." He turned abruptly to Domincea. "You may go now, Domincea. Your duties await you."

The Minorcan woman turned away, ignoring my polite, "Until tomorrow, Domincea."

"Now then, Miss Anderson." Dr. Vonfeldt's voice had been dictatorial when he dismissed Domincea but his tone went from sandpaper to butter when he spoke to me. "Please sit down. I think we should take time to get acquainted, don't you?" His warm eyes added a suggestive meaning to the words. He motioned toward a settee but I pretended I didn't notice the gesture and took a parlor chair opposite it.

He sat down on the settee closest to me and leaned slightly forward so that there was a suggesting of physical intimacy between us. "Mr. Danzel speaks very highly of you, Miss Anderson. He sang your praises, and now I can see why he's so taken with you. You are a very attractive woman. He must be fond of you. . . ?"

I bristled at the insinuation that my employer and I were intimately involved. "Mr. Danzel hired me as companion to his sister because he liked the way I treated my father and other patients at Gray Oaks. Nothing more."

"Of course, of course," he said smoothly. "I did

not mean to suggest anything else." The glint in his eyes denied the apology. "I'm certain that Miss Danzel will be in good hands with you and I'm happy to allow Domincea to relieve you each day. You may adjust the time as you see fit. If you prefer her to come every afternoon, that will be fine, but there will be times, I'm sure, when you'll prefer to be free over the dinner hour." His white-toothed smile broadened. "A lovely woman like yourself must not be allowed to dine alone. Her gentleman friends . . ."

"I have no gentlemen friends.."

"A pity. But a lack which I'm sure might be quickly remedied."

"Dr. Vonfeldt, I would like to speak to you about Cassie," I said in a businesslike tone, angered at his scavenging remarks about my private life. "I'm wondering about her condition. Her medication keeps her drugged . . ."

"I know, and in my judgment her condition does not warrant continuous sedation. I will prescribe some different medicine for her. I have not seen her records from Gray Oaks, but from what her brother tells me, her physician recommended that she be eased back into normal living as much as possible—that's why she's been brought here." He gave a satisfied smile. His fingernails were manicured and a large diamond sliced the air as he talked.

"She seems very withdrawn," I said.

"I am confident that Miss Danzel will benefit from the therapies we offer in our program. Our Roman and Turkish baths help preserve the equilibrium between waste and repair." In a rather pompous lecturing tone, he continued talking about the health services of the Casino.

I wanted to challenge many of his statements but I managed to keep still.

"These remarkable baths induce mental clearness . . . freedom from lassitude . . . accompanied by a sense of physical elasticity. We have the latest equipment for hydro-therapy, mechano-therapy, electro-therapy—all of which successfully combat disease, whatever its stage or severity."

The hyperbolic claim made my spine stiffen. "All diseases?"

"I gather that you are a disbeliever, Miss Anderson. But no matter. You will observe many miracles yourself while you are here, I promise you. Our new electric light cabinets will revitalize Miss Cassie. I predict that a few treatments lying under the healing light of orange bulbs will bring about miraculous changes in both her physical and mental health."

"But how can it do that?"

"The mysteries of electricity. The mysteries of electricity." His diamond sliced the air emphatically. "We will schedule daily applications of these electrical baths, as well as massage, hot air cabinets, and hot and cold Nauheim baths. We have found these successful in alleviating heart conditions, anemia, disfunctions of the spinal cord, neurasthenia, and many, many afflictions of all kinds."

"Almost like the Lourdes shrine," I said, with a sweet smile to lessen the sarcasm. His boastful speech resembled the flamboyant claims made by patent medicine hustlers who promise miraculous cures for everything from snake bites to impotence. Their quackery was dangerous, I knew, because truly ill people believed them. Dr. Vonfeldt's smooth, oily, charlatan's pronouncements made my skin crawl.

A slight tightening around his jet black eyes told me that my sarcastic thrust had gone home. He tightened those soft, almost flaccid hands. "You obviously have reservations. I can only remind you that Vance Danzel has put his sister in my charge, Miss Anderson. And you will be required to carry out *my* directives." Then he softened his tone. "I'm certain that you will enjoy our facilities yourself. Please feel free to avail yourself of our wonderful massages." His eyes gleamed. "I have perfected a technique of massage that all our women bathers find . . . stimulating."

"How nice," was all I could think of to say. The idea of those thick hands touching my bare skin made me want to shiver. "I'm afraid my duties will keep me quite busy."

"I'd inferred from what Mr. Danzel said that you were his special . . . guest."

Once more my color flared. "I am Mr. Danzel's employee."

"Of course, of course . . ."

A knock at the door kept me from responding to Vonfeldt's lascivious smile. I opened the door—and Gavin Rodene stood there. For a moment, I couldn't summon the usual polite amenities. I stammered, "Oh, it's you!"

As he raised a questioning eyebrow, I knew that my flushed and disconcerted face had made him wonder if he had intruded upon a private tête-a-tête. He looked past me to Dr. Vonfeldt, who slowly rose from the settee. "I'm sorry. I can come back later," Gavin said stiffly.

"No. No, please come in, Dr. Rodene. This is Dr. Vonfeldt. I don't know if you two gentlemen know each other?" I said with a rush.

"No, I've not had the pleasure," said Vonfeldt smoothly, his ingratiating smile in place. "I'm in charge of the health facilities at the Casino, in the Alcazar Hotel across the street."

"Oh yes," Gavin acknowledged the introduction without holding out his hand. "I've heard of you, Dr. Vonfeldt. In fact, your name was recently mentioned during my stay in France. Someone said that you had found your El Dorado in St. Augustine, curing fashionable wealthy women of all their ailments."

Vonfeldt said stiffly, "Yes, I was at the Naurein

Institute for several years. When Henry Flagler decided to offer a European-style resort, my name came to his attention. And what brings you to St. Augustine, Dr. Rodene? A vacation?"

"No, work, I'm afraid."

"Oh? I'm the personal physician of guests while they are here at the Ponce de Leon. I assume that you are not making a professional call, since Cassie Danzel has been put in my charge." Vonfeldt's thick shoulders were stiff and his smile absent.

"I'm making a professional call," countered Gavin, "but not on Cassie Danzel. Yesterday I treated Miss Anderson for a head injury. If you will excuse us, I would like to confer with my patient."

It was almost more than I could do to smother a giggle as the officious German doctor left with no more than a cold nod to both of us.

"I hope you didn't mind my getting rid of him like that?" said Gavin.

I let out the deep laughter bubbling in my throat. "Mind? You have my deep-felt thanks. You should have heard the nonsense he was mouthing. According to him, his marvelous baths will cure everything from heart disease to anemia. Nobody believes that, do they?"

"The hotel's full of people who have come here to find health while they spend their money. Actually, it's a good place for some of them. They are cured of their vague ailments because they exercise and eat properly. It can only help someone like Lady Edwina."

"But someone like Cassie?"

His eyes were suddenly hard agates. "Dangerous. Warm and cold baths, massage, and a hocus-pocus of electrical apparatus are not going to cure Cassie Danzel of a serious mental disorder. I can't imagine any reputable doctor approving of such treatment."

"But her brother said that those in charge at Gray

Oaks suggested she accompany them to St. Augustine this year. My instructions are to ease her back into living normally."

"I know. And there's nothing I can do but warn you. I have no way of knowing the extent of Cassie's mental disorders. I am going to make some discreet inquiries, but I cannot breach any professional ethics by intruding on the case. Since you seem determined to hold on to this ill-advised job . . ."

"I told you before—"

"I know, keep my nose out of your business." He grinned. "But since you are my patient."

"I am not!"

"I treated you for a head injury, didn't I?" he teased.

"A bump on the head which I have completely forgotten."

"Have you? Well, I haven't. Under the circumstances, I feel that you have become my responsibility."

My temper flared. "What circumstances give you the right to interfere in my life?"

"My father was called to the house when the youngest Danzel plunged to his death from an attic window. There was no way to prove it wasn't an accident. The screen could have been loose. The two-year-old could have climbed out on his own. It could have happened that way."

"But you're saying it didn't."

"I'm saying that my father suspected that the child was already dead when he went out that window. There was evidence that there had been a struggle before he fell. Cassie was found in that attic, huddled up in a tiny space under the stairs. I do not like the idea of an untrained young woman living here with a possible killer."

Chapter Four

I sat down abruptly on a gaudy parlor chair. The impact of Gavin's statement brought a physical reaction as well as an emotional one. I had not given any credence to Amelia Dorcas's vicious remarks, but now Gavin Rodene was saying the same thing. "You think Cassie killed her little brother and threw him out the window?" I said in a hushed, cracked voice.

"I don't know what happened. Nobody does. When they got Cassie out of her tiny hiding place, her mind had already retreated from the world. There were scratches on her as if the child might have fought her. She was institutionalized immediately. That's why I'm concerned, Brianna." He sat down where Dr. Vonfeldt had been sitting. "You should have known all this before you took on the responsibility of caring for Cassie. She's not to be trusted."

"You don't think a small, weak person like Cassie is going to throw me out a window?" I countered with more lightness than I felt inside.

"No. But she might decide to jump herself!"

My mouth lost all moisture. "Do you think she's suicidal?"

"I don't know, but I wouldn't trust her for a minute. Vance didn't tell you anything about the tragedy, did he?"

"No." I realized then how little I knew about the

Danzel family. My only contact with them had been at Gray Oaks and I had simply accepted them as a family suffering from the deterioration of a loved one, just as I had been. I had not looked beyond the surface. My financial plight had made me vulnerable to their offer of a position. "But I can't believe the doctors would have let her go if . . . if . . ."

"A family has the right to seek help wherever and whenever they wish. Apparently, Vance and his sister decided on St. Augustine."

"Dr. Vonfeldt? And his baths and electro-therapy?" I shivered in spite of myself.

"I tried to talk with Vance about it yesterday on the train but he politely told me to mind my own business," said Gavin wryly. "There's nothing I can do about Cassie, but I will not rest until you are out of this situation. You have to leave. Give up this dangerous and ill-advised responsibility, Brianna."

"And go where?" I had accepted the position because it put some order in my life. I couldn't go on living in the tiny rented room near Gray Oaks. I was twenty-three years old. My education had not been aimed at providing me with a means of supporting myself. When my father was well, he had absorbed all my time and attention and I had been happy to bask in his position and prestige. I had only a few friends because he had discouraged any activities that took me away from him. After he became ill, all of my energies went into making him as comfortable as possible. When he died, I had little money left, no future, and as many prospects as a capsized vessel floundering without oars. I tried to explain that Vance Danzel had put some structure back in my life, some purpose, and a means of supporting myself.

"I understand. But you are a bright, capable woman, Brianna. And I think the Danzels are misusing you. I told Vance so."

"You had no right to do that!" I stood up and

angrily walked out on the tiny tower balcony just to get away from him. Why couldn't he leave me alone? I resented his authoritative badgering. And I hated the way he sent my emotions into a swirling devil's wind.

Arched shadows fell upon my face as I leaned my head against one of the pillars. I was angry, frightened and confused. I had no resources. My home, along with most of the family possessions, was lost to creditors. Until my father's illness, my life had been protected, patterned, and secure. Now all of that was gone. It was easy for Gavin Rodene to think I should give all of this up and be on my way—but to where?

He came up behind me, not touching me and yet filling my senses with his presence. I stiffened, waiting for him to put his hands on me but he didn't.

"You can't stay here," he said quietly.

"I have nowhere to go." My words floated out into the open air, mingling with the laughter and gay chatter coming from the east and west wings of the hotel.

Below us, fashionable guests moved about among the gardens. Pastel summer gowns, waving fans, and splashes of color dotted the landscape like the brilliant plumage of tropical birds. Carriages rumbled by, and idle ladies and gentlemen made their way across the street to the landscaped gardens of the Alcazar to enjoy the amusements offered in its sporting palace, the Casino. Everything in the luxurious, elegant atmosphere was a contrast to my leaden, sterile feelings.

"Surely you have family . . . someone who will provide for you."

I shook my head. "My mother died when I was little and my father did not keep up any contact with her family. But even if I discovered a distant aunt or uncle I would not go groveling to them now." My chin came up. "For three years I was alone in the battle to save my father; no one offered me help then, and I don't intend to ask for it now."

"Then you must secure another position."

"I have no savings, no income except the wages that have been promised me. Finding something else will take time."

"Then you must let me help."

The offer was quietly seductive. How easy it would be to say yes, I thought. Please take care of me, solve all my problems, extricate me from this situation. Even as the possibility crossed my mind, it jolted me out of the deceptive reverie. I allowed myself a small laugh. Turning and looking him directly in the face, I said stiffly, "Thank you for the offer, Dr. Rodene. But this is my problem and I will solve it."

"Don't misunderstand me. I did not mean to imply that there were any obligations," he said quickly, noting the proud thrust of my chin. "It simply would . . ."

"Put me in your debt," I finished curtly. "No, thank you, Dr. Rodene, though I appreciate your concern. It's true I didn't know the extent of the responsibility I had assumed. Nevertheless, I must follow through."

"Then you're a fool!"

I was startled by the unbridled rage in the accusation.

"That's your professional opinion?" I asked testily.

He had lost his soft, persuasive tone. I saw that his gray-green eyes had suddenly hardened. "You must do as I say, Brianna. I don't want you around Cassie Danzel. It's dangerous."

As I stared at his clenched jaw, a barbed suspicion sprang full-blown into my mind. *He wanted me to leave for some nefarious reason of his own!* It was not my safety he was concerned about. He didn't want me around Cassie Danzel. He had been openly upset on the train when he discovered the girl was no longer institutionalized. Had he thought Cassie Danzel safely behind locked doors? He had probably tried to persuade Vance to send her back to Gray Oaks. Did he know more about the tragedy than he was admitting?

He reached out and touched me and I jerked back.

"All of you were there that day—the day the little boy died. Amelia Dorcas said so!" I lashed out at him, unable to still my rising suspicion.

"Yes." His glower was so threatening that I backed up against the railing. "And I'm trying to warn you that you could be drawn into something ugly and dangerous by remaining here."

"Nevertheless, I intend to stay!" When I tried to move past him, he grabbed my arm. "Brianna!"

"You're hurting me!"

"Better that than breaking your stubborn little neck, which is exactly what I feel like doing!"

"Let me go! What are you afraid of? What do you think I'll find out?" I snapped angrily. "What do *you* have to hide, Dr. Rodene?" The minute the challenge was out, I wanted to call it back.

For a moment, I thought he might strike me but he abruptly dropped my arm. "I can see that it has done no good to warn you. You are stubborn, belligerent, and very, very foolish." With that he turned and left me staring after him as he shut the suite door behind him with a final bang.

My heart was racing and my mouth was dry. I did not know what to believe. My instincts told me that Gavin Rodene was lying to me. I would have to be on guard against him. The memory of his face bent close to mine haunted me. Sudden tears filled my eyes and I didn't know why I was crying, but I did know that it was for the loss of something I never had.

I woke up that night in a cold sweat, my breath short and fast from a nightmare. In the dream, I had been struggling with Cassie, who was trying to attack me with some kind of instrument. It kept changing, from a stick . . . to a knife . . . and then a vicious swing of a bloody ax brought me straight up in bed!

I was fully awake with screams caught in my throat. My heart pounded wildly and it took several moments for me to shake off the terror that the nightmare had invoked.

I got out of bed, crossed the hall and checked on Cassie, reassuring myself that the girl was still sleeping quietly. Her tiny, passive figure clothed in a simple white nightdress and ruffled night cap mocked my nightmare. Cassie was the same languid, withdrawn person she had always been.

I went back to bed, but could not go back to sleep. I lay rigid, every muscle tense. A myriad of thoughts like sharp nettles swirled with unanswered questions and speculation. I wanted to believe that Gavin Rodene was concerned for my welfare, but I knew it wasn't true. There was something more, much more, behind his attempts to remove Cassie from my care, and I was stubbornly committed to finding out what it was that he wanted kept hidden.

When Domincea arrived to relieve me in mid-afternoon, I felt like a caged bird about to be set free. I had dressed carefully for my sight-seeing trip with Jack, choosing a summer frock of soft yellow foulard that flowed in gathered flounces from my waist and was drawn into a modest bustle in the back. I tied a lace-trimmed white scarf over my burnished brown curls, regretting the destruction of my one summer bonnet. I flushed remembering the incident which had put me in Gavin Rodene's arms for those few minutes on the train.

I told Domincea that I would be back in two hours. The servant nodded and took up her guard position beside Cassie's bed.

I left the tower—by means of the stairs. I didn't feel

up to arguing with Ira Deitz.

Jack Harvey was waiting for me at the same spot in the garden but this time without his easel. The artist wore clean, but paint-speckled work shirt and pants; his head was bare, allowing the sun to lace his red hair with copper and deepen the freckled tan on his face.

"Ready for a tour of the city?" His warm grin eased away the weighted mesh that had tangled my thoughts since yesterday, and I found myself laughing back at him as we wandered down King Street to a grassy plaza in the heart of the city.

I saw many people with the same facial features as those in Jack's painting. They stood around in companionable groups, chatting and gossiping. Shops were filled with customers wandering in and out of the Spanish-style buildings. It was easy to identify the townspeople as their simple attire was in sharp contrast to the fashionable winter visitors who rolled by in carriages on their way to a day of amusement, or leisurely strolled along the streets.

"How's the job going?" asked Jack. "You looked a little tense when you arrived."

"It's fine." I took a deep breath and smiled. I wasn't going to tell him about Dr. Gavin Rodene and his warnings.

We walked all the way down St. George Street to the city gates, a rock arch that had at one time been part of a protective wall built around the settlement. The narrow street was filled with pedestrians, hand carts, and horse-drawn vehicles fighting for passage.

"You must have a souvenir," announced Jack, drawing me into a little shop which offered a variety of items aimed at enticing tourists to part with their money: alligator skins made into writing desks, slippers, wallets and belts; fragile shells and coral in pastels and vibrant colors. I had never before seen fish-scale jewelry, delicate and durable, fashioned in brooches, hat pins, and combs. Despite my protests, Jack purchased a small delicately carved white pin, carefully set with tiny pink shells. With a flourish he presented it to me, grinning at the flush I felt mounting in my cheeks.

"I . . . I really don't know if I should accept it," I stammered.

"Of course you should," he said, as if that settled the matter.

I pinned it on my white lace collar, thinking how nice it was to be with someone so openly friendly, not dark and foreboding like Gavin Rodene. I wondered if he ever let that professional barrier down and enjoyed himself. Then I chided myself for wasting my time thinking about him. I promised myself that I would ignore him as if he didn't exist.

"You're awfully pensive," Jack said, watching my dark eyebrows draw together.

I gave a little laugh. "It's nothing. I'm really enjoying myself. Thank you for taking the time to show me about. How big is St. Augustine?"

"About five thousand. The city is less than a mile square." We wandered through narrow alley-like streets. Overhanging balconies on both sides almost touched each other. White coquina houses were shut from view by high walls, but I glimpsed gardens, palm trees, and masses of luxuriant foliage inside the wrought iron gates.

"What is that?" I pointed to a huge fortress which Jack identified as Fort Marion, a sprawling fortification which he said had been started by the Spanish on the San Sebastian River, as early as 1672. "It has changed hands and been renamed several times as the French and English and Spanish vied for possession of Florida."

Turrets and battlements fortified with cannons still stood guard, and a detachment of United States soldiers was stationed there. Even in the bright sunlight and warmth of a pleasant day, I shivered as I looked at it. It didn't help when Jack began describing in detail his visit to the dungeons and torture chambers, dank, windowless cells where prisoners had lived without a glimpse of the sky. "Would you like to take a tour?"

"No," I said quickly. "Just looking at the outside is enough."

"Oh, I'm sorry. I didn't realize . . ."

"It's all right." I gave a foolish laugh. "My father always said I let my imagination run away from me." I wanted to mention the feeling I had of being an unwanted intruder in the tower suite, and the things the elevator man had told me about Liz Chantilly—but I didn't. I suspected that Jack had his two big feet planted firmly in reality and would laugh at such nebulous uneasiness.

"Come on, let's walk along the seawall," he said. "That will put some color back in your cheeks. That's Anastasia Island over there. Some afternoon we can row across and visit the lighthouse and hunt for shells on the northern beach."

"There are so many lovely things to see here. Tell me about the town."

"Well, the millionaire, Henry Flagler, came down here with his wife five years ago and decided the place was worth commercializing. He's been at odds with the town fathers ever since because they won't follow through and spruce up the place for his hotel guests. Don't know how it's going to turn out," said Jack. "Have a feeling the town's people are hoping this tourist thing is just a cockleburr in their side that will go away. In spite of the tourist dollars, I think they'd rather have the place to themselves."

At that moment a tallyho rumbled by filled with a bevy of brightly dressed women holding protective umbrellas. Their high pitched chatter and laughter broke the quiet lapping of water against the rock embankments. "Where are they going?"

"Probably over there." He pointed to a large ship anchored at a nearby wharf. "Shopping aboard a Bahaman ship seems to be an amusing pastime. Every time one anchors here, its captain and crew turn salesmen, hawking artifacts, jewelry, coconut trees, skins, tortoise shells, and novelties to the rich ladies. They leave the ship with their arms loaded with things that they don't want or need." He gave a short laugh. "The wealthy shoppers give the stuff away or throw it out when they return to the Ponce. Their lives are organized around buying, buying, buying, not in evaluating the worth of their purchases."

It was the first time I had seen a resentful, tight line to his mouth. Maybe Jack's easygoing, amiable manner did not go bone deep, I thought, with something of a surprise.

"They do the same thing on Wednesdays and Fridays when they make the rounds of the artists' studios," he said in that same angry tone. "They gawk and chatter and simper, acting like art patrons when they have no appreciation for a good painting. They buy indiscriminately because it's fashionable. Sometimes, when I'm forced to listen to their stupid chatter, I feel like ramming my paint brushes down their throats."

"If you hate it so much . . . ?"

"Why do I stay?" The freckles on his face stood out like ugly blotches. "Because I've sold out to the commercial market place. Living under the auspices of Henry Flagler, I'm provided with all the pleasant necessities of life and have the freedom of time to paint and paint while the money flows in. And that, my dear, is why I put up with it."

His tone suddenly made him a stranger. I had glimpsed a dark, raging anger in him, and I was uncomfortable. "I think I'd better be getting back."

"I'm sorry. I didn't mean to be so critical," he apologized quickly. "I'd planned on treating you to a glass of Italian wine."

"Another day, perhaps. I shouldn't overstay my time."

"You don't have to jump when they pull the string, do you?" he objected rather impatiently.

"I have a job, if that's what you mean." My steady gaze made him look away.

We walked along in silence and then he took my arm as we crossed the street at the corner of the hotel. "The Ponce de Leon Hotel is really a tale of two cities," he said, his conversational tone returning. "I think you've found that out already. It's made up of elite, affluent guests and a hidden army of people who keep it running. The hierarchy in the staff is unbelievable. I haven't found anyone that I can talk to—until I found you. You're such a wonderful listener, I guess I got carried away. Sorry if I offended you. Thanks for spending time with me."

I smiled back. "I really enjoyed it. And thank you for the lovely pin. It'll always remind me of St. Augustine."

"And of me?"

I laughed. "And of you." I bade him a quick goodbye and started toward the side entrance of the hotel. I had only taken a few steps when I looked up and saw Gavin Rodene standing in the middle of the curved garden path, waiting for me.

"Who was that?" he demanded with a hard flatness in his eyes as he watched Jack disappear into the back gardens of the hotel.

"A friend of mine."

"You haven't been here long enough to make a friend."

"It doesn't take long to make friends, Dr. Rodene, nor *enemies* either," I retorted, my glaring expression including him in the last category.

He flinched as if the barb had gone home. "I'm

sorry, Brianna. I apologize for my behavior yesterday afternoon. And I fear I'm getting off on the wrong foot today." He actually smiled at me, and for a moment his gray-green eyes deepened like shiny rocks under water.

He wanted something. Yesterday he had tried the autocratic approach, today it was going to be something different. I stiffened against the persuasive charm of his smile. It would be easy to lose one's perspective when his expression and eyes softened like that, I thought. "If you will excuse me, I must get back to Cassie," I said briskly.

"She's fine. Lying placidly on her bed when I was up there. That woman, Domincea, didn't know where you had gone. I checked the dining rooms, went over to the Alcazar, and was searching the grounds when I saw you returning with your . . . friend."

"He *is* a friend," I snapped. "Jack Harvey, a resident artist. He showed me some of St. Augustine and I had a lovely time." I didn't know why I was defending myself to this arrogant man. It made me angry that I was accounting for my time as if he had some kind of jurisdiction over me. "I must get back and relieve Domincea. My time is almost up."

"I told her that you would be taking an extra hour." He took my arm in a proprietory manner. "What I have to say to you is important. We'll have tea in the dining room while I explain."

"Oh, I couldn't. I'm not dressed properly."

"Take off that horrid scarf and smooth your hair. Your gown is perfectly presentable. You'd like to have tea in the main dining room, wouldn't you?"

My hands nervously smoothed the yellow dimity of my full skirt and I picked at the lace trimming around the modest neckline. It was nothing like the gowns I had seen parading through the hotel.

"Relax." He gave me a smile that was tinged with amusement. "The simplicity of your dress mocks the elaborate trappings of other women who strive for the grace of your figure, Brianna, and your natural beauty."

The compliment befuddled me for a moment. I forgot that he was after something and I couldn't find an easy retort. I stammered, "But everyone else will be wearing a hat . . . and mine got squashed on the train."

He ignored my protests as he guided me firmly through the center courtyard, up the front steps and through the arched entrance of the hotel. We were going in the front door! I gulped back a sudden urge to flee around to the back entrance. I didn't belong here, and I knew it.

Unperturbed, Gavin led me across the rotunda to a wide, impressive span of marble steps which led to the main dining room. Despite my efforts to act unimpressed, my eyes widened with disbelief as we stood at the entrance of the magnificent hall.

The formal dining room was as large as some opera houses. Pillars of antique oak supported a vaulting ceiling lavishly decorated with designs of the sixteenth century. At each end of the oval-shaped room, bay windows of stained glass added prisms of light to the illumination provided by shimmering crystal chandeliers.

A maitre d' nodded to Gavin and seated us at a small table overlooking a grove of orange trees outside the west windows. The Spanish Renaissance spirit was carried out in baroque high-backed chairs and heavily sculpted tables. The stained glass windows spread color upon white damask tablecloths and napery, and splashes of rainbow hues were reflected in gleaming silver and hand-painted porcelain.

I did not hear the order Gavin gave to two hovering waiters in formal attire who appeared instantly at his side. My senses were bombarded with the lavish detail evident in everything from the monogrammed linens to the frescoes upon the ceiling. "It's lovely," I breathed in the kind of awed whisper one might use in a cathedral.

Because of its mammoth proportions, the dining hall appeared almost empty at this late afternoon hour. I brushed aside the knowledge that I should have been wearing a hat, spotless white gloves, and an afternoon gown appropriate for tea with a gentleman. I was here and that was a miracle in itself, so I gave myself up to enjoying every minute of it.

Gavin seemed amused as he watched my eyes dart about, taking in every nuance of the elegant room. Sweet strains of violins playing a romantic Strauss waltz floated down from one of the galleries above the room. "Shall we dance?" he asked facetiously.

"But of course. After we've had our tea," I answered in a falsetto voice, and then laughed from the excitement of it all.

"Now, aren't you glad I insisted?"

"Yes," I answered honestly.

For a moment our eyes met and held. Something happened to my breathing. His eyes were a soft caress and I felt a bewildering warmth seeping through me. Time was caught in a suspended moment. It was all I could do to look away from him and give a feeble smile to a waiter who at that moment had arrived with a silver tea service on a cart and several trays of delicate French pastries.

"I hope you see something that pleases you." Gavin's lips curved in an amused grin as the waiter waited for my selection. He seemed to delight in watching me.

Nervously, I chose two small cream puffs filled with chocolate mousse. Gavin chose hot mincemeat pie with a froth of whipped cream swirled like a snow drift on top. "I've been out at the school all day. Missed lunch completely." He sighed. "There is so much to do and so little time."

"What are you doing at the school?"

For a moment he hesitated as if judging whether or not my interest was sincere. "Setting up an adequate testing program for deaf children. Often a deaf child is considered mentally deficient just because he or she lacks language and attention skills. These children are then treated as if they're mentally retarded. Such a waste. In Europe, diagnostic techniques are more advanced. I learned much when I was over there."

I asked him questions about his recent studies abroad. The exchange was like those I used to enjoy with my father when he was engaged in some academic or intellectual pursuit. I realized then how barren the last three years had been. I had been isolated, almost as much a prisoner at Gray Oaks as he had been. My own intellectual activity had ceased with my father's and I had suffered a sterile existence for the years that he had been ill.

"Do you think you would like working with the kind of children I've been talking about? Helping them learn?" he surprised me by asking.

I know I looked blank. "I'm not trained for such a responsibility."

"That didn't keep you from accepting your present position."

I stiffened. Suddenly the pleasing rapport between us was gone. I had known from the beginning that there was a purpose in his invitation. If he couldn't control me one way, he would try another. The atmosphere and congenial conversation had been only a front, and I had almost been fooled. Yesterday he had tried the arrogant, demanding professional approach. Now it was a deceptively gentle, caring tone.

"I've talked to Helen Matley, the director of the school, about interviewing you," he said. "She's a friend of mine."

I recalled the feminine voice coming from the

buggy at the depot. The memory made me stiffen. Vance had insinuated that Dr. Rodene had found someone to take his mind off Lynette Talbot. How many women did he need under his control? "That's kind of you . . . and of her . . . but I've never wanted to be a teacher. My father was always a little disappointed that following in his footsteps never held any charm for me. And since I have no brothers or sisters, I have never been around children."

"Then you really don't know whether you would like it or not. You haven't had any experience by which to judge the matter."

"I know that I would feel inadequate working with normal children, let alone those with special needs. I appreciate your interest but . . ." my voice trailed off.

He laid his napkin on the table in an impatient gesture. "Your attitude is exasperating, Brianna. You won't accept financial help. I offer you a chance at different employment so that you can get out of a dangerous situation and you politely say no, thank you. You haven't given the matter any thought! How can you turn aside a perfectly acceptable solution? I've been honest with you about the dangers you're courting by staying with Cassie Danzel. Haven't I made myself clear? You're walking on the dark edge of disaster." His hands tightened as if he'd like to wring my neck. His tone was almost threatening. "Of all the stubborn fools, you take the prize!"

"Thank you, Dr. Rodene, for your kind words," I said stiffly, bristling at his tone. How dare he try to get me to accept a position under a woman who was in all probability his paramour? "I find your manner insulting and presumptuous. You have no right to tell me what I should and should not do."

"Someone has to!"

"I appreciate your concern, but I intend to make my own decisions. Now, if you will excuse me, I must get back to my duties." I rose to my feet, blinking rapidly against a fullness threatening to spill into my eyes.

Without waiting for him to escort me, I walked haughtily across the dining hall and was going down the bottom step of the wide marble stairway leading into the rotunda when he caught up with me. "Brianna, wait . . ."

At that moment someone called his name. "Gavin! Gavin, darling."

I followed his startled gaze. A pretty blonde woman stood at the registration desk. She waved gaily. With a lilting laugh, she swept across the marble floor toward him, a soft pink gown of flounces and satin trim flowing around her. Her bowed mouth curved in a smile that matched the sparkle to her sky blue eyes. A small hat dipped over one eye and gave a view of silken golden curls that bobbed as she walked.

"Lynette!"

"Surprise, darling!" Her voice was soft and musical. She leaned up and possessively kissed him on the cheek.

"When . . . when did you get here?"

"Just now. I decided there was no reason you couldn't combine business with pleasure." She looped her arm through his. "I'm so glad you were here to meet me. What a lovely surprise. Come and help me get my things collected." She laughed again at his astounded expression as she drew him away. He gave me a quick, apologetic look over his shoulder.

I stared at their retreating backs. Lynette Talbot. His fiancée. I swung around and came face to face with Amelia Dorcas who suddenly was standing right behind me.

The woman's smirking expression was all-knowing. She hadn't missed anything of the dramatic little scene. Apparently, her bright eyes had been picking out the new arrivals, hoping to collect bits of gossip here and there. From her expression I knew the appearance of Lynette Talbot had been an unexpected morsel. Amelia's smile was almost juicy.

"I didn't think Lynette would let him get away," she said in a whisper. "They've been matched since they were youngsters." She put her claw-like hand on my arm. "And she's been wearing his ring for over a year now." Her beady eyes gleamed. "I'm betting St. Augustine will see a fashionable wedding before the season's over." Her gaze slid maliciously over my hatless head and modest frock. "These men," she sighed sympathetically. "Always bent on amusing themselves, aren't they?"

Her rasping chuckle echoed in my ears as I fled to the servants' stairway and climbed the five floors to the tower suite.

Chapter Five

As I made the vigorous climb, my thoughts centered on the pretty, affectionate young woman who had greeted Gavin so possessively. Lynette Talbot was nothing like the woman I had imagined. Her cupid-bow mouth, fresh, almost translucent complexion, and round sky blue eyes were an artist's dream. And she had the kind of petite, rounded body that was depicted in fashionable magazines like *The Delineator* and *Godey's Lady's Book.* Lynette's lovely fair coloring was a sharp contrast to my dark hair and almost black crescent eyebrows, which now seemed utterly and totally unattractive. At the moment, I wanted to be anything but what I was, a twenty-three-year-old spinster attracted to a man engaged to someone else.

Even though I had known from the first day I met Gavin Rodene that Lynette Talbot existed, I had chosen to think of her as some high-nosed New York socialite who somehow had temporarily snared the doctor's attention. Now I knew that was not true. Gavin Rodene cared for his fiancée. It was evident in the gentle way he accepted her kiss on his cheek and the meek way he allowed her to take command of his attentions. Darn him . . . darn him . . . darn him, I swore. Even though I detested Gavin Rodene's high-handed autocratic attitude and was half-afraid of him, the moments I spent with him were charged with excitement and a bewildering swirl of emotions.

When I reached the tower suite and opened the hall door, I found Vance Danzel waiting for me. He was not smiling. With uncharacteristic briskness, he dismissed Domincea and then took out his gold pocket watch. He looked at it pointedly. "Domincea tells me you've been gone since two o'clock." His manner was stiff and his usual easy smile was absent from his handsome face.

"Yes, I . . . I'm sorry." I was still breathing heavily from my flight up the stairs. I took a quick intake of air and tried to collect my fragmented emotions. "I was . . . delayed."

"Domincea told me that Dr. Rodene was here earlier looking for you." Then Vance seemed to notice my distraught expression. "Is something wrong, Brianna?"

I forced a smile to my lips. "No, not at all. I'm afraid I allowed Dr. Rodene to persuade me to have tea. I am sorry . . ."

"Tea?"

"Yes, in the dining room," I said with a slightly arrogant toss of my head. I remembered that Vance had told me about the employees' dining halls.

"I hope that this isn't going to become a problem. I didn't realize that you and Dr. Rodene were on such . . . social terms."

"We aren't!" I said quickly. "And it won't happen again. His fiancée just arrived."

"Lynette Talbot?" A suppressed eagerness in Vance's voice surprised me "She's here . . . at the Ponce?"

I nodded. "She just checked in."

"Well, well. It will be pleasant to renew our acquaintance. She was always such a pretty thing. Well, now." As if the news had restored Vance's good humor, he gave me his people-management smile. "Dr.

Vonfeldt sent up some new medication for my sister. Domincea gave Cassie one dose and another is due at bedtime. Tomorrow Dr. Vonfeldt would like to start some therapeutic treatments. He thinks that by then Cassie should be alert enough to walk across the street."

I swallowed. "You think I can handle her by myself?"

"Oh, I think so, but I'll accompany you the first time, if you wish."

"Yes, thank you. I think that would be best." I had no idea how Cassie would react to the new medicine. Just the thought of managing her outside these rooms was frightening.

"Fine. I'll see you tomorrow then. Once the daily routine is set, it will be better for everyone. I'm sorry if I was a bit abrupt with you a moment ago, Brianna. I want you to enjoy yourself as much as possible but your first consideration is Cassie, of course."

"I understand and I apologize again for my tardiness."

"If you feel uncomfortable about any of the arrangements, please come to *me* and not anyone else. This is really a family affair . . . and you are one of the family now, Brianna. The less information outsiders like Gavin Rodene have, the better for all of us. I would prefer that you not talk to him about our private matters. Agreed?"

I nodded. "It was *not* at my request that Dr. Rodene spoke to you in the first place."

"I understand. A lovely young woman like you arouses protective urges in all of us. I am not immune myself. And I will share the responsibility of Cassie's care as much as possible." His smile matched a glint in his eyes which bordered on the flirtatious. He twirled his hat in his hands like a little boy who wants to make a confession but is afraid to reveal his thoughts. He must have decided against speaking. "See you tomorrow, then . . . about ten o'clock?"

"We'll be ready. I appreciate your confidence in me." And, I added silently, you are not like Gavin Rodene, who makes me feel completely inadequate. "I'm certain I can handle Cassie," I said as much to myself as to Vance. It was Gavin who was undermining my confidence with his dire predictions, making me fear that some tragedy was waiting in the wings.

"And I'm certain you can," assured Vance. His departing smile was the kind to turn a woman's heart upside down, but its sensuous overtones were lost on me.

I closed the door after him, then leaned up against it and pressed my hands against the panels. It was time to come to terms with reality. Those tender moments in the dining room with Gavin had instilled an excitement in me that refused to dissipate—even when I knew they represented self-torture by my clinging to them. I could not forget the crazy, wonderful, heart-stopping excitement when our eyes had locked in that wordless contact.

I walked over to a chair and sat down, putting my head in my hands. The scene in the lobby came back to me, bringing a peculiar pain under my rib cage. *It doesn't matter, it doesn't have anything to do with me.* The holier-than-thou Dr. Rodene had called me a fool and, oh, how right he was. I reached out for anger to replace the sickening emptiness I felt. I *was* a fool! From the very moment I had opened my blurred eyes and saw his lips wavering seductively close to mine, I had allowed myself to become entangled in his spell. How many women did he need to dominate? Lynette Talbot and the sweet-voiced Helen Matley were only two that I knew about, but there were probably others. I had almost allowed myself to accept the physical attraction between us that pulverized my will. A promise was there in his eyes that never would be fulfilled. At least the arrival of his fiancée had brought some sanity back into my behavior. Now, more than ever, I vowed not be manipulated by him. He claimed that he had my welfare at heart, but there was much more to his insistence that I leave my position as companion to Cassie—if only I knew what it was!

For some stupid reason, tears eased down my cheeks. I brushed them away angrily. I had promised Vance that I wouldn't talk about Cassie outside the circle of the family and I intended to keep that promise. Not that the handsome Dr. Rodene would have any time to issue invitations to tea or make solicitous visits to the fifth floor to see how I am doing, I reminded myself. He had professional duties to discharge and a beautiful fiancée to squire around St. Augustine.

What if I had accepted his offer to be interviewed by Helen Matley for a job at the school? And what if his sweet-voiced lady friend had hired me? Then I would have been obligated to him. What a tortuous position that would have been, enduring a sudden swell of desire every time he touched me, agonizing over his attentions to his fiancée, Helen Matley, and others. No, it was better that I carry out the duties I had accepted and put Gavin Rodene, M.D. out of my mind! If he tried to communicate with me, I would simply cut off all contact between us.

Having affirmed this decision, I went about my duties in a mechanical, regimented way. All that evening, Cassie remained docile but less lethargic. She had stopped her guttural whimpering and in some ways her muted silence was more distracting. I had the uneasy feeling that somewhere in that silent frame lay a cunning animal ready to spring. Her half-lidded eyes were deceptive. There was more tone in her muscles now, and she held her head straight.

That evening when Cassie opened her mouth for

the food I was spooning into it, her heavy eyelids lifted and she stared directly into my face. As always, the direct eye contact was a jolt, and I smothered a gasp. Cassie's brown eyes were a deep, empty abyss with no sign of life flickering there. They lowered as quickly as they had opened.

My hand trembled as I set down the spoon. My mouth was suddenly dry. "You did well with your dinner tonight, Cassie," I said in what I hoped was a steady voice. "Now we'll get you ready for bed. We have a busy day tomorrow. Your brother is going to take us for a walk. Won't that be nice? And then, when you feel like it, we'll take some strolls in the garden. They're lovely . . ." I kept up the monologue as I settled Cassie in bed. "This medicine is going to be much better for you. You won't sleep all the time."

Cassie lay still in bed, not responding in any way, and yet I felt that she was not oblivious to what was going on. Impulsively, I squeezed the thin, emaciated shoulders, so small and slight under her white night-dress, and even placed a kiss on her forehead. I smoothed back a fringe of hair that had escaped from her night cap. "Sleep well, Cassie. Remember, you're not alone. I'll be in the next room."

There was still no response from the huddled figure. I sighed, turned out the light and went out, leaving the door slightly ajar. The rest of the evening, I tried to work on needlepoint which I had started while sitting with my father at Gray Oaks, but I found myself just staring at it as it rested in my lap. It was a picture of two flying ducks and I had almost worked all the feathers on the two birds. I had never really enjoyed needlework but it had given me something to do while I sat at my father's bedside. Now I looked at the half-finished ducks and realized how much I hated the hand work and everything it stood for. I had been wrong to bring it with me.

Very deliberately I gathered up my yarn, needle,

and the unfinished needlepoint and dumped the whole thing into a wastepaper basket. Let one of the hotel maids fish it out if she wanted to save it, I was done with it. It was a foolish gesture but somehow it stiffened my resolve to take charge of my future and let the past go.

I was restless. It had begun to rain so I couldn't go out on the balcony. The uncomfortable feeling I always experienced in the oppressive sitting room seemed especially heightened. I felt a disturbing pricking at the nape of my neck that made me turn quickly to see if someone stood behind the chair watching me. Then I chided my foolishness. I was alone. No ghosts, no intruders. Darn Ira Deitz! He had filled my ears with tales of the woman who had gone mad here. Liz Chantilly. I wished I did not know her name. Now she seemed real and it was easy to believe that perhaps her tortured spirit remained in these rooms. I gave myself a mental shake. Stop it! You're too sensible to give in to such imaginings.

I undressed and put on a soft, cambric gown and then brushed my hair vigorously. The long tresses reached halfway down my back. As I held my head down, rich, deep strands like polished wood fell over my face in a shiny cascade. I brushed my hair until it glistened and snapped, and then I braided it in one plait down my back. I delighted in the daily fresh linens of the sweet smelling bed and wondered if I would ever get used to the efficient housekeeping services of the hotel. I turned off the light and then lay stiff with my eyes wide open.

I had slightly opened a window and I could hear faint laughter like the soft tingling of a distant bell coming from the garden below. The sound was a cue to loneliness. The huge hotel palace was filled with people and activity and yet none of it touched me. I was isolated, alone. Tears threatened to overflow the corners of my eyes. I could not lie to myself. I wanted to be downstairs, in the magnificent dining room or elegant parlor, or out in the gardens. I was too healthy and vibrant to be shut off from everything like a pariah. My young body mocked the spinster life I had accepted for myself. I tried to keep my thoughts away from Dr. Rodene but failed. I tortured myself with speculation about where he and Lynette might be this evening. Dressed formally for dinner, I mused, or perhaps sitting at the same table I had shared with him in the afternoon. The possibility hurt more than I wanted to acknowledge.

I closed my eyes and let my imagination have its way. What would it be like to be with him, to belong by his side, to savor his smiles and his loving touch? My body tingled as I imagined myself in his arms. My sworn admonitions to forget him mocked the rising longing in my body. If he were here now, in bed beside me, what would I do? Lost in the fantasy, I let the dream develop. He would kiss me with the same intensity he brought to everything else. He had touched only my hand, but that contact had sent my emotions reeling. As I dreamed, half-awake, half-asleep, his face formed before me. His eyes softened in passion; he smiled gently at me and his hand traced the soft contours of my body. I was afraid. I had never known a man's touch but I could feel a spiraling heat surging through me. We would be lovers. Lovers. The word lingered in my mind—then I awoke in terror.

A hand on my face! The fright was paralyzing. I couldn't move. My frantic gaze took in a shadowy form bending over me. Screams choked in my chest. Cassie with a knife? A bloody hatchet? Was I having that horrible nightmare again? I knew I wasn't: the heavy breathing was no illusion. The hand touching my face was real as it covered my mouth and claw-like fingers bit into my cheek. Cassie! The girl stood there like a statue, silhouetted against the moonlight.

I waited, not daring to breathe. What was she doing? For an eternity Cassie'a hand remained pressed against my mouth and cheek. I knew that any sudden movement on my part might precipitate an attack from the motionless girl. If those fingers closed down upon my throat—!

"Cassie?" I whispered through the fingers splayed over my mouth. "Cassie?"

Her slender hand began moving upward, going over my face like a blind person feeling my features.

"What is it, Cassie?" My heart thumped loudly and my breath was short.

Cassie did not answer. As quietly as she had come, she took her hand away from my face and drifted out of the room like a shadow. By the time I had grabbed my wrapper and followed her, Cassie was back in bed, curled up in the usual fetal position as if she had never left her room.

I was shaking so badly that I hugged myself to keep from falling apart. Being jerked out of sleep by feeling a hand on my face had nearly paralyzed me. I couldn't understand what had happened. What had driven Cassie to my bed? Why did the disturbed girl seem to be reassuring herself that I was flesh and blood?

I sat down in a chair beside her bed. The fright Cassie had given me had wiped out all semblance of sleep. I felt helpless and frustrated. What was happening inside that irrational mind of Cassie's? Was it possible that she had killed her little brother and thrown him out the window?

My confidence was being sorely tested, I admitted to myself, and my dogged determination not to heed Dr. Rodene's warning began to weaken. Even though I was more than a match for Cassie physically, the girl could have attacked me while I was sleeping. For the first time I gave some credence to the idea that my own life might be in danger.

I dozed only fitfully the rest of the night. Dark shadows tinted my cheeks when I dressed the next morning and I knew that nerves made the muscles around my eyes and mouth taut. Even my usual one-sided chatter was strained. I didn't know what to expect of Cassie as I anxiously kept to the morning routine. Even though Cassie accepted eating and being dressed in her usual docile manner, I could sense a change behind those half-closed lids.

I administered the medicine Dr. Vonfeldt had sent. It smelled different and I knew that it didn't contain laudanum. I could tell that it was not a sedative, for Cassie no longer moved with the heavy, slow motion of a drugged person. Several times I was startled by a flicker of sharp movement, as if Cassie were being directed by some inner command.

I was relieved when Vance arrived, as he had promised, to walk with us over to the Alcazar and the attached building called the Casino. I told him about the incident in the middle of the night with Cassie. He didn't seem to find it disturbing—but he wasn't the one jerked out of a deep slumber with a human hand on his face, I thought testily. "Why do you think she did that?"

Vance smile reassuringly. "I guess Cassie was trying to reassure herself that you are real." His eyes traveled appreciatively over the pink moiré dress I had chosen to wear. "I wouldn't mind reassuring myself of that . . ."

His flirtatious manner irritated me. I was tired and worried, and needed reassurance that the change in Cassie's behavior was expected. He dismissed all my questions with an amused wave of his hand. "Don't look so worried, Brianna. Of course, Cassie is improving. That was the idea behind bringing her here. She's ready to enjoy herself, aren't you, honey?" He slipped his arm through his sister's but Cassie did not look up at him or give any indication that she was aware of his presence. "Now, let's be on our way. It's a lovely morning for a walk."

We took the elevator down and I was too upset even to send Ira Deitz a gloating look. My spirits didn't begin to lift until we were outside the hotel. The beautiful morning was balm to my shredded nerves. I breathed deeply. A crisp freshness in the air floated in cool breezes off the water. Perhaps Vance was right. Perhaps I had over-reacted, been put too much on my guard now that Cassie had shown some independent action. I decided to accept Vance's confident reassurances. After all, he knew his sister's condition better than anyone.

Vance was an entertaining, charming escort. He described all the wonderful facilities that Henry Flagler had provided for his guests in the Alcazar Hotel and the attached Casino. The Alcazar was not as grand as the Ponce de Leon, I saw. Vance said that Flagler had built this second hotel to provide accommodations for less affluent visitors to St. Augustine. The Alcazar followed the same general architectural design as the more prestigious Ponce de Leon, and though it was more modest, this hotel was still resplendent. It had towers, pavilions, and arcades, and was trimmed with the same red brick patterns and red Spanish roof tiles. Fountains sprayed glittering streams of water into the air and walking paths wandered through lush gardens laid out in elaborate patterns.

I saw that the Casino was joined to the Alcazar, making the two seem like one building. Vance explained that all the health facilities were located in it, as well as a grand ballroom, bowling alley, a magnificent swimming pool, game rooms, and gymnasium. As we climbed a curved staircase and entered the Casino, my appreciative gaze followed tall, fluted columns upward to the wide graceful arches that made the interior dramatic.

I was startled to find myself on a balcony looking down upon an immense swimming pool, a giant marble basin filled with translucent green water. Eight arches rose from the floor of the pool giving the massive structure an effect of great strength and beauty. A vaulting glass roof spanned the enormous heated pool and allowed sunlight to make sculptured patterns on the mirrored water.

"It's unbelievable," I breathed.

"Some one hundred feet long and fifty-six feet wide," Vance told me. "Six feet deep at the east end and slanted to about four feet at this end." He grinned. "It's fashionable to go bathing at high noon, so my sister says."

I smothered a smile. Lady Edwina dressed in bathing attire would be something to see—long stockings, bloomers to the knees, long sleeves, high neck, and a balloon cap over her hair.

"Perhaps you and Cassie can join her some day soon," he suggested.

"I don't swim well enough for that," I said quickly, my silent mirth dissipating. Cassie in that huge expanse of water? A cold shiver went up my spine.

"Oh well, Cassie will probably enjoy the Turkish baths more, anyway. Come, we don't want to keep Dr. Vonfeldt waiting." Vance ushered us away from the pool and led us into a waiting room that featured the same grand architecture, with high arched doorways, thick carpets, and gold-trimmed ivory-colored walls.

A receptionist sat sedately behind a small French provincial desk. Very prim and straight, she wore a black dress relieved only by a small white lace collar and jet black buttons which sparkled on her rather expansive bosom. When Vance gave her Cassie's name, she glanced at her appointment book with a slight flaring of her nostrils and then lightly touched a desk bell.

I was startled when Domincea instantly appeared; I

had forgotten that this was where she worked.

"I'll amuse myself in the billiard room for an hour," said Vance. "And then walk you ladies back to the hotel." He gave me an encouraging smile. "I know Dr. Vonfeldt's treatments are going to do wonders for Cassie in no time at all."

It seemed to me that Cassie's withdrawn behavior was at odds with such encouraging remarks.

"Come this way," directed Domincea.

As we walked down a marbled hall, I glimpsed signs reading "Steam Room," "Cold Plunge," "Turkish Baths," "Electro-Therapy Room." I heard the high-pitched squeal of someone who must have found the water unexpectedly cold.

Domincea led us into a dressing room which had been tastefully decorated *a la femme*. Gilded mirrors, dainty dressing tables, velvet chaise longues, and silk screens were provided for milady's toiletries. While I sat and waited in one of the pink plush chairs, Domincea took Cassie behind a screen and changed her clothes, dressing her in a simple white Grecian gown. I wanted to ask all kinds of questions about what was going to happen but the woman's immutable expression did not invite conversation. Curious, I let my gaze scan the walls of the room.

A poster of a beautiful, dark-haired nude woman lounging in a marble hip-tub held the caption, "Ladies retain perfect physical beauty and abundant health through the use of cold and hot Turkish Baths." I decided it should have read "Rich ladies." The charge for a bath was about what the hotel employees earned in one day.

I read a framed message from Professor Erasmus Wilson, Royal College of Surgeons, London. It extolled the virtues of hot and cold baths for both men and women, as a means of bestowing health and alleviating disease. He recommended such baths for curing kidney, heart, blood, Bright's disease, diabetes, chronic indigestion, and insomnia.

But what about a deranged girl who has lost touch with reality? I was suddenly frightened for Cassie. A dark presentiment was like the warning rush of bat wings in my ears. I wanted to take the white-robed figure and run out of the building. It was all I could do to stifle my melodramatic urges.

Domincea led us down a hall where heavy moist air held the faint acidic smell of sulphur and rubbing alcohol. I could hear the release of steam and the sound of running water. Muted voices reached my ears.

The health facilities were extensive: small sunken marble pools with built-in benches under the water for hot and cold plunge baths, sitz tubs, metal showers, vapor cabinets, lounging rooms, and a gymnasium. The halls and rooms had been built with high ceilings and were heavily decorated with elaborate moldings. The marble floors were softened with huge, imported rugs. Wide arches and thick pillars framed balconies circling airy rooms where people could retire after their various activities. The Spanish Renaissance architecture was harmonious with the impression of a palace where leisure was king. I had never imagined anything like it, and I could not help but be impressed with the luxurious surroundings as I followed Domincea and Cassie into Dr. Vonfeldt's office.

"Good day, ladies." His white teeth flashed.

I was surprised to find his office quite modest. My expression must have been readable for he quickly explained, "We are in the midst of remodeling. My office is not quite ready so we must make do . . ." His white hands made an apologetic gesture. A dark, shiny wave of hair rose above his broad forehead and his white attire dramatized his well-conditioned figure.

I suspected that females of all ages might find him

physically attractive but I couldn't imagine letting him touch me for any reason. I resented his way of undressing me with his black eyes, and his smile was almost moist. I felt myself stiffening.

"The facilities were not adequate for handling all the new electro-therapy equipment," he explained as if wanting to impress me. "In the year that I have been here, I have doubled the number of services. My predecessor was content to offer only the traditional baths, but I see St. Augustine becoming the health capital of the world."

With himself as the emperor! The expectation was unspoken but evident in his stance and imperious bearing.

"And how are we today?" He reached out and lifted Cassie's chin so he could look into her face. Those lidded eyes closed even more as if deliberately shutting out his gaze. "Taking our medicine regularly, are we?" He looked questioningly at me with a patronizing tone that I hated.

"Exactly as you prescribed, doctor," I answered crisply.

"Good. We'll be seeing a big difference in her."

"She was up . . . in the middle of the night and came into my room. I woke with her hand feeling my face." I tried to give the information in a matter-of-fact tone but the residue of fright remained. I couldn't forget the terror of finding the figure bent over my bed, the panic that had blended with my earlier nightmare of Cassie attacking me with a hatchet.

"I see. Did she say anything?"

"No. I asked her what she wanted but she didn't answer."

"Well, I'd say we're making some progress." He beamed. "She certainly is handling herself much better."

"But I'm concerned that she may try to do something . . . irrational."

"It's your job, Miss Anderson, to see that she doesn't harm herself."

"But they kept her heavily sedated at Gray Oaks . . ."

"And that's why her brother brought her to me. He wants her to resume normal activity. The first step is to allow her mental faculties to operate without drugs. The daily treatments we provide will restore her physical health, increase her appetite, and make her stronger." He predicted a robust, healthy young woman in a matter of a few weeks.

"And her mental health?"

"We will begin our electro-therapy today. We are using one of the bathing rooms to accommodate our new equipment until a special room can be designed." He led us into a nearby room which still held pipes, hoses, and water spigots, though the steam cabinets had been removed. It was empty of furniture except for two strange looking cabinets, the length of a human body. Electric light bulbs covered the curved roof of the enclosed bed. There was just enough space for a body to lie straight without touching the yellow bulbs. A head rest was provided outside the box. It made the contraption look like an electrified coffin with one end open.

I had heard about innovative uses of electric light since Thomas Edison's invention only two years earlier, but I had never imagined anything like this. Could an electric bath really help physical and mental disorders? I wanted to talk with Gavin Rodene about it and then promptly brushed aside the thought. He had already aroused my suspicion about everything connected with Cassie Danzel.

"Ozonizing light beams into the tissues of the body," explained Dr. Vonfeldt. "Its effects are extremely agreeable to patients and efficacious in many stubborn cases which do not readily respond to other remedies. These electric light baths are particularly recommended for gout, rheumatism, and heart disease—and, in Cassie's case, neurasthenia."

"Neurasthenia?" I echoed. That was a currently popular, broad term used with nervous people, usually women suffering from vapors. Did Dr. Vonfeldt really classify Cassie as suffering from a mild case of nerves? Once more I felt deep fear as I watched Domincea install Cassie in the cabinet.

The girl lay there passively. Then, with a quick flip of his white hands, the doctor turned on switches and all the lights inside the cabinet came on.

Instantly, the most horrible scream came tearing out of Cassie's chest. She threw up her arms to try and cover her face from the sudden outpouring of light from the yellow bulbs.

I bolted to her side but the doctor shoved me out of the way. "Stay back. She's perfectly all right! There's absolutely no sensation of any kind from the lights. Only a slight warmth."

"But she doesn't like it! Take her out. She's terrified!"

"I am in charge here. Please wait outside, Miss Anderson." His eyes were points of anger.

"I want to stay!"

"Domincea, hand me the straps. Show this lady to the reception room."

There was no way for me to resist Domincea's bull-like strength. The woman propelled me down the hall, through an arched doorway, and back into the carpeted waiting room. She shoved me toward a chair in a corner, beside a potted tropical plant. "You wait here." Then she turned her broad back on me and disappeared down the hall.

For a moment I considered following her back to the treatment room, but I knew any protest would be useless. Vance had put his sister under Dr. Vonfeldt's care. There was nothing I could do. I clenched my fists and tried to get my anger under control. As I sat there, the large fluted leaves of the plant half-hid me from the parade of people coming and going. I tried to blot out the scene I had just left. I wanted to believe Vonfeldt—but had he been telling the truth? Was the cabinet nothing more than a warm, dry bath? If so, how could it cure anything except perhaps a mild case of nerves? Surely he didn't expect a benign light bath to do anything for such a deranged mind as Cassie's? Who knew what dragons Cassie was fighting in the dark recess of her torment?

I could not still my anxiousness about what was happening to her. Vonfeldt had strapped her down. Was she still screaming? When he had turned the lights on, she had shrieked as if someone were tearing her limb from limb. It must have been the sudden flash of light that bothered her, I thought. I had already discovered that Cassie was less agitated in a darkened room.

What shall I do, I asked myself, not content to accept the obvious fact that I needn't take responsibility for what happened to Cassie under a doctor's supervision. I doubted that it would do any good to take my concerns to Vance. Any charges that I might make accusing the German doctor of being a charlatan would be instantly dismissed as my own personal prejudice. Who was I to question his credentials? I had been hired to see that his orders were carried out. No, I was in no position to question the treatment given Cassie. Maybe heavy sedation wasn't the answer. Maybe improving her physical well-being would put her in touch with reality—but I doubted it!

My whirling thoughts were broken when Lady Edwina and Amelia Dorcas swept into the reception room. As always, Lady Edwina's bulk was startling. She must weigh two hundred pounds, I thought. Undoubtedly baths and exercise would be good for her.

Both women wore elaborate day dresses decorated

with a profusion of silk flowers and edged with satin and velvet ribbons. They wore the latest fashion in wide brimmed hats, heavy with veils and feathers. Their expressions were those of the pampered rich, their interest turned inward. They were so engrossed in their own conversation that they did not see me sitting in the corner.

"Have you told Vance that you are not going to indulge him any longer?" asked Amelia in her raspy voice. "It seems to me that you have been more than patient with him."

"Well, my patience is at an end, believe me. He had best find himself a rich wife and soon! Vance's ability to hold on to money is like that of a sieve."

"But your investments in England? Are you still sinking money into your husband's family estate? The returns on that have been disappointing, haven't they?"

"Like money sucked into a bottomless hole. You know how the English are, holding on to some old house as if it was worth all the expensive upkeep. That's why we're here and not abroad. I told Sir William that he would have to forgo the Riviera this year. And Vance had no choice but to come along with us so Cassie could pay the bills for all of this."

"You two are just like your mother," simpered Amelia. "She couldn't hold on to money, either. If Cassie were well, I bet her trust fund would be gone too."

"Well, it isn't. She hardly uses up the interest. It's really not fair. Daddy should have given me the power of attorney over her affairs instead of that old, tight-fisted lawyer. Vance is trying to get the will changed so he can handle her money, but so far he hasn't been able to. I'm the oldest, and with a better business head than he'll ever have. I should be the one handling Cassie's money."

"What if she gets well?"

"She won't." Lady Edwina's lips were set in a hard line.

"How do you know? Maybe Dr. Vonfeldt will work a miraculous cure."

Lady Edwina's heartless scoff chilled my blood. "Don't be a fool. Our poor little Cassie will *never* get well, you can depend on it!"

Chapter Six

The two women disappeared down the marble hall in the wake of an attendant. Almost immediately I was put under further duress by the arrival of Lynette Talbot and Gavin Rodene.

"You will wait, won't you darling?" Lynette pleaded as her small, rounded figure leaned seductively towards Gavin. Her forehead was slightly furrowed and her eyes anxious. "I just couldn't put off Dr. Vonfeldt last night. He insisted that I visit the baths this morning." Her laugh was a soft twitter. "Foolish man, promising me that the fountain of youth was his personal domain. My curiosity got the best of me, I'm afraid. You're such a darling to give up a morning's work for me. I promise to let you abandon me this afternoon and get back to your precious school. Last night was so wonderful I want to hang onto it. I really can't believe I'm here . . . with you. I'm not dreaming, am I?"

"No." He smiled patiently. "Now hurry a long. I'll wait for you." He guided Lynette over to the desk and gave her name to the receptionist.

"Ah, yes, Dr. Vonfeldt made the appointment himself." The woman's scrutinizing eyes appraised Lynette as she briskly tapped her bell to summon a female attendant.

In another moment Lynette was gone, having given her fiancé a warm, parting smile.

I drew back behind the potted plant so Gavin wouldn't see me. The conversation, laced with intimacy I had overheard, had brought an empty ache into my chest. My heart had quickened the moment I caught sight of his bold, strong figure and heard his voice. I didn't want him to see me. I was conscious of my simple moiré dress, with its narrow edging of ecru lace trimming a modest neckline. My head was bare except for a wide velvet bow I had placed on top of my hair in lieu of a hat. In this place of luxury I felt like a colorless wren, ugly and plain, and when Gavin walked directly over to where I sat and looked down at me, I gasped, "I didn't think you saw me."

"I have extrasensory perception where you're concerned, Brianna Anderson. I have to talk with you. Let's take a walk around the balcony."

My refusal was immediate but before I could voice it, he said, "Please. I know there's no reason for you even to be polite to me, but I have to explain. Please give me that chance." He was not the arrogant, commanding Dr. Rodene this morning.

I knew I was a fool but I rose to my feet.

"Thank you." He put a guiding hand on my elbow and tingling warmth spread under his touch. I could feel his thigh slightly brushing my full skirts as we left the waiting room and began walking around the broad balcony circling the pool. Other couples were taking the same walk and several hotel guests were at the railing, looking down at swimmers cutting the mirrored water with clean, crisp strokes.

My quick glance at Gavin's profile was measured and puzzled. What did he want to say to me? His countenance at the moment was in sharp contrast to the expression he wore when he looked at Lynette. His mouth was held in a tight line, his cheekbones accented by taut facial muscles, and his gray-green eyes narrowed in a frown as if wintry thoughts were responsible for his expression. Once more I was aware of the strength in his well-molded, straight nose, his firm chin. He was not handsome in the current vogue of debonair masculinity, I admitted, and his attire was conservative—dark trousers and a morning coat of gray and black twill. His impeccable white linen, gold cufflinks twinkling in starched cuffs, was in quiet good taste. Yet—he could dominate any gathering with his presence, I thought.

"I think your fianceée is very lovely," I said, as if I enjoyed inflicting barbs into myself. "I understand you have known her for along time."

He nodded. "We spent summer holidays together on Cape Cod as children, and attended social functions as adolescents and adults. Vance and Edwina belonged to that group, too. I can't remember when Lynette has not been a part of my life. She's five years my junior and I've always been protective of her," he confessed with a wry smile. "She used to call me her knight in shining armor. Anyway, when her father lost everything in a collapse of his shipping industry, he committed suicide. He left very little for Lynette and her mother to live on, and I promised to take care of her. We didn't see much of each other while I was in medical school but she was always there when I needed her. Even when there were other women in my life, Lynette seemed to understand, and she was always there when the casual romance was over. She's adept at mending a broken heart."

I felt sick to my stomach. "You fall in and out of love quite readily, it would seem," I said with false levity.

"Just the usual search for the right woman, I suspect." His eyes leveled on my face and the same kind of frozen moment I had experienced yesterday in the dining room overtook me again. I was caught in a sudden swirl of emotion that defied control. I didn't want to react to him but when he looked at me like that, the whole world disappeared and he dominated my thoughts, my emotions, and diluted my will to resist him.

"I have to get back," I said in a breathless rush. "Cassie should be through with her treatment in a few minutes." I did not want to discuss Gavin Rodene's love life. It had nothing to do with me.

"You haven't given me a chance to apologize for yesterday. I'm sorry for my behavior in the dining room. I didn't mean to pressure you."

"Then you're going to quit interfering?" I flashed out rudely, my whirlwind of emotions finding release in anger.

"No. I can't."

"Why?" I turned and faced him. "Why is it any of your concern? Cassie is not your patient. You hardly know me. What is it, Dr. Rodene, that disturbs you so much about my being in charge of Cassie Danzel?"

"Everything about this situation bothers me. Removing Cassie from Gray Oaks to bring her here. Expecting the great Dr. Vonfeldt to work his magic on someone as disturbed as Cassie." He shook his head. "It's an explosive situation—and you're right in the middle of it!"

Because he had voiced my own concern about Dr. Vonfeldt's treatment, I told him about the electric bath and Cassie's reaction to it. "Is there any danger?"

"From a few light bulbs?" His laugh was bitter and short. "No danger . . . and little benefit either. Oh, for a normal person, someone who is tense or overworked, lying in a warm cabinet might soothe the nerves, but nothing more. Same thing with the Turkish baths and massages. They are nice and relaxing and provide a pleasant way to spend time and money. But in Cassie's case, I'm afraid more harm than good will come of it."

I forgot my decision not to tell him anything. He seemed to be the only one willing to listen to me. Without analyzing my impulse, I told him about Cassie coming into my room and how I had awakened in terror with the girl's hand on my face. "What—what do you think made her do that?"

He didn't answer for a moment. "It's hard to say. There's so little we know about the human mind. According to Breuer and others who have made a study of hysteria, in cases like Cassie's perception becomes so distorted that everything seems flat, without dimension—like cardboard! Cassie may have been testing her perception when she felt your face."

"She didn't seem agitated. She just pressed her hand against my face like a blind person feeling it. Then she went back to bed. She still sleeps almost all the time."

"Lethargy and deep fatigue are also symptoms of mental disorders. The neurotic is constantly fighting an inner battle. Conflicting forces rage within their minds. At the same time, there seems to be an impersonal lucidity that allows these people to be aware of what is going on around them."

"You mean Cassie hears and understands everything I say?"

"Hears, yes. Understands—not in the accepted definition of the word. She has turned away from outer reality. It seems obvious that Cassie is responding to an inner reality. And that's where the danger lies. Keeping her heavily sedated is one way to control her outward behavior so she doesn't hurt herself or someone else . . ."

"But Dr. Vonfeldt has changed her medication. I'm positive it doesn't contain laudanum."

"Perhaps some other sedative instead?"

"I don't know. She's more alert, holds her head straighter. This morning she looked directly at me."

He swore under his breath. "The situation's a runaway train heading for disaster. No telling what will happen even if she returns to normality. She might remember—." He cut himself off short.

"Remember what?" The skin had begun to crawl on the back of my neck. *What shocking secret did Cassie hold in that dark, tormented mind of hers?*

We were back at the door of the reception room. Gavin ignored my question. "I would like to take you out to the school, Brianna. You could talk with Helen and see for yourself what it's like there. The children are happy and well cared for. It's not a depressing place—thanks to Helen. I know you two would get along. She's very special. I want you to meet her. Can you take your free time about three o'clock this afternoon?"

"I'm sorry but I've promised to meet my friend, Jack Harvey," I answered rather haughtily. I wasn't about to get involved in meeting another one of Gavin Rodene's ladyloves. The man was impossible!

Before Gavin could reply, Lynette came out of the waiting room and looked at us in surprise. "Oh, there you are, darling," she smiled at Gavin. "There was going to be a delay so I told Dr. Vonfeldt I would rather come back another time. I really don't think those hot and cold baths are my cup of tea." She laughed with a toss of her golden curls and velvet feathered hat. Then her eyes slid to me.

Gavin took the cue. "Lynette, I would like you to meet Brianna Anderson. . . ."

"I believe I heard Vance Danzel mention your name. You're a friend of his younger sister?"

"Paid companion," I corrected. I wasn't flying under any false colors. I kept my eyes steady and my chin firm as I returned Lynette's appraising gaze.

"Oh, yes. I remember now." Lynette gave a light apologetic laugh. "They are delighted to have found someone like you. Vance spoke very highly of you. It must be such a worry for all the family. I've had some experience because my mother has become rather senile. It's very taxing to be around someone who is afflicted like that. Thank heavens, Gavin provides a nurse for mama. I don't know how I'd handle the emotional strain. I don't envy your responsibility."

I searched for some sign of insincerity but if it was there, it was carefully camouflaged. There was nothing on the surface for me to dislike. And that made the situation even more intolerable.

"Perhaps we might have tea some afternoon, in my suite," invited Lynette. "It would be my pleasure. Don't you think that's a good idea, darling?" Lynette's eyes flickered to Gavin's face and waited for his reaction.

For a split second, I saw a glint of speculation in Lynette's sky blue eyes. So the sweet, peaches-and-cream Lynette was shrewd as a pretty spider spinning a web, I thought with some satisfaction. This was the second time Lynette had caught us together—she must have noticed me the day she arrived. Maybe she was prepared to pick up the broken pieces after another one of his love affairs the way Gavin said she had done in the past. I could have set her mind at ease. There was absolutely nothing going on between the dictatorial Dr. Rodene and me.

"I think Miss Anderson's time is all spoken for," said Gavin pointedly. "She just refused an invitation to visit the school. I wanted her to meet Helen."

"She's a delightful person. You really should go. Perhaps we could make it a threesome some afternoon?"

A masculine voice floated over her shoulder. "Why not a foursome?" Vance appeared at my elbow. "Where are we going? To the beach?"

"No, the Deaf and Dumb School," laughed Lynette.

"Count me out," grimaced Vance. "No offense, Dr.

Rodene, but it's not on my list of things to see in St. Augustine. You really should spend more time showing Lynette the sights. There's a pleasant boat ride to Anastasia Island."

"I'm afraid I don't have time," said Gavin crisply.

"Then allow me. I would be happy to escort your lovely fiancée around in your absence."

I saw Gavin's eyes flare. He had already admitted his protective leanings where Lynette was concerned and undoubtedly considered Vance a flirtatious rake, dallying with anyone who caught his fancy.

Before Gavin could answer Lynette said sweetly, "That would be very nice, wouldn't it, darling? Then I wouldn't feel so guilty taking you away from your work. I would love to take a carriage ride around St. Augustine. I do hate to stay inside the hotel all the time while you're busy."

"Then it would be my pleasure to oblige," Vance smiled warmly.

I saw Gavin's hands tighten. He looked as if he wanted to plunge his fist into Vance's smiling face but he said evenly, "If it pleases you, Lynette, I have no objections."

"Perfect," said Vance. "I'll see you this afternoon then, Lynette? Say two clock?" Vance bent his handsome, tawny head in her direction.

"Two o'clock," she agreed, peeking at Gavin as if to satisfy herself that she had raised his jealousy.

Vance watched Lynette's rounded, petite figure until it was out of sight as she and Gavin left the room. He gave a sigh and turned back to me. "Well, how did it go this morning with Cassie?"

"I really don't know. Dr. Vonfeldt wouldn't let me stay. She seemed to be passive and accepting until he turned on the lights. Then she screamed!"

"I was afraid she might go into one of her fits."

"Fits?"

"Well, not really 'fit'," he qualified, laughingly.

"Just odd behavior. She used to talk crazily about chairs trying to destroy her and things turning into enormous shapes."

"I don't believe you've ever told me exactly what her diagnosis was at Gray Oaks."

He shrugged. "I can't understand all that psychological nonsense. I don't think labels mean anything, do you? People shouldn't be branded. Like your father . . . what kind of a label did they put on him?"

He had touched a vulnerable spot. I remembered the evasive answers I had been given until his death. "I don't think they really knew."

"Well, I don't think they really know about Cassie, either. So let's not worry about putting a name on her problem." His smile was the kind that stilled any protests.

A few minutes later, when Domincea brought Cassie out to us, she passively let her brother guide her back to the hotel without showing any interest in where she was going.

I had lied to Gavin about having an afternoon date with Jack. Instead I had told Domincea that I didn't want to take my break until evening, thinking I might like to eat in the staff dining room. I stayed in the suite all day, watching Cassie sleep and moving restlessly from one room to another.

I went over and over my conversation with Gavin until it was worn threadbare. What had he started to say about Cassie remembering? Was he afraid that Cassie might have a moment of lucidity and tell me something he didn't want known? Was he trying to get Cassie sent back to Gray Oaks so she would be safely shut away from the world? He obviously did not want her here. He had been openly upset when I had told him on the train who my charge was.

What a maddening, unpredictable person he was. The fact that he was willing to take me to the school and introduce me to another one of his conquests was insulting. Lynette indicated that she was willing to accept all his lady friends for the passing fancies that they were, openly confident that no other woman could take him from her. But I was not Lynette! I would be insanely possessive of Gavin Rodene if he were my fiancé.

I decided that Lynette wasn't above giving Gavin a taste of his own medicine. Vance was obviously smitten with her—just the mention of her name made his handsome face glow. Why any woman would trade Gavin Rodene's company for Vance Danzel was something I couldn't understand. Vance was certainly more adept in social graces, but I found him quite shallow. The conversation I had overheard between his sister and Amelia Dorcas came back. "My patience is at an end," Lady Edwina had said. I couldn't quite remember what the reference to the family's investments had been, but I shivered remembering Edwina's malevolent laugh when Amelia suggested that Cassie might get well.

As if Gavin Rodene wasn't in my thoughts securely enough, that afternoon a gift arrived for me. I opened up a hatbox bearing the label of one of the hotel's boutiques. It contained a lovely midnight blue bonnet, decorated with peach silk flowers and satin streamers. The card inside read, "My apologies for crushing your other hat. Gavin."

My despondent mood evaporated like ice crystals under a warm sun. I wavered between sending it back with a haughty note and keeping it as the thoughtful gift it was. I tied the ribbon in a soft bow under my chin and preened in front of a mirror. Its fluted brim framed my face and deepened the blue of my eyes. My reflection in the mirror told me that foolish tears were running down my cheeks. Jack had given me a gift but it had not touched the deepest level of my feelings the way one from Gavin Rodene was able to do.

I went to bed happy but awoke in the middle of the night with a cold sweat on my forehead and the palms of my hands clammy. In a dream I had been reliving an experience which had terrified me when my father was at Gray Oaks. I had stayed late with my father one night and it was after midnight when I decided to go back to the small room I rented near the sanitarium. Wearily, I left my father's room and nodded at a night nurse who looked up from her station as I left the ward. My footsteps echoed in the hushed silence of the building as I took the stairs down to the front entrance. When I reached the front doors, I found that they were locked and all the business offices silent and deserted.

The attendant who was usually at the reception desk must have taken a break, I thought as fatigue overwhelmed me. The need to rest was compelling, but I knew if I sat down in one of the waiting room chairs, I would never want to get to my feet again. Frustrated by the locked door and the hours of emotional strain I had spent, I became frantic to get out of the building as fast as I could. I knew there was a side door on a lower level because I had wheeled my father out into the yard on several occasions. Wearily, I retraced my steps, went down another flight of stairs and reached a long, branching hall that led past the dining hall, storage, and supply rooms.

Everything was dimly lit and deserted at this midnight hour, and my footsteps echoed on the bare floor. The usual sounds of patients crying, mumbling, or thrashing about did not reach this isolated corridor with its hushed, waiting silence. I had grown used to the pitiful murmurings that constantly filled my ears in the wards; sometimes I thought I would scream just listening to them, but now their absence in this stark, isolated hall made the stillness like a silent scream. In spite of my fatigue, I quickened my pace.

Dark, possessive shadows gathered behind me, blotting out the way I had come. My own breathing, the swish of my skirts and the click of my heels were the only sounds. I seemed to be the only living thing in the gray stone structure. The hall went on forever.

Had I taken the wrong turn? It had not seemed nearly this long when I had pushed my father's wheelchair down this corridor, I thought with a rise of panic. Suddenly disoriented, I panicked. My gloved hands came up to my mouth to stifle a cry for help. I began running. My full skirts whipped around my legs, threatening to trip me. My fatigue had given way to terror.

Then I saw it! The outside door was as I remembered.

With a gasp of relief, I pushed it open, causing a loud alarm to shatter the waiting stillness.

For a moment I froze in the doorway. Then rational thought was lost as frayed nerves caused me to run forward, intent upon fleeing the building and its shrieking alarm. I stumbled down some steps and then a strong pair of arms reached out and jerked me to a stop!

"So you think you're going to take a little walk, do ye?"

I glimpsed a white coat as I struggled against a burly man who was trying to pin my arms down.

"Oh, a wildcat, hey?"

"Let me go—"

"Sure, I'll be letting you go all right. But not 'til you're back where you belong."

"You don't understand," I gasped. "I don't belong here . . . I . . ."

"That's what they all say." His coarse laugh matched his burly thick frame. "Don't you know there's no escape from Gray Oaks." He dragged me back into the building.

I screamed and fought him with every ounce of my

strength, but I was no match for him. In a few minutes I was secured in a confining straitjacket and locked in a stark white room. I cried hysterically and writhed against the restraining straps. It seemed an eternity before someone in authority came to explain the situation. I was finally released and given an apology for the mistake.

It was the memory of that traumatic experience that made the tower suite seem to reek of forced confinement. I knew there was no guard outside in the dim hotel corridor, no clanging alarm, and yet the sensation of being trapped was there. *There's no escape from Gray Oaks.* The words were a haunting echo in my ears as I sat in the dark in the isolated, fifth-story tower.

A high-pitched wail from Cassie's room jerked me back to the present. I took a deep breath and hurried to her.

She was sitting up in bed looking straight at me. Her haunted, dark eyes were vacant pits. They told me nothing. So much of what we know about other people is learned through reading their eyes, I thought with a sense of helplessness. Cassie's were void of expression or comprehension as she hovered on the dark edge of madness.

"It's time for your medicine," I announced in a strained voice because I didn't know what else to say. Cassie's complete withdrawal was different from my father's gradual loss of touch with reality. I had had time to adjust to the slow deterioration of his mind and I had known him when his mind was sharp and lucid. His mental disarrangement had not frightened me. I had treated him as a normal, rational person—even at the end. In my naiveté I had thought caring for Cassie would be much the same, but it wasn't!

My hands trembled as I spooned the medicine into Cassie's mouth. I knew nothing about this young woman. I had no past relationship with her to draw upon.

"Cassie Danzel! What in God's name is she doing in your custody?" Gavin Rodene's explosive words came back to me and I felt raw fear creep up my spine.

Chapter Seven

The next week passed without incident. I took Cassie to the Casino for her daily treatments and varied my free time so that Domincea sometimes relieved me in the afternoon and sometimes during the dinner hour, so I could eat in the dining hall with other employees. The congenial Jack Harvey provided companionship and some normalcy in my life. He had been right about the hotel encompassing two worlds. There were musical soirees, military balls, water carnivals, and formal dinners, and a variety of private parties which kept the hotel guests busily attending one affair or another. There was little compensation for the working class who made these functions possible. In my isolation in the tower rooms I rarely glimpsed the social whirl, but when I did, I felt like a child looking through a picket fence at some affair to which she had not been invited.

I heard nothing from Gavin Rodene. If he hadn't sent me the lovely hat, I would have been certain that he never thought of me at all. Every day brought new challenges in handling Cassie. The lack of sedation had made a great change in her. Most of the time the girl's eyes were fully open, yet completely vacant. Her passive behavior almost disappeared. Feeding her became very difficult when

Cassie wouldn't open her mouth. Her fixed stare at a tiny piece of bread crumb was like a hypnotic trance.

I sensed a dynamic energy warring in Cassie's stiff frame. Like a clamped down steam valve, Cassie seemed to be straining and building up to an explosive action. It worried me. The medicine Dr. Vonfeldt had prescribed seemed to have little effect upon her behavior, which became more bizarre.

One day she had been especially trying, and by evening my nerves were frayed. I knew I had to talk to someone about Cassie's change in behavior. Dr. Vonfeldt and Vance always brushed aside any concern I expressed about her building resistance to the routine of eating, dressing, and sleeping. I remembered that Gavin had warned me that Cassie might try to harm herself. As much as I hated to swallow my pride and talk to him, I decided that I really had no choice. He was the only person who would listen to me.

When Domincea arrived to relieve me after dinner, I hurriedly left the tower suite. I ignored the stairway and stubbornly rang for the elevator. Ira Deitz didn't work most evenings and the short, bald man in his place made no objections to my using the elevator.

As I emerged on the main floor, I met Sir Wilfred coming out of the Gentleman's bar. He was looking quite debonair, dressed in evening clothes with a silk hat and cane. Undoubtedly fortified with scotch, he was heading toward the parlor, where I could see Lady Edwina, Amelia Dorcas, and Vance sitting together. He passed me without a greeting and I suspected that he was already well on his way to becoming inebriated.

"Yes?" An imperious clerk responded in a frigid

tone to my presence at the front desk. He had a nose that seemed visibly to lengthen under his gold-rimmed spectacles. A deprecating and pointed glance at my modest attire indicated that he thought I was someone who should not be taking up his time.

I read his disdain but was not intimidated by it. He and Ira Deitz made a matched pair, I decided. "Please ring Dr. Rodene's room and tell him that Miss Anderson would like to speak to him in the lobby."

The desk clerk's thin lips curved nastily. "I'm afraid that won't be possible. Dr. Rodene left word that he will be at The Deaf and Blind School until tomorrow. He stays with Miss Matley, I believe. Is there a message?" The clerk's knowing smirk was insulting.

No doubt, he thought Dr. Rodene had ducked out on some prearranged tête-à-tête with a servant. "No, thank you," I answered crisply, hoping that color hadn't swept up into my cheeks.

With my head high, I walked across the rotunda and went out the carriage entrance. I needed to compose myself, to take a walk in the night air and clear my head before I would be fit for after-dinner tea in the staff dining room.

Spending the night at the school! With Helen Matley! He had even been so brazen as to leave her number. How could Lynette put up with it? The maddening Dr. Rodene flaunted his women with a casualness that brought nausea to the pit of my stomach. I strode angrily down a winding path that led through thick plantings of date-palms, leafy palmettos, creamy white magnolias, and scarlet flowers. Although scattered park lamps illuminated the hotel grounds, only shards of pale yellow light pierced a heavy grid of interlacing trees arching over the flagged path. On every side, thick glossy leaves were green-black against the night sky. As I walked, I could hear faint music coming from the dining room and the muted clatter of horses' hooves upon the cobbled driveways.

A distant trickling of water told me a fountain must be nearby but I could not see it. In the daytime, I was certain that the lush greenery made the grounds cool and refreshing, but in the shadows of night, the trees and shrubs lost their reassuring, recognizable shapes. Heavily laden branches moved in the breeze as if reaching out to entrap me. The night was suddenly sinister and threatening. The back of my neck began to prickle.

I stopped and swung around. Nothing. I stood there a moment, fighting a sense of rising uneasiness. Shadows laced the flagged walk but at that moment the moon came out from behind a swath of fast moving clouds and I could clearly see that no one was on the path behind me.

I started walking again. But the presentiment would not go away. A sense of urgency brought a cold beading of sweat upon my brow. What was the matter? Why this engulfing urge to run, to flee, or to scream? I had never been given to hysterics. But even as I mocked my sudden hysteria, I spun around and began walking rapidly back toward the hotel through the tunnel of trees.

When I emerged from the gardens I was in the shadow of the great hotel; it was ablaze with lights and activity. I hesitated. I had only been gone about fifteen minutes and all day I had been looking forward to my break. What was the matter with me? Why did I want to flee back to that horrible tower suite as if it were a sanctuary? Something beyond rational thought made me give in to an urge to return to the suite as soon as possible.

I hastened to the lobby and when the elevator arrived, I rushed into it almost like a threatened animal plunging into the safety of its burrow. I stayed at the back of the lifting cage, ignoring the guests who came and went on each floor. Their conversation about food, entertainment, and parties poured over me without making any imprint.

My stomach was knotted and I suddenly feared that I was becoming neurotic. Had the long years with my father taken their toll? Were my emotions out of control? My forehead was moist with sweat. *What was the matter with me?* For a frightening moment I wondered if I were losing my sanity.

As if someone were after me, I left the elevator and quickly traversed the short hall to the tower suite. I flung open the sitting room door—and froze.

The suite was in total darkness. Only dim light from the hall made a watery radius a foot inside the room. With a vibrating sixth sense, I realized that I had been running not *from*—but *toward* horror.

"Domincea! Cassie!"

What had happened? Where was everyone? I wanted to turn and run but a dogged strength made me move forward into the dark room. I blinked frantically, trying to adjust my eyes to the lack of light.

"Cassie!" My voice was high-pitched and jagged. My nose caught some scent which slipped away before I could identify it. In the waiting silence, I thought I heard someone breathing. A cry caught in my throat.

Then a wave of cool air hit my cheek. I swung around. The balcony door was open!

Dear God, no! For a moment I thought I was going to faint. I couldn't draw my next breath. Mounted against the night sky, a small figure stood upright on the narrow railing of the balcony with one hand touching a slender column.

Cassie was going to jump!

I controlled a frantic impulse to rush and scream at her to get down. I knew that rational words would not penetrate that other world where Cassie lived. Trying to talk her down would be foolish. It would have to be done physically. I wasn't sure I could hold her dead weight. Should I leave Cassie there? Go for help? Where was Domincea?

At that moment, I heard the hall door close. Someone had been in the sitting room! Who? Why hadn't they answered my cries? Were they responsible for Cassie being out on the balcony? But whoever had been hiding in the darkness was gone. There was no time to think about that or anything else. Even though I wanted to turn and run for help I couldn't. I had to act now; another minute might be too late.

I trapped my breath in a burning chest. Any sudden movement behind Cassie might send her over, some detached part of my brain reasoned as I eased forward. It was only a few steps to the railing but every one was an eternity. A calm voice within took charge.

Easy!

Slow!

Don't frighten her!

The orders came from somewhere beyond the shrieking clamor that fright had set up in my head.

One more step.

One more—then I was close enough! With a frantic grasp, I flung my arms around the girl's waist. Cassie swung around and surprised me by grabbing the column with both hands, and holding on fiercely.

"It's all right, Cassie. It's me! I've got you."

She let go so suddenly that both of us fell back on the floor of the balcony. I cradled her tightly, afraid that she might try to jerk out of my arms, but Cassie went limp. She whimpered and then her thin hands went up to my face which was wet with tears of relief.

"Cassie," I sobbed. I stroked her dark head as it pressed against my breast.

She began making guttural sounds. At first, they made no sense and then a phrase came through the incoherent babbling: "Made me do it!"

I was positive I had not misunderstood the words. "Who, Cassie? Who made you do it?"

She did not answer.

Chapter Eight

"Now tell me exactly what happened." Dr. Vonfeldt ordered when he came out into the sitting room where I sat with my hands clasped tightly together, trying to gain command of myself.

I had summoned him right after ringing for a hotel attendant to relight the gas lamps. As soon as Vonfeldt arrived he took charge of the moaning Cassie, giving her a hypodermic sedative, and staying with her until she was deep in sleep.

Before I could answer, he demanded, "Where is Domincea?"

I handed him the note I had found on a pier table near the door. "Domincea. Leave your patient. Return to the Alcazar at once," it read.

"Who wrote this?" The plain square of hotel stationery bore nondescript printing.

"I don't know but I . . . I think someone was here, in this room, when I came back." I told him that I had sensed someone in the darkness and had noticed an elusive odor which had escaped identification. "I wasn't supposed to be back for two hours but instead I returned after about fifteen minutes." I didn't tell him that I had felt danger in the garden and that some nameless urgency had driven me back to the hotel. He would have ridiculed my intuition. "When I opened the door, I couldn't see anything. Someone had put out the lamps."

"The whole thing is preposterous," he said impatiently. "I'm inclined to think that Cassie might have staged this whole thing herself. It's possible, you know. Emotionally disturbed people are diabolically clever. They like keeping everyone in an uproar."

"But she was about to jump off the balcony!" I said, aghast.

"Humph! That's what she wanted you to think. You told me she was holding on to one of the pillars."

"I think she was going to jump. I'm sure she said 'They made me do it!' "

"Who? Who made her do it?"

"I don't know. She wouldn't answer."

His smile was patronizing. "That's what I mean by cleverness, Brianna. I don't think she intended to jump at all."

"Do you honestly believe Cassie's capable of writing such a note, extinguishing the lights, and then climbing up on the railing to wait for me to come back and rescue her?" My tone was scathing and he bristled at it. "Someone was in this room. I heard the door close."

He shook his head. "I'm afraid, Miss Anderson, that you've given your imagination full rein. Mr. Danzel had assured me that you were a very sensible, dependable young woman. You must not put sinister connotations where there are none."

"I know that I left the door open when I came in. Someone closed it when I was out on the balcony with Cassie!" I countered belligerently.

"My dear, you are much too upset to remember anything clearly. I will talk with Domincea to ensure this doesn't happen again, and I will also inform the Danzel family of the unfortunate incident.

Now, I suggest you get some sleep. If you would like a light sedative . . . ?"

"Thank you. I never have trouble sleeping," I lied. I would have endured twenty-four hours of insomnia before I'd take anything from a man like Dr. Vonfeldt.

After he had gone, I let myself slump in the chair. Would I ever be able to forget Cassie's pathetic little figure wavering on that balcony railing? Even now my palms were moist with sweat. Dr. Vonfeldt's arrogant dismissal of the whole thing infuriated me. He acted as if I were somehow to blame for the whole incident. His suggestion that Cassie had staged the whole thing herself was ludicrous. Was he trying to cover up some responsibility of his own? After all, he had chosen Domincea to relieve me. Had the whole thing been carefully planned? Was Domincea a part of the conspiracy? Cassie had said very clearly, "Made me do it." Who? Dr. Vonfeldt and Domincea? But why? How would they benefit from her death?

They could have been paid to do it! The thought struck me with a glacial chill. Had my early return foiled their plan?

I arose the next morning with deep shadows under my eyes and a feeling that I was trapped in a neverending nightmare. When it came time to take Cassie to the Alcazar for her morning treatments, I tried to get command of a growing nervousness. I didn't know what to expect from Cassie or anyone else. I was relieved and surprised when everything went as usual.

I didn't see the Danzels, Lynette Talbot, or Gavin that morning. I wondered if the handsome doctor was still at the school, enjoying Helen Matley's company. If only he had been in the hotel last night—I shoved the thought away. I knew I could not depend upon Gavin Rodene's support when I needed it. It was a good lesson to have learned, and one I would not forget, I vowed.

When Domincea arrived at two o'clock, I tried to ask her about what had happened last night. She clamped her mouth shut and refused to discuss the matter. I decided that I needed Jack Harvey's easy-going, cheerful company more than ever. I changed into a light blue summer voile with lace-trimmed flounces, a dress that had been one of my father's favorites. As I set the new bonnet on my brown curls and slipped on a pair of white gloves, the stoic Domincea watched me. I gave her an uncertain smile. I didn't know why the large, expressionless woman made me so uneasy.

When I closed the sitting room door I felt like someone escaping from prison. In some ways the atmosphere at Gray Oaks had not been as depressing as this isolated tower, cut off from all the activity of the hotel. I was debating whether to challenge Ira Deitz and see if the pompous elevator man would allow me to ride the elevator down when I heard the cage rising. To my surprise the doors flew open on my floor, and unexpectedly I was face to face with Gavin Rodene.

"Good morning," he said in the most pleasant of manners.

I had difficulty maintaining a cool reception at this unexpected meeting. The nervous tingling sensation in the pit of my stomach was like the wings of a thousand erratic moths fluttering there. "Good morning." I managed in what I hoped was a light, casual tone. "Ground floor, please," I said to stony-faced Ira Deitz as I brushed past him.

"I'm glad I caught you," Gavin said, standing so close that his warm breath bathed my cheek and the faint spicy smell of a man's tonic teased me with his nearness. He was immaculately dressed as usual, and clean-shaven. His eyes held a warm friendly glint that only made me more determined than ever to keep a polite distance between us.

I kept my gaze fixed on the doors of the elevator as the cage descended. Was the popular doctor just getting back to the Ponce from his night away? I was angry that he had not been available when I'd needed to talk with him last night. Now he was acting as if I should be falling all over myself because he was ready to give me some attention.

As the elevator filled up with people from other floors, I was forced to move closer to him. He whispered, bending his head close to mine, "That's a very becoming hat." His eyes twinkled at me and his bold mouth curved in a soft grin.

I could not keep the heat from sweeping up into my face. I had forgotten I was wearing his present. How dare he embarrass me by mentioning it. He was no gentleman. I never should have accepted it. Never!

"I have a buggy waiting to take us for a ride." His voice carried to a pair of young ladies whose admiring eyes had already traveled over him as they entered the elevator. They exchanged questioning glances, noting my simple summer dress and rather worn white gloves. Their condescending attitude rankled me so much that for their benefit I smiled at Gavin and said sweetly, "How nice."

We left the elevator and had taken a few steps

across the lobby when I turned and said coolly, "Good-bye, Dr. Rodene."

"But you said in the elevator—"

"I lied."

"Brianna, you look terrible."

"Thank you very much. Is that your medical opinion or merely a rude personal observation?"

"Both. You've got dark shadows under your eyes and you're as taut as a bowstring. An afternoon ride will do you good."

"I tried to reach you last night," I lashed out, angry that he was so solicitous now yet had been cavorting with one of his ladyloves when I'd needed to talk with him.

He looked surprised. "I left a message . . ."

"Yes, I know. You spent the night at Miss Matley's apartment." My tone was bitter.

He swore under his breath. Without waiting for my consent, he firmly propelled me past the arcade of expensive shops just off the main rotunda.

"I don't want to go with you," I hissed.

"I know," he answered with infuriating arrogance.

There were people all around us, some of them nodding and greeting Gavin by name. I resented his high-handed manner but didn't have the courage to make a scene.

He helped me into a smart buggy with red wheels and dark maroon upholstery. Then he lightly sprang up on the other side and took his place beside my in the elevated seat. With a flick of the reins, he sent a small sorrel mare trotting out into the cobbled street and then south on Cordova Street.

As if this were the most pleasant and relaxed of encounters, Gavin politely pointed out some of the city's old landmarks, giving me an approving smile when I eased back into the seat and looked less like a porcupine ready to launch its barbs.

In a few minutes we had left the populated area of the town behind. Gavin sent the horse trotting down a narrow road leading through a tropical landscape of palms, shrubs, and grasses, and an occasional cultivated orchard. A heady mixture of lush foliage, wild flowers, and moist ground combined to create a pungent natural perfume.

It was a bird watcher's paradise, I thought, catching sight of a colorful woodpecker loudly excavating a cavity in a cabbage palm. All along the narrow road, Florida blue jays darted about, squawking loudly as the horse-and-buggy intruded upon the tropical landscape. A flock of tiny birds which I could not identify darted in and out of wax myrtle bushes, looking like feathers tossed in the air from the shaking of a pillow. I couldn't help but give a deep sigh as my taut muscles began to relax. The sun was brilliant, the air freshly laden with moisture from the nearby water. It was warm but not hot.

"Are you ready to tell me what has happened to deepen the violet shadows under your eyes, Brianna?" His tone was soft and inviting.

I bit my lip. Now that he was here, offering to listen, I hesitated. So many suspicions, so many unanswered questions. How could I sort them all out? I was confused, and frightened about trusting anyone.

"Please, Brianna. Won't you think of me as your friend?"

"No," I said bluntly, and then softened my answer with a feeble smile.

"I see. You prefer Jack Harvey?"

How could I tell him that he wasn't at all like Jack? There were no spinning tops gyrating lopsidedly in my stomach when I was with the redheaded artist. We had an easygoing, friendship, whereas with Gavin Rodene, I felt as if I were being drawn into an undertow. His nearness diminished everything else, and a bewildering tide of emotions swept over me.

"It seems to me you could use more than one friend at the moment."

That was certainly true, I had to admit. Gavin's offer of friendship promised support and understanding, two commodities I desperately needed at the moment. It was obvious that Dr. Vonfeldt was going to protect himself and Domincea in the incident. The terror and the deliberate viciousness that could have sent Cassie to her death caused me to tremble even now, in the warmth of a brassy sun.

Gavin must have felt the tremor in my body, for suddenly he reined the horse into the shade of a tall, gnarled magnolia tree. He turned in the seat and put his arm around me. "Now tell me about it," he ordered.

I moistened my dry lips. "Last evening, I took my free time after dark . . . after the dinner hour. I was gone about fifteen minutes, taking a walk in the west gardens, trying to clear my head. Cassie had been especially difficult and I was worried. I thought the night air would relax me but I . . . I was uneasy in the garden . . . I sensed that something was wrong. I thought someone was following me—I felt some kind of danger. This feeling built up until I could ignore it no longer. I decided not to continue my walk." I swallowed hard. "I know now that the danger was not outside the hotel, but inside. Shaken and upset, I decided to cut my break short. My intuition impelled me upstairs."

Gavin's arm tightened on my shoulder. "Go on."

"When I got to the hall door, I opened it and

found everything in darkness, the lamps extinguished. I called out as I entered. In the shadowy darkness I sensed someone there . . . in the sitting room. There was a slight whiff of something I was too upset to identify, and then a wave of cool air hit me. The balcony door was open. There was Cassie! Standing on top of the balcony railing, wavering—as if she were about to jump." I put a gloved fist up to my mouth. The memory was too real to be borne again.

Gavin drew my hand down and held it tightly in his own.

"I wanted to scream but didn't. Somehow I managed to reach Cassie. She was staring straight ahead as if she were hypnotized. When I grabbed her, she twisted round and held onto a pillar with both hands. I tried to reassure her, and when she seemed to recognize my voice, she let go. We fell to the floor and . . . and then she touched my face . . . just as she'd done in the middle of the night. She held onto me tightly and she said . . ." I gulped. Tears were flowing down my cheeks now. "She made guttural sounds and then I'm positive she said, 'Made me to it'."

I buried my face against his chest and he stroked my head as he encircled me protectively in his arms. My breath rose and fell in deep gasps. "No wonder the stress showed in your face." He gently lifted my chin. "It's all right," he soothed, easing away wisps of hair clinging to my wet cheeks. "It's all right."

His face was poised close to mine as it had been that day on the train. I had wanted him to kiss me then, and the desire had not gone away. From the moment I had felt his touch upon me, he had inflamed a need to be in his arms.

He bent his head, kissed me gently on the lips,

and then placed butterfly kisses in a circle around my mouth before he claimed my lips again. My response was not practiced; I knew nothing about kissing a man. Somehow my arms found their way around his neck and my fingers slipped into the thick waves of hair lying on his neck. His mouth tugged at mine, as if he were tasting the sweet desire rising between us. I don't know how many kisses he drew from my lips before he lifted his head and lightly traced the curve of my cheek with his fingertips. "You shouldn't do that to a man, Brianna," he said half-chiding, half-serious.

My lips were still softly parted and he seemed to summon all his will power not to kiss them again. He pulled me back into the crook of his shoulder and rested his cheek against mine. For several moments, we sat quietly in the shade of the thick copse of trees.

"Feeling better?"

I nodded. "You were right. I should never have accepted this position."

"It's not too late, Bri. You can resign immediately."

"You would like that, wouldn't you?" I said thoughtfully.

"Yes. I'll notify Vance immediately."

I wanted to hold the ugliness of the world at bay and remain suspended for a few more minutes in a quiet, loving contentment, but something in his voice made all the questions and suspicions rush back. "That's what you've wanted from the very beginning," I said, withdrawing from his arms. My euphoria had vanished. *Did Gavin Rodene always get what he wanted—one way or another?*

"I've told you, Helen Matley will take you on. I've already talked to her. She's a darling."

I stiffened. "I'm sure she is." Maybe Lynette could accept his other women, but I wouldn't. "Thank you, but I'm capable of handling my own affairs," I said testily. "I don't need the help of your paramour."

Gavin looked as if I'd slapped him. "I see. What exactly are you accusing me of?"

I bit my lip. "I don't have the right to accuse you of anything. I'm not your fiancée. But if I were, you wouldn't be spending the night with Helen Matley or embracing someone else on a buggy ride!" I was angry that his kisses still burned on my lips. "How do you sort your women out, Dr. Rodene? By days of the week?"

His eyes glinted with cold fury and for a moment I thought he would take me by the shoulders and shake me. Instead—he turned away, angrily jerked on the reins, and set the horse trotting back toward town.

I had expected him to take me to the hotel, but he headed the horse-and-buggy south on St. George Street until we reached San Marcos Avenue.

"Where are we going?" I asked indignantly.

"You'll see." He was not the gentle lover who had held me close and kissed me with a passion that sent my head reeling. His jaw was tightly clenched and a vein pulsated in his forehead.

"Please take me back to the hotel," I asked, suddenly frightened.

"No."

I was about to protest when he turned into a wide driveway in front of several white buildings set in a wide expanse of grass and trees. A sign swung over the arched gate: "St. Augustine School for the Deaf and Blind." I could see small children playing in the spacious grounds. Each group was accompanied by a woman supervising the laughing, chattering boys and girls.

"Why did you bring me here?" How dare he! "I told you I'm not interested in changing positions."

He ignored me as the buggy rolled along the circle drive to the front of the main building. He reined in the horse and jumped down. When he came around to my side to help me down, I remained seated. "I'm not going in."

"Yes, you are. Either on your feet—or over my shoulder. Which do you prefer?"

"You wouldn't dare!"

"Wouldn't I ?" His tone left no doubt in my mind that the threat was not an idle one. I had no choice but to alight from the buggy.

I suffered his touch until my feet reached the ground. Then I tried to pull away from him, but he cupped my elbow firmly and led me up the front steps. We entered a large vestibule. A wide, polished oak staircase mounted on one side and I could see a series of doors opening off a long corridor which ran to the back of the building.

"Good afternoon, Dr. Rodene."

"Nice day, Doctor."

He nodded and smiled as people who looked like staff members greeted him.

I was seething with indignation but my escort didn't seem to notice. Halfway down the long hall, he led me into a spacious office filled with dark mahogany furniture smelling of freshly applied turpentine and beeswax. A large English-style desk was flanked by deep leather chairs which matched a long couch placed along one panelled wall. I had never seen so many leather-bound volumes crowded together in tall bookcases. Sun filtered through curtains made of intricate lace and cast shadows on the wide-plank oak floor. A bouquet of pansies sat on the desk in the midst of books, papers, and a white quill pen.

"Wait here," Gavin ordered without ceremony. "I'll get Helen."

"No. Please don't." I touched his arm and send him a pleading look. "I'm sorry. I spoke out of turn. It's none of my business, really."

"Isn't it?" He pulled me against him and kissed me with a fierceness that had not been there before. Plying my lips, he roughly parted them and his questing tongue flickered in excruciating sweetness. A wild jolt of sensation raced through me and made me lean against his commanding body. When he lifted his mouth, his tone was mocking. "I think the way you kiss me makes it your business, Brianna."

He turned and left the room. I abruptly sat down on the couch. His kisses had sent me into a dazed insensibility. Now more than ever, I didn't want to meet Helen Matley. It was difficult enough having to endure Lynette's sugar-and-cream loveliness. Undoubtedly Helen Matley would, in her own way, be every bit as attractive as his fiancée—and she would have brains as well!

What was I doing here? My lips burned from his kisses. My body was reeling with a hunger that was bewildering. I was not ready or willing to meet another woman he so obviously cared about. I wanted to turn and run. A knife plunged through me when I heard a remembered, sweet voice and light musical laughter outside the door.

I took a deep breath and stiffened to meet the woman who could bring a soft shine to Gavin's eyes whenever he said her name.

"Brianna, I want you to meet Helen Matley."

I gaped openly at a pink-faced, gray-haired lady who sashayed into the room with the energy of a young girl. A full smile put laugh lines around her eyes and across her cheeks.

This was Helen Matley? Relief and happiness brought a wavering smile and a flush of embarrassment to my face. I couldn't bring myself to look at Gavin as I greeted the director of the St. Augustine School for the Deaf and Blind.

"And you are Brianna," Helen said as she took my hands and squeezed them. "Gavin has been so concerned about you. He told me about your father. I'm so sorry. It is a terrible cross to bear, seeing someone you love fade away like that. Please sit down. I've so wanted to meet you." Her round, soft brown eyes frankly surveyed me and seemed pleased with what they saw. She sent a wink of approval at Gavin who stood watching us. "She's as lovely as you said. Now, I see why your mind has been going six directions at once, my boy." She gave a teasing chuckle and then sobered as she turned back to me. "He's been so worried. I hope you have decided to follow his advice and remove yourself from that impossible situation. Gavin feels that the girl is a danger to herself and others." She patted my arm. "You must let us help."

I couldn't find any words. Finding out that Helen Matley, the seductress, was only a figment of my imagination was such an embarrassment that I couldn't organize my thoughts.

"Brianna is very stubborn," offered Gavin. "Once she gets an idea in her head, it's like trying to pull out a weed with a ten-foot root. I had to bring her here to prove a point."

I looked at him then, and as I flushed, laughter bubbled up in my throat. I felt such a fool. I had let my imagination endow Helen with all the traits of a femme fatale. No wonder Gavin had been angry and brought me here to dispel such mistaken ideas. "I apologize," I said softly. "You proved your point."

He grinned in satisfaction and his greenish eyes were soft and caressing as they gazed at my face.

"And what point was that?" Helen cocked her round head to one side.

"No matter," said Gavin, sitting down in a leather chair near us. "Helen, I'm hoping you'll persuade Brianna that there's a place here for her. She had a traumatic experience last night . . . and I'm afraid there's more to come." He told Helen what had happened.

"Oh my!" Helen put a plump hand against her pink cheek. "It does sound ominous. You're certain someone was there when you came back, Brianna?"

"Positive."

"That could only mean—" Helen's voice trailed off.

"Whoever it was did not expect her to return so soon," Gavin finished grimly.

My hands tightened into fists on my lap. "Dr. Vonfeldt seemed to dismiss the whole thing as something Cassie might have done herself, but the note directing Domincea to leave the apartment would seem to rule that out. I do know Cassie behaves differently now that she's no longer sedated. She's more willful, more belligerent, and sometimes she seems to be watching me. Dr. Vonfeldt says that you can't trust someone as far removed from reality as Cassie."

"That's true," agreed Gavin readily.

"You don't think that she—"

"I don't know what to think at this point," confessed Gavin. "You told me that Cassie mumbled 'made me do it.' She could have been referring to inner voices."

Helen nodded. "There are cases which indicate that the mad hear voices within their own minds which force them to do things—even harm themselves and others."

"I'm sure I heard the hall door close while I was easing up behind Cassie."

"In your state of fear you could have been mistaken," cautioned Helen.

"I could have been—but I wasn't!"

Gavin smiled wanly at Helen. "See what I mean? She won't give an inch. What are we going to do with her?" Helen looked concerned.

"Somebody on the outside must have slipped the note under the door, knocked, and left, perhaps by the servants' staircase so they wouldn't be seen," I insisted.

"Oh my goodness," said Helen. "I just can't believe someone would deliberately make that poor girl get out on that railing. Who would do such a thing . . . and why?"

"Yes, why? Who would have gained if she'd fallen to her death?" asked Gavin in a tone which showed he already had the answer.

I stared at him. It seemed to me that shadows from the past flickered behind his eyes, giving them a haunted look.

"Could Vance have done it? To get control of Cassie's money, perhaps?" I prodded.

"Doesn't he have money of his own?" asked Helen.

"Tony Danzel left a will leaving everything to his children, but I don't know exactly what the division was," said Gavin. "That was almost four years ago.

Vance could have spent all of his inheritance. Edwina has a better business head than Vance. She's probably held on to her money."

"She has some holdings in England," I said quickly, remembering the snatches of conversations I had overheard between Amelia Dorcas and Lady Edwina. "But I got the impression they hadn't turned out very well. Both Sir Wilfred and Lady Edwina said that they were here in St. Augustine because they couldn't afford to go abroad. I heard her tell Amelia that she was going to quit indulging Sir Wilfred . . . and that her brother had better find himself a rich wife."

"So it could be money," said Gavin.

"But didn't they bring Cassie to St. Augustine to get better?" asked Helen.

I remembered Lady Edwina's chilling laugh when her friend suggested that Dr. Vonfeldt might cure her. "Maybe not. Maybe nobody wants her to get well." My eyes settled on Gavin. "She might be safer back at Gray Oaks."

"That could be why they brought her here—so she wouldn't be safe," mused Helen. "Well, I do think Gavin is right about getting you away from there, Brianna. We can always use an extra pair of hands here at the school."

"But what about Cassie?"

"She's not your responsibility, dear. You're not a member of her family."

I remembered Cassie's small head pressed against my breast. For several brief moments when she hugged me, I had felt close to that tortured spirit. How could I explain my reluctance to turn my back on the situation? If someone was planning harm to Cassie, I needed to be there to try and prevent it. Some of these thoughts must have been visible in my face for Gavin's eyes took on that hard gray hue. "Be sensible, Bri. Cassie needs professional attention—"

"Like Dr. Vonfeldt?" I countered. "Why don't you talk to him, instead of badgering me?"

"I want you out of that damn situation! Please, Brianna . . ." His voice softened, his eyes pleaded, and I felt myself going soft all over. My lips were still warm with remembered kisses, and I might have agreed to anything he wanted, if a rustle of skirts and Lynette's lavender perfume had not announced her presence as she floated into the room.

"Naughty boy," Lynette greeted Gavin affectionately. She was a vision in baby blue taffeta trimmed with velvet lavender bows that matched her plumed hat. Her smile was open and friendly, and Gavin immediately rose when she came in and took a couple of steps toward her.

Lynette stood on tiptoe to kiss him lightly on the cheek. "I was waiting for you to come back to the hotel and decided that the best thing to do was to come and get you myself." She slipped an arm through his and smiled at Helen. "The two of you are simply impossible, Helen, but how nice to see you again. When Gavin told me he was going to St. Augustine, I decided to pack up and follow him. I so enjoyed meeting you when you visited New York, and I was dying to see the school. That's all Gavin talks about, you know. He says you're doing marvelous things."

"With his help, we are. Thank you for loaning him to us."

Lynette's eyes flitted to me sitting beside Helen and a small frown creased that lovely white forehead. "I hope I'm not intruding?"

"Not at all," assured Helen, graciously. "Brianna

was asking some questions about the school, and I was trying to persuade her to join our staff. I'm afraid Gavin and I have been bragging about it. You know how we are. We feel that Brianna would fit in very nicely . . . and I think she was about to say yes." Questioning eyes went to my face waiting for an affirmative answer.

The impulse to give in to Gavin's pleas had faded. My smile wavered but my tone was quite firm. "I came to St. Augustine to look after Cassie Danzel. I don't think I can turn my back on that commitment," I said evenly. "But thank you, Miss Matley, for the offer."

"I heard what happened last night," said Lynette, easing down in the chair Gavin had vacated. She settled her full taffeta skirts around her and smoothed her embroidered gloves. "Such a frightening thing. I wouldn't blame you at all, Miss Anderson, for not wanting to remain as a companion under the circumstances. I really can't understand why Vance brought her here. Why did he?" Her round blue eyes fixed on me questioningly as if very much interested in my answer.

"Apparently the doctors at Gray Oaks thought she was ready to ease back into living normally. At least, that's what Mr. Danzel told me when I accepted the position of companion."

"Vance certainly has a lot of confidence in you." Lynette smiled at me. Her pretty face was like a doll's, wide baby blue eyes and a mouth pretty as a pink rosebud. "He told me that he's never seen anyone as good with his sister as you are. Such a relief, he says, to have someone capable of handling a trying situation."

The compliment was in sharp contrast to Gavin's insistence that Cassie would be better off in someone else's hands. I looked up at him as he leaned against Helen's desk. Unwittingly, my eyes followed the long sweep of his legs, conscious of the firm muscle of his thighs and the memory of the pressure of his arms holding me against his chest. Before I raised my gaze high enough to meet his eyes, I looked away.

Lynette's presence strengthened my resolve not to accept Helen's offer. Taking a job at the school would bring a different kind of torture into my life—namely, Dr. Gavin Rodene. How could I keep my dignity and integrity if forced to sit in the same room with him and his fiancée, and pretend that there was nothing between us? I couldn't. Even now, I felt out of place.

Lynette had quietly engaged Gavin in a private conversation, turning her back upon Helen and me as if we didn't exist. "Please, darling, I promised we'd be there. There'll be an orchestra and dancing after dinner. I know you must be tired but I really couldn't refuse the invitation. Even Henry Flagler and his wife will be there. I'm dying to meet her. I understand she's trying to show everybody that she fits into society despite her background as servant to his former wife. Amelia says she throws temper tantrums. Can you imagine? You won't disappoint me, darling? I really haven't seen anything of you since I arrived. I try to be patient but . . ." Her wide eyes were wistful. "Though I enjoyed my excursion with Vance it's you I want to be with."

"I don't like you seeing Vance," Gavin said, frowning.

"Then you'll go? Good. I just came for your promise. I have a hansom waiting . . . unless you want to take me back to the hotel?"

There was a weighted moment. For once Gavin's

usual aplomb deserted him. I broke the silence. "If you don't mind, Miss Talbot, I'd like to make use of your hired hansom. I've already overstayed my time."

"Oh, are you sure?"

"Quite sure." I stood up, bid Helen goodbye and, without looking directly at Gavin, left the room. I had reached the front steps when Gavin caught up with me.

"Brianna! Please listen to reason. Go collect your things at the hotel and come back here. Let Domincea take over."

"Don't try and order me about, Dr. Rodene," I said stiffly. "You may have your doubts about my ability to do my job but I have made a decision. I'm going to stay until I'm discharged—"

"Or until something disastrous happens!"

"Don't try to frighten me!"

"I'm trying to pound some sense into that stubborn head of yours. Please, Bri, stay here. Now that you've met Helen . . ."

"I apologize for my insinuations. I can understand your anger. But the fact remains that you have a fiancée who is very much in love with you—and I never could stand crowds!"

I climbed into the waiting hack and gave the driver an order to take me to the Ponce. I bit my lips and blinked back tears as I left a stiff, motionless figure glaring at the departing cab.

Chapter Nine

I had no sooner returned to the hotel and settled Cassie for a nap, when I had visitors. Lady Edwina and Amelia Dorcas swept into the sitting room, deposited themselves on the high backed sofa, and ordered late tea. Then they ever so politely told me they were here to question me about the incident the night before.

"You understand, Miss Anderson," said Edwina in her lofty, lady of the manor tone, "that my sister's welfare is of utmost importance to me. I will not tolerate any dereliction of duty. My brother, Vance, chose you for this position without my approval. He was impressed by the devotion you showed your father at Gray Oaks and he expected you to show the same kind of dedication in caring for Cassie. Last night's incident is intolerable!" The censure in her tone could not be missed.

"I agree," I responded, my spine stiffening. Amelia had a malicious smirk on her face as if she were relishing the impending clash of personalities. Her aquiline nose actually twitched.

"Then why did you allow it to happen?" Lady Edwina demanded. "If Cassie is not safe in your hands, perhaps we should engage someone else who is more competent." She was wearing shades of bright purple in a gown fashioned with layered skirts, and she looked like an overblown chrysanthemum spread out over the settee.

I bristled under the unfair attack. Surely Dr. Vonfeldt had told her what had happened? "I don't understand, Lady Edwina. It was Domincea, the attendant Dr. Vonfeldt provided, who left Cassie alone, not I. When I left, Domincea was here, and when I returned less than fifteen minutes later, she was gone—and Cassie was standing on the balcony railing. Didn't the doctor tell you what happened?" I felt a cold trickle down my neck. Had Dr. Vonfeldt lied about the incident to protect Domincea?

"Of course he told me," she said haughtily. "Domincea was called away by someone who wanted her out of the room. There was a note slipped under the door, while you were supposedly taking a walk." The implication was clear.

For a moment I couldn't speak.

Amelia leaned forward, wetting her lips as if savoring some sweet morsel. "Dr. Vonfeldt suggested that you might have slipped the note under the door yourself, Miss Anderson."

"But that's absurd," I choked. "Why would I do that?"

"Why indeed?" Lady Edwina popped a sweet biscuit into her mouth and her jowls moved in rhythm as she masticated it. In a weird sensation I imagined myself caught between those relentless teeth. A surge of fear made me tremble.

Amelia's small dark eyes settled on me with a greedy gleam, as if enjoyed the sudden drain of color from my face and the trembling of my lips. "Dr. Vonfeldt suggested that the emotional strain of your father's illness might be showing itself in . . . some abnormal tendencies," the hawk-faced woman explained in that grating voice of hers. "Or perhaps your father's malady might be an unfortunate tendency that runs in your family."

The malicious suggestion that I might be suffering from mental imbalance took away my breath. Amelia's sly smirk was like a grappling hook and I felt myself being pulled into a murky pool of vicious innuendoes and untruths. How did one defend oneself against such treacherous lies? I was so appalled by the accusations that for a moment I could find no words to contradict them.

My consternation and stunned silence obviously delighted Amelia. She was expert at fanning the smoldering sparks of a scandal. "You can't blame Lady Edwina being concerned for the welfare of her sister . . . if what the doctor says is true," Amelia simpered.

"It is *not* true!" I heard the hysterical rise in my voice. I mustn't give way to any display of emotions, an inner voice warned me. I must keep calm, though I felt like screaming my protests for all to hear. Why would Dr. Vonfeldt tell such lies? These vicious accusations were the product of a diabolical mind. Why had he laid the blame on me? Aloud I said, "The suggestion is absurd!"

"No need to be defensive," countered Lady Edwina, as if an accusation of madness should be borne with quiet submission. "Dr. Vonfeldt was looking at the matter from all angles, as I must do. You *could* have arranged the unfortunate incident last night. We have only your word for what happened. Poor Cassie cannot corroborate your story. You might have made the whole thing up, just to cast yourself as some kind of heroine."

"Is that what Dr. Vonfeldt thinks?" I managed to ask coldly.

"He suggested it as a possibility, that's all. I confess that it seems more likely to me than your story about a mysterious visitor coming in here, turning out all the lights and coaxing Cassie upon the balcony railing. You must admit that the whole incident is rather bizarre, Miss Anderson."

"Yes, but it happened!" I was astonished and frightened by the dark clouds of suspicion settling upon me. How could I combat such insidiousness?

"Do tell us about your father's illness," Amelia invited. Her smile was gluttonous. "You've been under a strain for several years, practically living at Gray Oaks, haven't you? Your father went mad, we understand? Such a shame . . . a professional man like that, losing his mind."

"My father's illness has nothing to do with this matter!"

"That remains to be seen, doesn't it?" Lady Edwina countered.

"I don't know what you're implying. Someone came in here last night, arranging for Cassie to fall to her death. That is the person in need of Dr. Vonfeldt's attention—"

"And who might that be?" Amelia waited like a sharp-toothed shark about to clamp down on some unsuspecting prey.

"I don't know. But I do know that someone was here, in this room when I returned. I heard the door shut while I was on the balcony with Cassie."

"It could be your imagination," said Lady Edwina with a wave of her fat hand. "Unless you're lying about the entire matter."

"I didn't imagine it and I'm not lying! Someone planned for Cassie to fall to her death last night!"

Amelia leaned forward. "Do you really think so? Poor Cassie. Why would anyone want her dead?"

"I should think the family could better answer that than I," I answered stiffly.

"Well, I never!" Lady Edwina's double chins bounced with indignation. "How dare you insinuate that my brother or I know anything about this unfortunate affair? I find your attitude offensive, Miss Anderson. My brother will hear of this."

"Yes," I agreed. "And so will Dr. Vonfeldt!"

Amelia gave a rasping chuckle. "Obviously someone is lying."

"Well, I suppose there's nothing to be done," said Lady Edwina in a tired voice. "Of course, Miss Anderson, if you feel that the strain of caring for Cassie is too much for you, we would understand if you decided not to continue . . ." Her voice trailed off.

With that statement, Lady Edwina made it impossible for me to withdraw from the situation. If I left now, Amelia Dorcas would see to it that a shadow hung over me for the rest of my life. *The poor thing, unbalanced, you know. The Danzels had to let her go. There was an incident—* I shut out the malicious inner voice and smiled at both women. "I feel perfectly capable of caring for Cassie. You may be certain that when I am on duty, I will devote myself to protecting her from harm. And I intend to speak with Dr. Vonfeldt about his unwarranted suspicions."

"I would be careful, my dear," smirked Amelia. "It is not wise to challenge a qualified doctor about his professional diagnosis. He is the physician in charge and an emotional outburst would only prove his point. I should hate to see that happen."

"I'm sure you would. You may rest assured, Miss Dorcas, I have no intention of helping Dr. Vonfeldt prove his point."

After they had gone, I gave in to anger and the frightening sense of impending disaster that their visit had brought. I felt as though a net of lies and innuendoes were about to entangle me in a terrifying mesh from which there was no escape. The vicious suggestion that I was the one responsible for last night's terror had shaken me.

I paced the room. I had never liked the white-toothed Dr. Vonfeldt, but I would never have expected such blatant untruths from him. *Madness!* Because of my father, they were questioning my own sanity. I was certain as I could be of anything that I was healthy and rational in my thinking. I was sure that, whatever malady had felled my father, it had not tainted my own mental acuity.

"There is nothing wrong with my mind!" I said aloud. I had been bombarded with reasons why I should not continue in the Danzels' employment. These ran the gamut of being in danger myself, according to Gavin, and now the danger I posed for Cassie, as suggested by Dr. Vonfeldt and openly expressed by Lady Edwina. A pattern of treachery had been set in place . . . but I didn't know why. Nor by whom! I had only one choice, to stay and try to protect myself and Cassie from someone who had placed a frame of violence around us.

After we had finished an early evening meal which I scarcely tasted, I gave Cassie her medicine and then led her into the sitting room. She seemed content to sit on the couch and stare at the floor as if mesmerized by a spray of flowers in the carpet. Her placid expression gave her thin face a smooth, serene look. She might be pretty, I thought, if she had some flesh on her bones and some animation in her face. Had she always been different, strange, hovering on the edge of madness? Or had the incident with her little brother been the precipitating event? I went to the couch and sat down beside her. The present situation tied us together with a Gordian knot. And I did not know where the danger lay for either of us.

As was my habit, I began talking to her as if she were an attentive listener. "Someone is trying to make it look like there was no one here last night." Talking aloud, I went back over everything that had happened. "We'll have to watch our step, Cassie. I don't know what is going on but—" A knock at the door suddenly cut off my monologue.

Very cautiously, I opened the door, and then let out a weak laugh of relief. It was Jack Harvey. His friendly, freckled face was a wonderful sight. He ambled into the gaudy sitting room and normalcy instantly returned.

"Good Lord!" he exclaimed as the impact of vines and roses and patterned rugs and furniture hit his esthetic sensitivity.

I laughed, already feeling better. "It's awful, isn't it? Some woman named Liz Chantilly moved in when the hotel first opened, and they let her furnish it the way she wanted. But she went mad—"

"And I can see why," he said with a wry grin. "This decor would put anybody into a squirrel's cage." Then he looked chagrined, as if he'd said something wrong. "I'm sorry. This is Cassie, isn't it?"

I nodded.

"She's different from what I expected . . . more vulnerable, somehow. Does she hear us?"

"I don't know. She just sits like that—and stares. Dr. Rodene says she's responding to some reality within her own head."

"She looks harmless enough but—" he shook his head. "I don't know how you can take it."

"It's difficult sometimes," I said, and weariness crept into my voice.

"Hey, you don't look so good yourself. What's the matter?"

"Nothing." I forced a smile. I wasn't about to spread the story of last night. I'd leave that to Amelia.

"I decided you must be avoiding me. I've painted the same damn bush in the garden a dozen times waiting for you to show up. Am I such poor company that you don't even want to have tea with me?"

"No, not at all. In fact, I intended to look you up this afternoon—when something else came up," I finished lamely.

He raise an unruly, reddish eyebrow. "Some*thing* or some*one*?"

"Someone," I admitted. "But I promise that tomorrow I'll come."

"Good. And don't forget Wednesday afternoon. That's the day the hotel artists will have an open house. Remember? Guests of the hotel are invited to stroll in and out of the studios to view our paintings. I'd be pleased if you came and looked at some of mine."

"I'd love to!"

My enthusiasm was so sincere that he colored at the roots of his red hair. "Guess you think I'm forward, coming up here like this and everything . . . but I was worried about you." He looked down at Cassie and his thick eyebrows pulled together. "I don't think you should be up here in this isolated tower all by yourself."

"Not you, too!" I said sharply.

"Oh. Sorry. I hit a sensitive nerve, I believe."

"Yes, you did. And I'm fine . . . just fine. This is my job. And I can handle it!"

"Sorry." He spread his hands in a helpless gesture. He turned to leave. "Just remember—I'm a friend. In case you ever need one."

I spent a restless night fighting off specters of all kinds as I drifted in and out of one disturbing dream after another. Everything was mixed up in a ghoulish mass: Gavin and Lynette laughing at me with mocking faces; Dr. Vonfeldt's white hands reaching out to snare me; Amelia Dorcas's sharp nose pecking at me like a woodpecker's bill. When I awoke my hair was moist from nervous sweat and I felt as if my whole body had been put on a washboard while I slept.

I went wearily into Cassie's room to begin the day's routine.

She was gone!

The covers were pulled back and an empty bed and rumpled sheets stared back at me.

My voice rose with sudden panic. "Cassie, where are you?" I fled down the short hall to the bathroom and threw open the door, hoping to find the missing girl there even though I always accompanied Cassie to the facilities. It was empty. I didn't know what I had expected but my rounded eyes stared at the high claw-footed bathtub to reassure myself that it was empty of water—and Cassie.

I rushed out into the sitting room. Both the hall and the balcony doors were locked with skeleton keys I kept in my bedside table. I checked. The keys had not been disturbed.

"Cassie, where are you? No time for games," I

said in a mock cheery tone, knowing the girl would never answer me even if she heard. I went through the suite again, looking into every nook and corner, under beds, behind floral drapes, every place where Cassie might be huddled out of sight. I couldn't find her.

She couldn't have disappeared. Not into thin air. Both doors had been locked—unless someone else had unlocked them with another key!

I froze in the middle of the bedroom floor. My mouth went dry. Had the same person who failed to send Cassie to her death the first time come back? Had he or she spirited Cassie away in the night? Even though I hadn't been sleeping very soundly, they could have let themselves in without my knowledge and taken Cassie. Or opened one of the doors and allowed her to wander away into danger.

The balcony was still locked and empty.

The stairs!

Caught in a frightening scenario, I ran down the short hall to the narrow stairwell and leaned over the railing to stare down into the vaulting stories below. The noise that floated up to me was the normal bustle. I could hear maids going up and down the steep steps and I knew that if a crumpled body lay there, someone would be screaming. No, Cassie did not lie at the bottom of the staircase. If she had left that way, she was gone!

I went back into the suite and shut the door, leaned up against it, closed my eyes and forced myself not to give in to pure panic. What should I do? Careful, an inner voice cautioned. Whatever had happened to Cassie, it would be charged to me. Dr. Vonfeldt's vicious innuendoes had set me up for instant culpability. I must not raise a hue and cry until I was certain that Cassie was not somewhere in the suite. And then, if someone had taken her away in the night—!

I swallowed a hard knot in my throat and very systematically went through the rooms again. In desperation, I jerked open the door of a small wardrobe in Cassie's bedroom, too small and crowded to be a hiding place but—

There she was!

Crammed into the tiny space under all the clothes, Cassie lay hunched up in a ball. At first I thought she might be dead but as light flowed into the wardrobe, she moved and I sobbed with relief.

"Cassie!"

The girl put her hands over her eyes. She whimpered, "Brites . . . brites."

"It's all right, Cassie. It's all right. Don't be afraid. Come on, now . . . let's get back into bed." She did not want to leave the dark closet but very firmly, I coaxed the girl out of the cramped hiding place. Only someone as small as Cassie could have hidden there, I thought, wondering if she'd been there all night. What silent terror had sent her there?

As I led her back to bed, Cassie continued to whimper "brites" and kept her head buried in arms thrown up over her head. Even the filtered morning light edging the drawn drapes seemed to bother her. When I spread a cover over her, she buried her head under it. I wondered if the electric light baths had driven her to this. I sat on the bed, comforting her, and in only a few minutes, Cassie was fast asleep.

I went out into the sitting room and slumped down in a parlor chair, weak and spent. Fright had drained my energy, leaving me as limp as wet paper. I resisted the impulse to put my head in my hands and sob.

Nothing had happened, I silently reassured myself as I sought to get my trembling under control. Only my imagination had put a sinister overtone on the incident. Something in Cassie's tormented mind had sent her into the wardrobe to hide from the light. I breathed deeply. Thank heavens I had not gone running to anyone making a spectacle of myself!

My hands remained unsteady as I went through my morning toiletries. The shadows in my cheeks had deepened and a tight line around my mouth remained even when I tried to relax my facial muscles. The morning's fright lay on me like a heavy cloak. If I hadn't learned to handle the pressures of my father's illness, I might have admittted defeat, but my resolve remained strong even as I admitted to myself that it was taking its toll on my nerves and health.

Cassie awoke in about an hour and the daily routine proceeded normally. She didn't seem any the worse for having spent an undetermined number of hours cramped up in the small wardrobe, and she accompanied me docilely across the street when it was time for her treatments.

We walked slowly through the landscaped gardens in front of the Alcazar, allowing my frayed nerves to heal as I watched the lazy flight of yellow butterflies among the green-gold leaves and vivid rainbow blossoms. Jets of water from the fountains caught the sunlight like streams of multi-colored beads. Arm in arm with Cassie, I engaged in my usual monologue, talking to her in soft tones about the loveliness of the morning. Under the shade of her bonnet, Cassie's eyes were nearly closed in that narrow squinting fashion of hers, but her muscle tone was firm as she moved by my side. Several times I thought she seemed to be listening like a blind person receiving stimuli through her other senses.

By the time we reached the stairs to the Casino's front doors, my mental equilibrium had been restored. I was ready to confront Dr. Vonfeldt about the vicious innuendoes which questioned my own mental health. I steeled my courage as we went in—but he was not there. Neither was Domincea. An unfamiliar gray-haired woman took charge of us when the receptionist rang her bell.

"Where is Dr. Vonfeldt?" I asked.

"Called on an emergency."

"And Domincea?"

"She accompanied him."

I had been steeled for a confrontation and now it had to be postponed. Cassie disappeared with an attendant, leaving me to return to the waiting room. When I heard Dr. Vonfeldt's name mentioned by two elderly ladies sitting near my chair, my ears immediately became attuned to their conversation.

"An unfortunate affair. Miss Delany had been a patient of Dr. Vonfeldt ever since he took over the health facilities. Everyone thought he was making progress with her. She was so young and pretty."

"Committing suicide like that right in her room at the Alcazar. Terrible. I guess she was in a lot of pain."

"She left a note, but no one knows what it says. Guess they'll be calling the family."

"I understand that some New York physicians recommended surgery but she refused. Dr. Vonfeldt assured her she had made the right decision. I wouldn't be surprised if she bequeathed a considerable amount to him in her will. He's quite ambitious, you know."

"Well, she had all the faith in the world in Dr. Vonfeldt."

All the faith in the world in Dr. Vonfeldt. The words were like soft-footed spiders trekking up my spine. I couldn't still a rising presentiment that Cassie was going to be another of the young women sacrificed to the saturnine doctor's ambition. What plans did Dr. Vonfeldt have for Cassie Danzel—and what would happen to Brianna Anderson if she got in the way.

Chapter Ten

On Wednesday afternoon, I waited for Domincea to relieve me as arranged, but she didn't come. My promise to Jack to attend the artists' open house made me especially anxious when four o'clock came and there was still no sign of her.

Cassie refused to take her nap and was more alert than she had been since I had taken charge of her. The girl kept her head erect now, and there were times when she seemed to be spanning between reality and the confusion in her mind. There was no sign this afternoon of the whimpering huddled creature who had hidden in the wardrobe all night.

"Let's take a walk," I said impulsively. Vance had wanted his sister to resume normal activities, I rationalized. Maybe this would be a good time to give it a try.

After I had brushed Cassie's dark hair and made a thick braid twist on her neck, I tied the streamers of a straw bonnet under the girl's chin. A simple fashioned white frock made Cassie look young, innocent—and normal. Those dark disturbing eyes were in shadow under the wide brim of her bonnet, and I was satisfied that a casual glance at Cassie's appearance would not bring undue attention upon her.

I wore a cream-colored summer gown with the same shade of peach lace as the silk ribbons on my new blue bonnet. A peculiar warm feeling spread through me as I tied the streamers. Thinking about that first day when I had tumbled into Gavin's arms on the train brought a smile to my lips. I was like a miser when it came to hoarding the memories he had given me. I couldn't forget the way he had held and kissed me in the carriage. If his fiancée hadn't shown up when she did at the school, I might have been persuaded to do as Gavin and Helen wanted, but reality had swept in with Lynette's silken skirts and lavender perfume.

Cheerful and confident, I took Cassie out of the hotel and we joined a stream of guests drifting through the hotel gardens. Ladies with parasols strolled languidly along the flagged walks or sat in shady arbors, chatting with friends or laughing coquettishly in the company of some admiring swain. I kept Cassie close at my side as we made our way along the east side of the hotel to the artists' quarters.

The two-story brick building which housed visiting artists had been built at the edge of the hotel property bordering on Valencia Street. Although it was roofed in the same Spanish red tile as the hotel, its rectangular lines were straight, broken only by the loggias running the length of the building on both floors. Climbing vines like rampant green cobwebs trailed over a staircase leading to the second floor, and tubs of flowering plants added color to the same grayish-white coquina stone used in the rest of the hotel facade. The back of the building faced the street but the front opened onto a pleasant courtyard.

In honor of the Wednesday open house, easels had been set up on the lawn to display the various artists' works. I quickly scanned the people milling about but failed to see Jack among them. Waiters passed through the crowd offering drinks and light refreshments. A hum of laughter and congenial conversation blended with the soft tones of a violin played by a man seated unobtrusively in the shadows of one of the arches. The gathering was festive, and I felt completely out of place. If I hadn't promised Jack to come see his paintings I would have deemed the outing a bad idea and gone back to the hotel.

With Cassie's arm looped firmly through mine, I joined a slow moving parade along the first floor loggia. We went in and out of several studios. A combination of styles and subjects were offered, all the paintings discreetly marked with exorbitant prices. Numerous floral oil paintings by George W. Seavery seemed to delight the female viewers. The ladies made cooing sounds and tittered their appreciation as each artist personally conducted them around his studio.

I completed a tour of the first floor studios without finding Jack so, lifting my skirts with one hand, I guided Cassie up the steps to the second-floor loggia. The soft, moist coolness under the arched roof was refreshing and I realized the day had become quite warm.

In the first studio, oil paintings depicting St. Augustine's quaint streets and houses were receiving rapt attention from milling viewers. These, Frank Shapleight's canvases, had the highest price tags of any I had seen. I wondered if Jack charged that much for his. I had nearly despaired of finding him when we reached the next to last studio and I glimpsed his red head through the doorway. There were few people in the room and he saw me immediately.

"I had about decided you weren't coming," he greeted me with a broad smile.

"Domincea didn't show up today. So I decided to bring Cassie."

He looked down at Cassie standing at my side like a blind person waiting for some indication whether she was supposed to walk or sit. "How is she?" He scrutinized the small placid face framed by the bonnet. "She's so . . . fragile looking." He took her hand in his big one and held it firmly. "Hello, Cassie."

Her eyelids flickered but she did not raise her gaze to meet his.

He looked at me questioningly. I shook my head. "I don't know how much she hears . . . or understands. I think she takes in what is happening around her but not in the same way we do; she handles it differently."

"Comes up with different answers?"

"Maybe." I told him about finding her hidden in the wardrobe. "It scared me to death when I found her bed empty. I didn't know whether she was in the suite or not. The doors were still locked but . . ." I swallowed the rest. I hadn't told Jack about the other incident so I didn't want to tell him that I'd suspected someone of taking Cassie away in the night. "Anyway, I found her huddled in a small wardrobe, hiding from the 'brites.'"

"'Brites'?"

"I think she means 'lights.' She covers her head as if to shut it out."

"Maybe that's why she keeps her eyes half-closed?"

"Maybe."

Several people who had been looking at the canvases wandered out and there was only one person left in the room, a plump young woman who sat in a corner sewing buttons on Jack's shirt. She snipped the thread with a pair of scissors and gave Jack a smile of satisfaction. Then she folded up a pile of mended garments, set the sewing basket on them, and stood up.

"All done." She smoothed a hotel maid's uniform that stretched tightly over her full bosom and ample hips. "That should be holding you for a few days," she told Jack with the lilt of an Irish brogue.

"My thanks, Molly. I don't know what I'd do without you."

"Ye'd be falling out of yer clothes, that's what." She winked at me and gave us a hearty wave as she left.

"Heart of gold," said Jack. "Decided I needed some mothering, I guess." He seemed embarrassed and added gruffly, "Well, did you come to see my work or not?"

Sunshine coming through a series of windows at the back of the building made the studio light and airy, and I could see why he had been persuaded to accept Henry Flagler as a patron for the privilege of working in such pleasant quarters. The telltale odors of turpentine and fresh paint perfumed the air. The studio was fairly crowded with old, but comfortable looking furniture. Every corner was stacked with drawings or frames and stretched canvases. A half-finished picture stood on an easel with a messy palette smeared with fresh paint, and a pile of brushes and tubes of paint.

With Jack on one side of Cassie and me on the other, we walked around the room, looking at framed and unframed canvases. Jack's paintings were different from anything I had seen in the other studios. No pretty flowers or romantic tropical gardens, nothing executed with a romantic touch. Jack painted figuratively, sometimes just a woman's face and sometimes groups of people, olive-skinned with the Mediterranean features he'd identified as Minorcan. The backgrounds were bold, almost harsh; bright yellows, oranges and sepia were thickly applied on the canvas with a palette knife. The painting which caught my eye was on an easel placed in a secluded corner. I stood and looked at it for a long time. The portrait was of a woman who looked strikingly like Domincea. She was older, with gray in her hair, but the dark eyes and strong, bold features could have been hers.

I was about to mention the resemblance when I heard the commotion of people coming into the studio. I turned around to see five visitors enter the room—all of whom I knew.

"Well, for heaven's sake! Look who's here," laughed Vance. He had a guiding hand on Lynette, who walked by his side, the epitome of loveliness in a soft azure silk gown and matching bonnet. "Brianna's brought Cassie to see the paintings."

"Do you really think she should have?" questioned Lynette, a worry line spoiling the ivory smoothness of her forehead.

"Of course. It's exactly what I wanted," Vance assured her as they crossed the room.

Lady Edwina gave a groan and flopped down in a chair, her bulk oozing over the sides like soft bread overflowing a pan. "I told you I didn't want to climb those steps," she lashed out at her husband. Sir Wilfred immediately patted her thick shoulder which was covered by a lace fichu that allowed a glimpse of her ample neck. He murmured something apologetic which Lady Edwina ignored. She kept up the tirade of complaint even after he had eased away from her side.

"Here, Edwina, use my fan," said Amelia Dorcas. "You never seem to remember yours." The tall angular woman was dressed in bright green and looked about the studio with her nose arched as if smelling something a little distasteful. "I can't say that I approve of his subject matter."

Edwina gave a languid wave of the fan. She said in a loud hiss that could be heard clear across the room. "I thought the artists' open house was for hotel *guests,* not hired help. What is Miss Anderson doing here?"

I flushed in the sudden, embarrassing silence.

"She is a guest," snapped Jack. "Mine!"

Amelia smirked. "Oh, I see. Another . . . friend of Miss Anderson. She doesn't seem to lack for male companionship, does she?"

"I think I'd better go," I said quietly to Jack. I didn't want to create a scene and I doubted that I could continue to keep my temper under control.

"No, stay. You haven't finished seeing everything."

I hesitated. Vance had taken Cassie's arm as if he were going to guide both her and Lynette around the room. I couldn't very well hurry Cassie away if her brother wanted her to stay.

Jack began talking to me about a new technique he was using to get depth in his water scenes. He showed me some paintings depicting fishermen on Matanzas Bay. As he talked I glanced at Cassie and saw that Vance was keeping her safely at his side.

Across the room, Sir Wilfred and Amelia viewed a painting with Fort Marion in the background and exchanged some heated words. The argument appeared to stem from some disagreement about the British occupation of St. Augustine. Sir Wilfred seemed bent on upholding the British right to command St. Augustine at some point in its turbulent history.

At that moment a richly dressed matron with a small dog clutched in her arms entered the studio. Dressed in a Parisian-styled gown, her flat breast was weighted with ropes of pearls and a diamond brooch. Dangling earrings sparkled in her ears and the flowered brim of her hat was almost a foot wide, with a high crown that made her head look off balance.

"Mrs. Bouchard," cooed Lady Edwina excitedly, getting to her feet. Apparently she was someone worthy of Lady Edwina's attention, I thought, watching the fat woman's obsequious manner. "How nice to see you. I should have expected you to be here. Everyone knows your reputation as an art patroness," gushed Lady Edwina.

Before the socialite, Mrs. Bouchard, could reply, the white ball of fur that was her lap dog leaped out of her arms and landed in the middle of a portfolio of drawings piled on a table, sending them all over the floor.

"Bicky! Bicky! Come back to mother this instant!"

But Bicky tore around the room, darting under chairs and knocking over the pile of cartons Jack had stacked in the corner.

"Get that dog out of here!" he roared. Several times he dived for the yapping creature, but missed.

"Bicky! Bicky! Naughty dog!"

The dog darted through Vance's legs and headed for the door.

"Stop him!" shrieked his mistress as three people appeared in the doorway to see what was happening. A young man reached down to scoop up the obstreperous Bicky and handed him back to Mrs. Bouchard.

"Oh, thank you. Thank you," she gushed. "He's such a willful little pixie. I didn't want to bring him, but he always bites at my shoes if I don't consent to take him."

The furor was over and Mrs. Bouchard left the room, scolding Bicky for his lack of manners but making no apology for the scattered drawings or the disorder left behind in the studio.

I had just stooped down to pick up a portfolio when Lynette screamed. I saw that her eyes were rounded in horror. She pointed at the painting of the Minorcan woman whom I had thought resembled Domincea.

My God! My breath caught. A pair of scissors stuck out of the woman's throat. The blade had been covered with red paint to give the illusion of blood gushing from an open wound.

My frantic eyes turned to Cassie.

She was pressed against a wall with a smear of red paint on her virginal white dress.

Chapter Eleven

Lady Edwina lashed out at everyone for subjecting her to such a deplorable, embarrassing situation, and she placed the blame directly on me. "We're paying *you* to look after my sister, Miss Anderson. Why weren't you watching her? Mooning over your artist instead of keeping Cassie under control!"

"That's unfair," I countered. "Cassie was surrounded by her *family!*" I shot a look at Vance. He had been escorting his sister and Lynette around the studio.

"That's true," said Vance readily. "It wasn't anybody's fault, Edwina. That stupid little dog took everybody's attention away from Cassie. I got involved in trying to catch it. I'm as much to blame as anyone."

"No one's to blame," said Lynette with her usual sweetness. "It is not fair to Miss Anderson." She smiled at me. "Gavin was worried that something like this might happen. The present arrangements are not adequate. Surely you now see the wisdom of finding a different position, Miss Anderson . . .

perhaps at the school?"

I stared at her. *Not you too!* Was Lynette a part of the conspiracy to get me away from Cassie?

Amelia's sharp eyes were taking it all in. "Doesn't Dr. Rodene think you capable of handling Cassie, Miss Anderson?" she prodded, like someone throwing timber on a fire.

"Nonsense!" snapped Vance, his usual congenial manner gone. "Brianna is not at fault here. She's doing a good job. You can see how Cassie has improved—"

"Improved!" shrieked Lady Edwina. "How can you say such a thing? After that—!" She touched her flabby hands to her own thick throat as if she could feel the blades of the scissors sticking there.

Sir Wilfred hovered over his wife. "There now, dear . . . no harm's done." He was obviously embarrassed by Lady Edwina's crude remarks and lashing tongue but was unable to stem the tide of her accusations.

"We were wrong to bring Cassie to St. Augustine," Lady Edwina lashed out at her brother. "We should have left her at Gray Oaks."

"Weren't you the one who first suggested the idea?" Vance flung back at her. "Don't try to put all the responsibility on me."

The conversation I had heard between Lady Edwina and Amelia came back. I remembered the way Lady Edwina had dismissed the idea of Cassie getting well under Dr. Vonfeldt's care, *as if she'd expected something like this to happen.*

And what about Vance? He made an outward show of caring about his sister, but did he? I couldn't keep from wondering how he would benefit from all of this.

"It's all right, honey," I murmured, keeping Cassie close to my side in a protective manner. Everyone looked at the two of us as if we were conspirators in this ugly act. The animosity in the room was palpable.

Jack must have felt it, for he came over to my side. "What in the hell is going on?" he whispered as Vance and Lady Edwina continued lashing out at each other.

"I don't know."

He frowned. "The girl is really dangerous, Brianna. It could have been blood and not paint spilled. Where'd she get the scissors?"

I nodded at the sewing basket sitting on the pile of mending. "They look like the ones your friend was using when we came in." I told him then how I had been struck by the resemblance of the woman in his painting to Domincea. "She's an attendant at the Casino, the one who cares for Cassie during my daily breaks. She didn't come today and that's why I brought Cassie along."

"You don't think Cassie was striking out at her, do you?"

"I don't know. Cassie hates the treatments. Maybe she thinks Domincea is responsible for them."

Jack's freckles stood out on his face like spots of black soot. "Thank God she struck out at a painted canvas and not a real person. I don't like it, Brianna. I don't like it at all!"

At that moment the family fight subsided. Vance began insisting that they pay for the painting.

"A very generous offer, Vance," said his sister in a scathing tone, "when you know who will end up paying for it. I'm the one who must foot all the bills. You and Sir Wilfred see to that!"

"Cassie has money of her own! It's her trust

that's paying our expenses here, not yours!" A moment of stunned embarrassment echoed his words. Color swept up into Vance's fair cheeks. He looked at Lynette and stammered, "Please excuse the family hysterics. I'm afraid we've let our emotions get out of control. We must pay for the damage that Cassie—."

"Forget the damn painting," said Jack.

"No, Mr. Harvey." Vance's charm was back in place. "You will receive proper compensation for the painting. Now, I suggest that Brianna take Cassie to her room. As for the rest of us, I'm sure an afternoon repast would not be amiss at this point." He smiled at Lynette in that persuasive way of his.

"A glass of . . . refreshment . . . would be very nice," said Sir Wilfred wistfully, licking his thin lips.

Lady Edwina glared at him. "We'll all have *tea* and forget this unfortunate affair!" she said, ignoring her husband's downcast expression which made it plain that tea was not what he had in mind.

I let them leave and then made my apologies to Jack. "I'm sorry . . . I really am. I never dreamed something like this would happen."

"It's not your fault. The whole thing is bizarre! I never realized that you were caring for someone so disturbed. I'm worried. There's no telling what she'll do next."

At that moment Cassie began stroking her hands in a peculiar fashion. As I noticed their pale whiteness, my mind lurched to a sudden stop! How could Cassie have put red paint on the scissors . . . on the painting . . . smeared on her dress—*without getting any on her hands?"*

I knew that if I didn't sleep, my eyes would be

sunken dark holes in my face by morning. I hugged myself as I paced the living room in my cotton nightdress and matching high-necked peignoir. A quickening wind caught under the roof tiles. Rain pelted against the windows and the sound of the storm rose and fell in haunting crescendos, blanketing the night with a starless sky. For some reason I had kept my startling observation to myself and had not mentioned the absence of paint on Cassie's hands to Jack. Perhaps it was the paint on his own hands that kept me silent, though I knew it was foolish to put any kind of sinister interpretation on the lingering red stains on his fingers. He might have been painting earlier and not removed it all. Still, I was silent about the evidence that proved Cassie was not the one responsible for ruining his painting.

Someone else was guilty! I was certain of it, and the ramifications were terrifying. Cassie had been exposed in public as a crazed lunatic, capable of jabbing a pair of scissors into someone's throat; the malicious setup had been deliberate. The mending basket was in full sight and tubes of paint were all over the place. The fiasco with the dog had produced such confusion that anyone in the room could have done it. Cassie did *not* have paint on her hands—who did?

The question would not let me rest. I went into Cassie's bedroom and found the girl lying on her back staring wide-eyed up at the ceiling. My heart lurched up in my throat. Cassie always slept on her side in a fetal position, curled up, hugging herself in a protective ball.

"Cassie?" I touched her arm gently and sat down on the edge of the bed. Cassie's thin, small frame hardly made a hump under the covers. "Are you awake?"

No answer, but a slight frown furrowed her pale forehead.

"I can't sleep either. It's almost one o'clock." I smoothed out the bedcovers. "I know you didn't do it, Cassie. Someone else stabbed that portrait and smeared red paint on your dress. Whoever it was wanted everyone to think it was you. When that dog was running all over the place, someone took the scissors out of the mending basket and a tube of red paint and ruined the picture." I was voicing my thoughts more for myself than for Cassie's enlightenment. "I've tried to remember. Everybody was wearing gloves except you and Jack. The guilty one could have taken them off, done the deed, and then put the gloves back on afterward. I'm positive someone was covering up red paint with a pair of gloves."

I sighed. I was silent for a long time and then said wearily. "There's nothing I can do, Cassie. I have to let them go on thinking it was you . . . but we know better." Impulsively, I put an arm around Cassie and held her close. "I'm not going to leave you, Cassie. They're not scaring me off." I bent my head against hers and closed my eyes to keep the tears from flowing. The sound of wind and rain cut us off from everything. It was just the two of us—alone.

Stilling an urge to stay there in Cassie's room, I got up, still looking at her pinched, pale face framed by a white night cap which kept the dark hair out of her eyes. The high necked gown and the ruffled edge of the cap made Cassie seem even younger and more vulnerable. "I wish you'd eat more, Cassie. You're too thin." I knew it was foolish to carry on such a mundane monologue with someone who was locked in a reality far removed from rest, food, and exercise. If my own loneliness had not been so acute I might have laughed at myself.

I went back into the sitting room. There was little I could see looking through the windows. All lights were blurred and faint, and this only added to my eerie sensation that the building was floating toward some murky waterfall that would soon sweep the elegant hotel off its moorings.

Night thoughts were dark specters all around me, and I was deeply conscious of my vulnerability. I had to be clever enough to protect myself and Cassie. At the moment, I felt anything but clever.

When a knock sounded on the hall door, I jumped as if a shot had sounded in the room.

"Yes? Who is it?" My chest rose and fell with quickened breath.

"It's me. Open the door, Bri."

Gavin! I clamped down on the sudden joy racing through my veins. "What do you want?" I answered in a measured tone. I couldn't let him in! I was in my night clothes, my hair was down.

"I want you to open the door."

"I can't . . . I'm in bed . . ."

"You are not. You're standing in the middle of the sitting room floor. Now open this door."

"I . . . it's . . . it's not a proper time for you to call . . ." I stammered.

"A doctor makes calls any hour of the day or night. Open up, or I'll have to get a key downstairs . . . and that might cause a lot of embarrassing questions. Open the door, Bri."

My mind refused to work. I wanted to see him. I desperately wanted to share the traumatic events of the day with him. Finally, the need to be with him outweighed all matters of propriety. I unlocked the door.

Gavin strode in without looking at me. "Where's Cassie?"

"In bed, of course!"

Without pausing, he went down the short hall and into the girl's bedroom.

Cassie lay curled up on her side, her eyes fully closed and her dark eyelashes lying tranquilly upon her wan cheeks.

"She's asleep," I whispered.

He nodded in satisfaction. "Good."

I followed him back to the sitting room. "What do you want?"

"I just got back from the school and decided to have a drink before turning in," he said. "Sir Wilfred was in the bar, having more than his usual intake of scotch. He told me about this afternoon's incident." Gavin looked at me then. "It's just as I thought. You're asleep on your feet. Well, I'm here now . . . go to bed, Bri."

He turned his back on me and began shifting pillows to one end of the long settee. His manner was so impersonal that I was unreasonably piqued. He didn't even seem to realize that I was embarrassed to be in my night clothes. In fact he hadn't given any indication that he had noticed me in any personal fashion. I watched him with open disbelief and resentment as he took off his fawn-colored coat and hung it on the back of a parlor chair.

"What are you doing?"

"Getting comfortable."

"You're not planning to stay here all night?"

"That's exactly what I plan to do." He loosened his soft tie. Without looking at me, he sat down. "Now get to bed. You can relax and get a good night's sleep. I'll keep my eye on Cassie."

He was so professional in his attitude that it was almost comical. He obviously was trying to play watchdog without causing me any embarrassment, but having him here was an impropriety that I could not permit.

"There's no need for you to . . . compromise my reputation," I said haughtily, not quite certain whether I was upset because he was so impersonal or because I didn't trust myself to maintain the attitude he had established.

"I'm not leaving you alone with Cassie. She's a killer. She proved that today."

"She's not a killer!

"All right—a potential killer. Sir Wilfred said she stuck a pair of scissors into the throat of some woman in a painting."

"She didn't do it. Someone else did it while our attention was on a little dog."

He looked at me then, searching my face. He must have seen conviction and the usual stubborn glint in my eyes. His jaw tightened as if to curb some emotion. "You'd better tell me exactly what happened."

I sat down in a nearby chair. I folded my hands in my lap and kept my head up, my eyes fixed on his. "I decided to take Cassie with me to the artists' open house this afternoon because Domincea didn't show up to relieve me . . . and because I'd promised Jack that I'd come. Cassie seems so much better now that I thought it might do her good to get out like that. Besides," I said defensively, "her brother has been encouraging me to try and resume some normal activity with her."

Gavin's steady gaze was impossible to fathom.

"Anyway, just after we got there, Lady Edwina

and Sir Wilfred, Vance and. . . ." I hesitated, "and Lynette came in." I took a deep breath and tightened the hands I had clasped in my lap. "We were looking at the paintings . . . Cassie was with Vance and Lynette . . . and then some woman, Mrs. Bouchard, came in with a little yapping dog that jumped out of her arms and began to wreak havoc in the studio, knocking over cartons, portfolios, drawings. There was bedlam for a few minutes trying to catch the beast. After she left . . ." I faltered.

"Yes?" His tone was still impersonal and it provided me with the rigidity I needed to go on.

"Lynette screamed and pointed at a portrait I'd noticed earlier. It was of a Minorcan woman who resembled Domincea. There was a pair of scissors jabbed in her throat . . . a smear of red paint . . . like blood around the cut."

"Cassie—?"

"That's what everyone thought. There was red paint on her dress, all right, and on the scissors—but none on her hands!" I said triumphantly. "None on her hands," I repeated, my heart leaping with suppressed excitement.

Gavin's dark eyebrows drew together.

"She wasn't wearing gloves," I told him. "Don't you see what that means? Cassie couldn't have handled the paint and scissors, and smeared it on her dress without getting a drop on her hands."

"Then who—?"

"I don't know. The guilty person must have taken off his or her gloves and then put them back on to hide any telltale paint smears."

"Was everyone wearing gloves?"

"Everyone but Jack and Cassie. There were paint smears on his hands, but that's the way they are all the time."

"Maybe someone hired him to do it?"

"What?"

"I said maybe someone—"

"I heard what you said. That's preposterous! He's a reputable artist and a—"

"A friend of yours. I know." He sighed. "All right, all right. But he did have paint on his hands."

"He's an artist! He always has paint on his hands and clothes!"

"You should have made everyone take their gloves off when you noticed Cassie's clean hands."

"They were already gone, but I'm certain they wouldn't have paid attention to me anyway. Lady Edwina was frying me in oil with her fiery remarks and it was agreed by one and all that I was somehow to blame."

"I told you someone was setting you up to be the scapegoat. Now maybe you'll listen to me and get out of this mess while you can."

"I can't leave now. Cassie needs me!"

"For God's sake, Bri! When are you going to get it through your head that she's not your responsibility? Your father was one thing but Cassie Danzel is another!"

"Someone's trying to make Cassie look like a dangerous lunatic—and she's not! She didn't do it. I'm not going to let others use her to carry out their own evil intent, as they did today. Next time they won't catch me unaware like that, I promise you!"

"So you are going to put yourself in danger over and over again. You're a poor, misguided fool—"

"So you've told me before," I snapped. "Now will you please leave?"

"No." His jaw was set. "You haven't convinced me that Cassie or someone else won't be after you in the middle of the night."

"I told you that she didn't do it!"

"Maybe she didn't, but you know damn well that something's going on! What good are you going to be to yourself or Cassie if you can't think straight? You need a good night's sleep and that's why I'm here. Now for heaven's sake, will you please take that delicious body of yours out of my sight!" His tone was gruff.

"You can't sleep on that sofa . . ."

"Doctors learn to doze anywhere. Please, Bri, don't argue. I didn't come here to force myself upon you . . . although the idea has its merits. You know how I feel about you and you know what the situation is at the moment, but I'm not going to let something happen to you while we're straightening it out. Now get out of my sight before I forget to act like a gentleman." He sat down abruptly on the settee and let his head fall back upon a cushion as he closed his eyes and stretched his legs out in front of him.

I hesitated. I knew I shouldn't give in but I really didn't want him to go. His presence had made the room seem cozy and warm despite the rain and wind outside. I wanted to sit beside him, brush the hair back from his forehead, and put my head in the hollow of his shoulder. Lines of fatigue deepened the cleft of his chin.

"You're tired," I said softly.

"Yes."

Sitting there with his eyes closed, his magnetism was greater than ever. My suspicions of him lost their validity in his presence. I knew that it was dangerous to trust him, but I couldn't help myself.

The fact that he seemed willing to stay up all night to protect me brought foolish tears into the corner of my eyes. What did it matter that he had committed himself to someone else? I wanted him to know that I appreciated his coming. Then, as if he sensed that I about to take a step toward him, he growled, "Don't! Go to bed . . . now!" He didn't raise his head or open his eyes. "Good night, Bri."

"Good night!" I swung around on my slippered heels and left the room. He was impossible! One minute gentle and caring and the next as abrasive as a cat's-claw bush. I'd never met anyone so infuriating.

I took off my robe, climbed into bed and pulled the soft covers up around my shoulders. I had to admit that the relief of having him within calling distance was unbelievable. Even though I had argued that Cassie presented no danger, I knew such a conviction was unfounded.

One thing was clear. Gavin was worried about my safety. He had come to protect me. The knowledge brought a soft smile to my lips. Well, at least for one night, I wasn't alone in this horrible, isolated suite. He was here with me and the knowledge began to ease the tension from my muscles.

I must have been asleep for several hours when the recurring nightmare of Cassie coming in and standing over my bed came back. This time the girl did not have a knife or hatchet in her hand, but a pair of bloody scissors. As she thrust them down viciously in the terrifying dream, I sat up, screaming and fighting the bedcovers.

The next instant, Gavin was beside me. At first, I lashed out at him as he tried to touch me. "No,"

I screamed.

"It's all right, Brianna," he said in that commanding voice of his. "You've had a nightmare."

I blinked wide-eyed at him and then crumpled, covering my face and sobbing. He sat on the bed and pulled me close, running his soothing hands over my trembling back. "Hush . . . hush . . . you're safe." "Cassie . . . scissors . . . she was going to stab me," I sobbed. I buried my head against his shoulder and my body shook uncontrollably as he held me against his hard chest.

"Cassie's sound asleep. You were dreaming."

"It was awful. So real." I gulped, trying to get control of myself.

His lips touched my wet cheek, brushing away my tears with light, silken kisses. "Don't cry. It's over now, darling. I'm here."

It seemed right for him to be there, to soothe and comfort me. Cradling me in his arms and gently trailing kisses along my cheeks, his strength and warmth eased into my trembling body. The love I had been trying to deny surged through me like a great river overflowing its banks, sweeping me along in its rising tide. I lifted my tear-washed face to his, raised my arms and locked them around his neck, pressing the ripe fullness of my breasts against his chest.

He kissed my eyelids, moist with tears, and murmured endearments. "My wonderful, precious, brave Brianna." He loosened my hair from its braid and his fingers laced the thick strands like a fan upon the pillow.

"I should go back to the living room," he said huskily.

"No . . ."

"If I don't go now—"

"I know . . ."

"Bri . . ."

"I know," I said again.

Soft moonlight touched my face and he searched it as if seeking some sign that would strengthen his resolve to leave me. I pulled his face down to mine. "Kiss me," I ordered. I had waited long enough for this dream to come true. My mouth parted under his and I welcomed the questing tongue that teased and aroused me. I let my hands trail down the back of his head, and then traced the smooth lines of his shoulders rippling under the white linen of his shirt. At some point, he discarded his clothes, eased in beside me and drew the length of my body against his.

"Don't go," I pleaded, fearful that the dream would fade.

He gave an amused chuckle. "No, darling I won't go." He slipped off my gown and his lips hovered over my breasts. His mouth and tongue teased the hardening pink buds and then returned to my lips to cover them with possessive kisses.

From my lips to my trembling thighs, he brought an awareness of my body that I had never before experienced. I felt totally and utterly desirable, a woman capable of receiving and giving deep passion. I was whole . . . complete . . . caught up in an experience that dwarfed all others. Circles of indescribable pleasure radiated outward from his touch, enveloping me in a bewildering rapture. I gasped his name and clutched him to me.

He parted my legs, smothering my mouth with a kiss, and soon the rhythm of his body swept me away from all pain to mounting ecstasy. I was a part of the rising crest of passion that became unbearable until I cried out in a culminating, exploding sensation.

Afterwards, we lay quietly, spent and fulfilled. Gavin kissed me lightly on the forehead and murmured with a wry smile, "Now you'll sleep, my darling."

Chapter Twelve

I stirred languidly the next morning as I began to awaken. If I had any more dreams, they were only the kind that brought a soft smile to my lips. I stretched out my long supple limbs under the rumpled covers and murmured contentedly. I had enjoyed a deep, refreshing sleep, the kind that had eluded me for so many nights. Shafts of light from an early sun pierced lingering rain clouds and promised a warm, bright day. Doves nesting in the high crevices of the hotel announced their pleasure as they cooed and flapped their wings to dry in the sunlight.

For a moment I stared blissfully at the ceiling, then the memory of last night brought me straight up in bed.

I was alone.

No sign of my lover remained. Had I been dreaming? No, I was naked. My nightdress was still in a crumpled heap on the floor. I covered my breasts with my hands and found that they still tingled. My nipples hardened with remembered caresses. Heat swept up into my cheeks.

In the light of morning, the remembered passion was indecent. I was shocked by what had happened—and I knew I was to blame. How could I ever look Gavin Rodene in the face again? I had clung to him, cried on his shoulder, and like a brazen doxy, I had invited him into my bed.

As I took a bath and then dried my body, still warm as from a lover's touch, I could no longer deny the truth. I was hopelessly in love with Dr. Gavin Rodene. There was no way to go back, and what lay ahead frightened me. He was betrothed to another. Endearments had fallen from his lips but no promises.

Why had he slipped out without waking me? Was he already regretting his behavior? Maybe he intended to pretend that it had never happened. I was not foolish enough to think that I was the first woman to spend the night with the handsome Dr. Rodene. Had he come to my apartment knowing exactly what would happen? He had not been able to persuade me to take his advice any other way; maybe he decided that making love to me would lessen my resolve to stay with Cassie. Had he used my foolish infatuation to further his own malevolent purposes? But even as the possibility taunted me, I did not believe it.

The breakfast cart had just been removed by a hotel steward when someone knocked at the door. A boyish hotel attendant held out a florist's box to me.

"You must have made a mistake."

"This is the only tower suite in the hotel with a lovely lady in it," he said with a grin, his frank gaze complimentary. "That's what the man said."

I accepted the box with as much grace as I could manage but I know my surprise had given me away. I had never received flowers from anyone, not even my father. A huge bouquet of red roses rested in the green tissue paper. With trembling fingers I opened the small card with "Tower Suite" printed on the outside. It had a simple, scribbled message: "Good morning." It was not signed.

I buried my nose in the sweet blossoms and allowed myself a foolish giggle. The flowers were the reassurance I needed. I stroked my cheek with one velvet rose bud. The only disturbing thing about the card was the fact that Gavin had not signed his name. This brought back the reality of his situation. He was engaged to be married and that tie must be broken before he was free to admit his love for me. In the meantime I could hold his love secretly, like a protecting armor, I told myself. I refused to question my innocent belief that, since he had made such passionate love to me, he would want to marry me instead of Lynette.

The dark shadows were gone from my cheeks. The mirror told me that my skin glowed with new translucent beauty, and I couldn't keep the sparkle from my blue eyes. Even my simple white lawn blouse and navy walking skirt took on a graceful lilt as I floated about, humming foolishly and talking gaily to Cassie as if we were confidantes.

In this blissful happiness, I took Cassie across the street to the Casino for her morning treatments. I was curious as to why Domincea had not come yesterday to relieve me, but my curiosity went unsatisfied. Domincea did not come forward to receive us as she usually did. Instead a slender young man answered the receptionist's bell.

The male attendant was dressed in white and his tall, lithe frame was a sharp contrast to Domincea's muscular build. As if aware of my scrutinizing gaze, he peered through thick lenses in gold-rimmed spectacles and said rather self-consciously, "I'm Ralph Winters. I usually work on the men's side but this morning I'm taking care of the electro-treatments. Will you please follow me?"

Apparently he didn't know that I wasn't allowed to accompany Cassie, and I wasn't about to enlighten him.

"As soon as she is ready, bring her into the next room," he said when we reached women's dressing room door.

I nodded as if I were familiar with the routine. Where was Domincea? I wondered as I undressed Cassie and helped her into a white robe. Did her absence this morning have something to do with the incident with the painting yesterday? That didn't seem likely. Had she been dismissed because of the woman who had committed suicide? Both she and Vonfeldt had been away after it happened. I was glad that a nice young man had taken her place even if it was just temporarily.

Ralph Winters was waiting for us in the Electro-Therapy room. Nothing had changed in the room since that first day I had brought Cassie here. It was still empty except for the two electric cabinets and the bare faucets and hoses left for the tubs that had been removed.

I watched Cassie carefully to see her reaction. If she started screaming again, I didn't know if I could hold my tongue even though I desperately wanted to find out exactly what they were doing to Cassie during these treatments. My resolve to keep my mouth shut was short-lived. When the young man began blindfolding Cassie, I gasped involuntarily. "Why are you doing that?"

"Blindfolding her? Because the lights seem to bother her. It's not unusual . . . patients of this kind usually prefer darkness."

I remembered the incident of Cassie hiding in the closet and complaining about the "brites!" I had noticed that the girl kept her eyes and head covered a lot of the time as if trying to shut out light.

He eased Cassie into the cabinet without any protest on her part. Apparently the thick blindfold was reassuring but still he took white straps and fastened her arms down securely.

I was relieved that Cassie did not wince or cry out when he turned on the numerous electric bulbs. The inside of the cabinet glowed with orange light. "She doesn't seem to mind it," I said, letting out my breath.

"No, it's just a pleasant warm sensation. Would you like to stick your hand in and see how it feels?" he offered, noticing my alarm.

"Yes, I would." I took off a glove and put my arm in the cabinet. It was just as he said, pleasantly warm and nothing else. I reasoned that it must have been the bright light that had caused Cassie's discomfort the first time. I couldn't see how lying under a couple of dozen light bulbs would do her any harm—or any good either.

After fifteen minutes, he took Cassie out of the cabinet and we went into another room where he put her in sunken marble tub filled with warm water. I remembered that at Gray Oaks water was used to quiet patients.

I watched Cassie as she sat on a marble bench that ringed the pool. She seemed quite tranquil. Her heavy-lidded eyes remained half-closed. I felt myself relaxing. I had been prepared to see Cassie as a victim but I could see nothing threatening about the daily treatments in this sunken bath nor in the electric light cabinet. The whole procedure seemed benign—as well as ineffective.

When we were ready to leave, Ralph Winters

bade us goodbye. I was tempted to ask him about Domincea, but I restrained myself. I didn't want him to think that I preferred the older woman when the exact opposite was true. I hoped he might be assigned to relieve me as Domincea had been doing. "See you tomorrow?" I asked, in a probing tone.

"Tomorrow, as usual."

His answer was disappointing. The daily two hours away from Cassie were necessary to keep my sanity, and I would hate to give them up.

On the way back to the hotel, I saw Amelia Dorcas in the Alcazar courtyard in time to avoid her. She was one person I didn't want to meet. I was afraid that the prying gossip would pick up on my heightened senses, look into my bemused eyes, and read the truth there. If she found out that Gavin had spent the night with me—! I turned pale just thinking about it.

As I started across the lobby, the officious desk clerk called my name and handed me a folded message. It read, "Will pick you up at two o'clock, carriage entrance. Gavin."

I could feel my cheeks burning as I turned away. My stomach was suddenly tumbling around like a nervous acrobat. I was going to be with him again in a couple of hours.

I was skittish as a young colt as I waited for lunch to be brought up. The hotel attendant was late with it. "Sorry. Everything's a mess in the kitchen. Two of the cooks walked out and orders are stacked up like leaves falling off trees." He left on the run.

I lifted off the silver covers. A salad of artichoke hearts, shrimp Florentine in golden pastry shells still steaming and aromatic, and a variety of dessert cheeses made a colorful display upon gold-rimmed porcelain plates. I spread a white damask napkin across my lap and Cassie's. As usual the food was very good. I tried to eat but a taut excitement brought a full feeling to the pit of my stomach.

As though Cassie had picked up on my nervousness, she became extremely belligerent and uncooperative. She even knocked the spoon from my hand when I tried to feed her a bite of pastry.

Exasperated because the food had splattered on the white leg-o-mutton blouse I was wearing, I said shortly, "All right. Here, feed yourself!" I thrust the spoon into the girl's hand.

Cassie stared at the spoon as if trying to recognize the object. She held it motionless in her hand. Her forehead puckered and her gaze never wavered from the metal object.

I held my breath and watched her. I sensed that something was going on in that dark fathomless mind of hers. What in the world was she thinking? It was the first time I had seen Cassie with such an intent expression on her face, as if trying to draw something out of her murky memory. I was breathless watching the change in her face. Cassie's dark eyes were no longer empty and glazed, but alive! They registered some inner perception.

"What is it, Cassie?" My tone was soft.

No response.

It was unnerving to watch her. How could Cassie continue to stare at that spoon with such a fixed, unblinking look? Just about the time I began to think that she would gaze at it forever, she moved her other hand and slowly began to stroke the smooth, rounded curve of the silver spoon. Deep in her throat came a noise like a soft crooning, similar to that of a lullaby. The sound was eerie, scalp-tingling.

Why was Cassie petting the spoon like that? She raised her eyes. "Bud . . . Bud . . . Bud . . ." Cassie said the word over and over in a monotone voice, looking directly at me!

My stomach muscles tightened. This was the first time that Cassie had ever tried to communicate with me. "Bud?" I echoed in a strained voice.

Cassie's eyes were fixed on my face with the same intense stare she had given the spoon. I didn't know what to say or do.

Then very slowly her hand reached out, and she touched my face with the same searching probing she had shown that night in the bedroom. I remained quiet and let the girl's fingers trail over my mouth and nose, and slip down my cheek. I remembered Gavin had said that in some mental cases everything became flat, one-dimensional, like cardboard. As suddenly as she had reached out, she dropped her hand. She seemed satisfied. "Bud . . . Bud?" she said again. This time there wsa a questioning tone.

"Bud," I repeated. Then I took Cassie's hand and kissed it. "I don't know what you're saying, but it's all right. Good, Cassie. Good." I blinked rapidly against a sudden fullness in my eyes. Cassie had reached across a dark chasm and touched me. An attempt at communication was there. "Good girl. Good girl." I took the spoon and this time Cassie let me feed her.

After lunch, I settled Cassie in bed for her nap, excitement over the new development racing through me. Cassie was getting better. I felt that she was drawing back from the dark edge of complete and irrevocable madness.

As I dressed I worried what I would do if Domincea didn't come. The woman's absence this morning indicated that she was no longer carrying out her daily responsibilities.

I considered contacting Vance. He had told me to call him if I needed him. But he had also expressed his disapproval the day I had tea with Gavin. I must not let anyone suspect anything. This new, wonderful ecstasy was too fragile. Being in love was like an opening blossom which a harsh wind could shatter in one cruel moment. I knew that the wrong person could carelessly destroy it. Even now I could not shake an uneasiness that warned me that such happiness was too precarious to endure.

I dressed carefully as if there were no question about keeping the rendezvous with Gavin, and at exactly two o'clock a knock came at the door.

Domincea! I jerked open the door. "Oh," I stammered.

Ralph Winters shifted his long, lanky body and looked through his thick spectacles at me. "I hope I'm not late?" He still wore his white coat and trousers.

"Oh, no," I answered, flustered. "I . . . I was expecting Domincea."

"I was just informed that I'm taking her assignments for the time being. May I come in?"

"Oh, of course," I said, stepping back. "I'm sorry. I didn't mean to give the impression that you weren't welcome. I was just surprised, that's all. And worried, too. You see I have an appointment that I don't want to miss." I knew I was babbling and gave an embarrassed laugh. "I'm glad you came."

He smiled and his face lost some of its plainness. "Is there anything I should know about Cassie?"

"She's asleep now. She needs her medicine when she wakes up. Since I didn't have my free time yesterday," I told him with a boldness that surprised even me, "today I will take a longer break than usual . . . if that's all right?"

His eyes slid to the bouquet of roses on a nearby table. "I understand." Were his eyes actually twinkling behind those heavy lenses? "Have a good time."

I put on my bonnet, looping the blue satin ribbon into a bow under my neck. I saw in the mirror that excitement had put a rosy hue in my cheeks and my eyes sparkled with the anticipation of seeing Gavin. My dress was a deeper rose color than the flowers on my hat and the tight bodice was fashioned with a lace inset which allowed pale skin to be seen under the delicate trimming. I had worn it to some of the faculty summer parties in the halcyon days when my father was well.

"You look very nice," Ralph said shyly, and then looked embarrassed by his compliment. He probably was not used to flattering young women.

"Thank you," I smiled graciously. I felt like laughing and chattering excitedly but tried to maintain my composure as I took my leave. I was a woman in love, and very much afraid that it showed on my face and in the way I floated over the floor with a joyous step. I looped the chain of my reticule over my arm, pulled on a pair of long ivory gloves, and nodded goodbye.

I boldly rang for the elevator. I felt invincible, my high spirits giving me confidence enough to take on Ira Deitz. When the doors flew open I was ready to do battle, but I didn't have to. A younger man was at the elevator controls and he bade me a pleasant "Good day."

He was obviously new to the job and had trouble leveling the iron cage at each floor, but I was glad the cantankerous Mr. Deitz was not around to break my mood. I took it as a good sign that I was about to embark on a glorious outing. This optimism was short lived. As I stepped out of the elevator on the main floor, a familiar raspy voice halted me. "Miss Anderson . . . just a moment, please!"

I turned to meet the woman I least wanted to see—Amelia Dorcas!

"My, don't we look attractive today," Amelia simpered. "Such a pretty flush on your cheeks. And such a flattering bonnet. Did you buy it in St. Augustine? I saw one just like it in the hotel arcade. A very expensive price tag. A gift, perhaps?" she smirked, as if she already knew the answer.

The obnoxious woman seemed to be ubiquitous and all-knowing. It would do no good to lie to her, I thought with despair. If Amelia hadn't already guessed, she would probably make it her business to go in the shop and find out who had bought the bonnet. "My other bonnet was ruined the day of the train incident. Dr. Rodene graciously replaced it."

"Such a generous person, isn't he?" Her beady eyes gleamed. "Always wanting to do the right thing. And Lynette is so understanding. Poor girl, she has no idea how devious men can be. Imagine not even suspecting that her fiancé is sending another woman flowers." The older woman cackled.

I wondered if I hid my sudden consternation. *She knew!*

"Don't worry, dear. My lips are sealed. I just

happened to be in the elevator this morning when the boy got in with the florist's box. I couldn't help seeing "Tower Suite" written on it."

"Oh, you must mean the bouquet of roses . . . for Cassie," I lied, in what I hoped was a careless tone. Amelia couldn't have seen the intimate message inside.

The woman's hawk-like nose quivered as she gave a rasping laugh. Amelia didn't challenge the lie, but I knew that she wasn't fooled. "Really, my dear, I've never seen you looking quite so—radiant."

It was just as I had feared. My emotions showed. Did the woman sense that my body still held the flush of a lover's embrace, that every nerve was tingling, waiting for his touch? "If you will excuse me, Miss Dorcas," I said with a rush. "I've been looking forward to a walk in the garden." I turned away and deliberately headed in the opposite direction from the carriage entrance. It would be just like Amelia to follow me and find out who was waiting there for me.

My heart was pounding loudly as I went down the hall and exited from the rear door. Once outside, I pressed up against the building and waited to see if Amelia was coming after me. I stiffened as the door opened almost immediately, but it was an older gentleman and not Amelia.

"Thank heavens," I sighed, letting out my breath. Jack had conducted me about the buildings and grounds so I was familiar with the passage that ran under the building to the other side of the hotel. Hurrying as if I were some kind of conspirator, I made my way around the building to the carriage entrance.

Gavin was there waiting with a small buggy. His

eyes were fixed on the other entrance, and he blinked with surprise when he saw me approaching from the back of the hotel.

"Amelia Dorcas," I said, in answer to his questioning frown as he helped me in the buggy. "She waylaid me in the lobby to let me know that she saw the flowers you sent this morning. I lied and said they were for Cassie, but I don't think she was fooled."

Gavin's jaw tightened and I knew he was swearing under his breath. "That vulture. Somebody ought to wring her neck. I suppose she'll go running to Lynette."

I was startled by the vehemence in his voice and I saw that his fists were white-knuckled on the reins. My euphoric happiness began to fade. *Gavin did not want Lynette to know about us.* Nothing had really changed, had it? I had been a fool to think that all his responsibilities for Lynette had been put aside. Reality was a harsh light destroying the rosy dream that had embraced me all day.

I bit my lip to keep it from trembling. "Where are we going?"

"Some place where we can talk."

Talk? Not make love? I desperately wanted him to hold me in his arms. I glanced at his rigid profile. It was hard to imagine his lips soft and yielding, kissing mine with a persuasive gentleness. I wanted to reach out and touch him but I was afraid. He was a stranger, angry and aloof, lost in his own thoughts. Stubborn pride made me want to lash out and crumple that aristocratic veneer of his.

"Cassie's getting well."

I couldn't have hoped for a more visible reaction. "What?" he swung his head around. His gray eyes were like honed steel. "What did she do?"

"She tried to communicate with me."

"My God!" He reined the horse near a slow moving inlet by the river. Some fishing boats trolled the waters near the rounded green island of Anastasia. He ignored the tranquil scene and swung around to me. "What did she say?"

"Bud."

"This is no time for jokes." He glared.

"I'm not joking. That's what she said. 'Bud . . . bud . . . bud.' All the time she was stroking a spoon. Do you know what it means?"

"No, but I'm damn sure that she knows. If she's started to bridge the gap between her inner reality and the outside world, it's only a matter of time before she can make herself understood."

"But isn't that wonderful? She is getting better."

"You're getting out of there, Bri. I'll arrange for someone to pick up your things."

Sudden anger overrode all my other emotions. "I'm not leaving. I've told you that a dozen times."

"I know." His eyes softened, and his mouth lost some of its rigidity. "But after last night—"

"Last night doesn't change anything. I'm sorry to disappoint you, but you miscalculated. Making love to me isn't going to make me change my mind—if that was your intent."

"It wasn't and you know it!"

"I only know you're hiding something from me."

"Bri—" he began in a patient, exasperated tone.

"Deny it," I challenged him. "Deny that you're afraid Cassie is going to reveal something about her little brother's 'accident.'"

Gavin worked his handsome jaw but did not deny it. "I want you to leave because I love you. It's not safe. It never has been. Cassie—"

"I'm not afraid of Cassie."

"You are a hard-headed, stubborn little fool."

My lips trembled. "Please take me back to the hotel."

"Not until you listen to me. We'll leave St. Augustine as soon as we can. You're getting out of that situation."

No declaration of love . . . no proposal of marriage . . . just authoritative orders.

I refused to look in his eyes and drew away from him.

"I love you, Bri. And I wish things were different at the moment, but they're not. I can't just withdraw from my commitment to Lynette. She's been my responsibility for too long. It's going to take time to settle things—and until I can, you must do as I say."

His declaration of love sounded hollow, as if he were trying to manipulate me again. Just how far would he go to get me away from Cassie Danzel?

Chapter Thirteen

Jack Harvey surprised me by joining me and Cassie on our way to her treatments a couple of days later.

"Where have you been keeping yourself?" He peered at me with a raised eyebrow. "You don't look so good. Is Cassie getting you down?"

"Not Cassie."

"It must be a man then."

I nodded.

"That handsome Vance Danzel, no doubt."

I looked surprised. "Why do you think that?"

"I overheard him doing battle with Lady Edwina over you. He was defending you against the old biddy's snide remarks. She wants you gone."

"I know."

Jack glanced down at Cassie. He seemed startled to see her walking with her head upright. "How is she?"

"Much better. Little by little, she seems to be fighting her way out of a dark morass."

"Is that a doll she's carrying?"

"Yes, Ralph Winters gave it to her. He's a male attendant who has taken over for Domincea, and he's marvelous with Cassie. He just arrived here from England, where he's had experience with the mentally ill. Apparently he'd worked with someone like Cassie and had success using a doll to help breach the gulf between mind and reality. Cassie strokes the doll and talks gibberish to it. It makes one shiver to watch. She covers up the doll's head with a blanket just as she does her own. It's impossible to figure out what she's thinking or saying, but at least she's coming out of that catatonic state. Ralph seems to have established some contact with her. He seems to understand what's going on in her tortured mind."

"He should have been in the studio when she jammed the scissors through my painting."

"I don't think she was the one responsible."

"What?" Jack looked at me as if he couldn't have heard correctly.

"It was somebody else. It had to be. Cassie didn't have any red paint on her hands, when it was all over the scissors, the painting, and her dress. Tell me, how could she have done it and kept the paint off her hands?"

"My God! She couldn't have. You just have to touch one of my paint tubes and you've got some on your fingers. I found that tube of red on the floor later . . . smeared and messy."

"Then that proves it! Someone deliberately made things look like Cassie had done it."

"Why would they do that?"

"I can only guess . . ."

"And?" he prodded.

I took a deep breath. "If something else happens—God knows what it might be—who is going to be accused of doing it?"

"Cassie."

I nodded. "I'm horribly afraid that somebody is deliberately setting Cassie up."

He let out a slow whistle. "I don't like it!"

"Neither do I. And I've got to make certain that it doesn't happen."

"But how are you going to do that? My God, you're putting yourself in danger, Brianna. You can't handle something as diabolical as this."

"Yes I can. Now that I have Ralph Winters' help, I feel even more confident."

"What happened to Domincea?"

"She was let go. Unfairly, Ralph says, but Dr. Vonfeldt had to have a scapegoat. A patient of his committed suicide and left a note that was critical of the care she had received. Since Domincea had been the one in charge of her treatments, Dr. Vonfeldt dismissed her as a public gesture that he had solved the problem. I never liked Domincea all that much, and Cassie is much better with Ralph, but I feel bad that she lost her job."

"It's you I'm worried about. You could be in danger. Brianna, you should get out of this while you can!"

"You sound like . . . like somebody else I know."

"But you're not going to listen to me any more than you listen to him. Right?"

"Right!" I gave him the full warmth of my smile. "I appreciate your concern, Jack. Really, I do."

"I see you're still wearing the pin I bought you."

"Of course."

"Don't forget what you promised. If you need me . . ."

"Thanks. You'll always be my friend, Jack."

"Good." He gave me a crooked grin and left me at the steps of the Casino. I didn't tell him that he was the only one who had had paint visible on his hands that day. He would have been hurt by the observation, and I wasn't about to jeopardize his friendship. But I hadn't forgotten it!

I looked up then and saw Vance waiting for us at the top of the stairway. From his expression, I thought he was displeased that I had been walking with Jack. My stubborn independence made me thrust my shoulders back as we mounted the curved staircase. I was ready to tell him that my choice of friends was my business when he took the starch out of my demeanor by saying, "I want to talk to you about Ralph Winters."

"What's the problem?"

"Perhaps none . . . but he seems to be having a lot of influence on Cassie. Giving her dolls, spending a lot of extra time with her. Every time I come to see Cassie, he has just come or is just leaving."

I felt my spirits sinking. I had been so grateful to have someone share the responsibility for Cassie that I hadn't even considered the possibility that Vance might not approve of the new attendant. *Didn't he want his sister to get better?*

"I think he's good for Cassie."

"What do we know of this man? Does he think he's some kind of doctor? How do we know he's not doing more harm than good?"

"One look at her answers that," I countered briskly. "She's no longer a limp marionette with all the strings cut. Now she moves around on her own. Her attention is not always centered inward. Sometimes I think she's even aware of me as another person."

At that moment Cassie raised her eyes and looked directly at Vance. "Bud . . . Bud . . . Bud!"

Her brother looked as stunned as if she had given him a vicious blow to the stomach. His mouth worked, but nothing came out.

Cassie lowered her gaze to her doll and began stroking it. "Bud . . . Bud . . . Bud . . ."

"You know what that means?" I asked, sudden excitement catching in my throat.

He nodded, as if swallowing against a sudden dryness. His voice was uneven. "My little brother, Teddy, had a stuffed bear he called Bud. It was found beside Teddy on the terrace when he fell to his death."

I put my arms around Cassie's thin shoulders and squeezed her. "Good, girl." I looked up at Vance. "Don't you see? That word is a slender thread stretching to the present!" My happy smile challenged Vance's ashen look. I told him about the incident when Cassie had said "Bud" for the first time. "She looked at the spoon as if it were a cue for remembering. Does that mean anything to you?"

He nodded. "Teddy used to throw a tantrum if Cassie didn't feed his bear at the same time she fed him. My little brother was spoiled. Threw a temper tantrum any time someone didn't do what he wanted. He made life hell at home, especially for Cassie. Our mother made Cassie responsible for keeping him quiet and out of her hair."

"She was like a mother to him then?"

Vance nodded. "Cassie was about seven years old when mother found out she was going to have Teddy. She didn't want another child, and as soon as Teddy was born, she turned his care over to hired help. Edwina and I were busy with our own lives and Cassie was the only one in the family who spent any time with him. We know now that Cassie was under a lot of mental strain; she was only a child herself and being responsible for a two-year-old was too much. Looking back . . . well, she had reached a breaking point and we didn't know it. My father tried to make it up to her by leaving her Teddy's share of his wealth."

I couldn't keep my eyes flaring from surprise. Cassie had inherited *double* what Vance and Edwina had realized from their parents' death! Getting control of that much wealth was certainly a motive for hoping that Cassie would not live too long. "And Cassie was found with scratches on her face in the same room where Teddy fell from the window," I said aloud.

"How did you know that?"

"Dr. Rodene told me."

Vance swore. "Those Rodenes take a lot upon themselves. His father had no business being involved. He wasn't even our family physician."

"But he was a good friend of your father's," I countered. "Isn't that why he was called?"

"I don't know. I . . . I wasn't there when it happened."

"You were away . . . at school?"

"No, I had moved back into the house. Edwina and Sir Wilfred were living there too, but I wasn't in the house at the time of the accident."

"Do you think it was an accident?"

"Of course," he said sharply. "Some more of Gavin Rodene's vicious speculations, I presume? What is he suggesting? That Cassie threw my brother out the window?"

"Perhaps not Cassie—"

"What is that supposed to mean?" His easy, affable manner was gone. "What are you insinuating?"

"Nothing," I said quickly. "I didn't intend to suggest anything. I am very fond of Cassie and I'm just trying to understand the whole situation as best I can. In my judgment, Ralph Winters is very good for your sister. You can see for yourself that she's more alert. You do want to see her improve, don't you?" My steady gaze challenged him. "That's your reason for bringing her to St. Augustine, isn't it?"

"Of course it is."

"Then I should think you'd encourage Mr. Winters to spend as much time with your sister as possible. He seems able to reach her better than anyone else."

"You don't think I should speak to Dr. Vonfeldt about him? After all, he is the physician in charge."

I knew what would happen if Dr. Vonfeldt found out that his attendant was getting credit for Cassie's improvement. Ralph Winters would be dismissed as fast as Domincea had been. All Vance had to do was repeat the glowing report I had just given of Ralph, and he would be on his way.

"I'm sure you and your sister want Cassie back to normal as soon as possible." I waited for his nodded agreement. "Then you shouldn't say anything to anyone. If you do, Cassie might lose the ground she has gained." With those words, I dumped the responsibility in his lap. If he had Ralph discharged, there would be only one conclusion to be drawn—he didn't want his sister to get well!

"All right." Vance forced his affable smile. "We'll let things remain as they are . . . for a while. Cassie may remember even more as time goes on." Was there a worried edge to his words? I sensed an undertone that made me wonder if Vance was happy with the prospect of Cassie regaining her memory.

Dr. Vonfeldt was back. He came out to greet us. Vance bid him simply "Good day" and turned and left, much to my relief.

"And what is this? A doll?" Dr. Vonfeldt asked.

I stiffened. Cassie was holding it protectively in the crook of her arm. If the doctor tried to take it from her, I didn't know what would happen. Ever since Ralph had given it to her, she had clung to it night and day.

Fortunately, Dr. Vonfeldt seemed amused but not much interested. His silky smile was for me. "You're looking lovely today, Miss Anderson. But there is a lack of color in your cheeks. Some of our warm sulphur baths would be most beneficial," he cooed. "I do wish you would take advantage of our facilities. Our ladies love the wonderful feeling that comes from an invigorating massage." His white hands moved slowly and languidly to punctuate his words and I stifled a shudder of repulsion. "Shall we set up an appointment for you?"

"Thank you, but I don't have any free time at the moment. Perhaps later," I said vaguely. I didn't want to antagonize him. I had changed my mind about attacking him for his vicious insinuation of my being responsible for the balcony incident. It would accomplish nothing—any emotional outburst could be turned against me. It was better to keep myself alert and under control.

At that moment Sir Wilfred arrived with Lady Edwina. I was saved from any further discussion as Dr. Vonfeldt was forced to give all his attention to the complaining Lady Edwina. Gallantly, Dr. Vonfeldt guided her down the hall, allowing Ralph Winters to take charge of Cassie. "Miss Anderson will wait here for Cassie," the doctor instructed Ralph, who looked surprised.

Vonfeldt obviously did not want me overseeing Cassie's treatments, but I felt I could relax now that Ralph was in charge. I sat down in my usual chair in the corner, half-hidden by the riotous plant. Lady Edwina's querulous complaints floated back into the waiting room, and Sir Wilfred was obviously relieved that it was the doctor's turn to listen to them.

He stroked his mustache and then tipped his hat to me, murmuring something about a game of billiards. I had to laugh at his quick exit, like a school boy suddenly released from the watchful eyes of his superior. It was obvious that Sir Wilfred enjoyed the good life, but I wondered if the money his marriage to Lady Edwina had brought him was really worth years of servitude. If Lady Edwina decided to economize, her husband would feel the pinch—her brother as well.

I let my thoughts sift through the things Vance had said about Cassie and their little brother. Vance claimed he had been out of the house when the tragedy occurred but I sensed that he was withholding a full explanation of where he had been. I wanted to question him about it, but at the moment I could not do anything that might result in Ralph Winters' dismissal. Better to keep my curiosity under control, I thought, confident that, piece by piece, I would be able to fill in what had happened to send Cassie into madness.

That afternoon when Ralph Winters arrived to relieve me, I decided to use my free time to do a little shopping. I had not been back to St. George Street, with its teeming shops, since that first sightseeing tour with Jack. Even though I knew I could probably find the artist in his studio or in the garden, I felt like being by myself. I couldn't throw off a weighted despondency that settled on me every time I thought about Gavin. I couldn't deny that I loved him. Just thinking about him brought an indescribable tingling racing through my veins. His touch, his kisses, his caresses, were bittersweet memories that threatened to tear me apart. I couldn't throw off the suspicion that making love to me had been an expedient, a way to exert pressure on me to do as he wanted.

As I walked the narrow streets, I was glad that it was a glorious day, bright and cheerful with a saffron sun. My leaden spirits were soothed by glimpses of shadowy, cool gardens behind wrought iron fences. These lovely green sanctuaries were accented with statues and musical fountains. Huge palmetto fronds hung over the walks and moved slightly in the breeze like giant fans. Bright spring flowers spilled out of window boxes and the branches of fruit trees hung heavy with bouquets of pink and white blooms, filling the air with sweet perfume.

From deep in one of the gardens I heard a mockingbird caroling "sweet, sweetheart," and for a moment it brought new pain. I blinked back a fullness in my eyes. If Gavin really loved me, he would share his secrets with me. He would help me carry out my responsibilities instead of angrily demanding that I leave Cassie without a backward glance. Didn't he realize how much I had come to care about the vulnerable young girl? If things went wrong and they sent Cassie back to Gray Oaks, I would be devastated. But that's what Gavin wanted. "She has no business being here with you or anybody else," he had said angrily.

I made a few purchases in the tiny shops; mostly sensible things that I needed. I bought a bottle of rose water to keep my hands soft, a broader hairbrush to quicken my nightly brushing, and a pair of white stockings to replace the loomed silk ones that had worn out at the heel. I passed up all the inviting curios which had caught my attention the day I had window-shopped with Jack, but I did give in to an impulse to buy Cassie a ruffled night cap and some new ribbons for her daytime wear. I was pleased with the way Cassie was filling out. She was greatly changed in appearance. If nothing happened to set her back, Cassie might recover from mental illness as other people recovered from physical ailments, I thought with a prayerful hope.

My shopping did not take up as much time as I had expected, so I decided to take a stroll down Avenida Menendez before going back to the hotel. As I walked along the water, I drew in the fresh air and watched sea gulls swooping down and pecking the beach for tasty morsels. I was so absorbed in my own thoughts about Gavin and Cassie and the future, that at first I didn't notice the woman walking slowly ahead of me. Then recognition startled me like a sharp report of a pistol.

I couldn't believe my eyes. Lynette—walking all alone! Her slumped dejection was a contrast to her usual bouncing manner and light steps. Her shoulders rounded, she stopped and leaned against the stone parapet, staring morosely across the water. As I drew closer, I could see deep lines etched in Lynette's usually smooth face and the hint of tears on her cheeks.

I didn't know what to do. My first impulse was to turn around and walk away as fast as possible. But this had never been a natural response for me. "Reckless and foolhardy" had been my father's assessment more than once, when a simple withdrawal from some unpleasantness would have saved me considerable heartache. I could have retreated without Lynette even seeing me, but something about that solitary figure drew me forward. Maybe Gavin had told her that he couldn't marry her, that he was in love with someone else. In spite of myself, my heart leaped with hope. Could it be that I had been wrong about him?

"Miss Talbot." I lightly touched the sleeve of Lynette's rose pink gown and felt her flinch in surprise.

Her sky-blue eyes swung around, her expression startled and stiff under her fashionable hat. The muscles in her face eased when she saw who it was. "Oh, it's you, Brianna." She sighed in obvious relief. "I'm sorry. You startled me." Her smile was fleeting but there was nothing censorious or accusing in her expression. She did not act like a woman who had just met her rival.

Gavin has not told her about me. Hope died as quickly as it had come. "Is something the matter, Lynette? You look upset."

Her pretty blue eyes filled with tears and she put a clenched gloved hand up against her mouth as if to stifle any words from coming out. She was obviously deeply distressed.

Impulsively, I put an arm around her soft, heaving shoulders. There was something childlike about her and suddenly I could understand Gavin's protective feelings. "Can I help?"

Lynette shook her head. "No one can help."

"Do . . . do you want to talk about it?"

She buried her face in a hankie for a moment and then gave me a watery smile. Her lips quivered. "I know I did wrong . . . but when Gavin got back from Europe, I was sure we would be married right away. I thought everything would be all right. And then Gavin came here without me . . . and I couldn't put it off any longer. I couldn't."

"What, Lynette?" It was someone else asking the question. I had already stiffened against a dream about to be shattered beyond repair. "What couldn't you put off?"

"Going to a doctor. I just came from his office. He says I'm three months pregnant." Tears spilled down those ivory-petaled cheeks. "And Gavin told me last night that he's changed his mind about marrying me. What am I going to do? What am I to do?"

I moistened my dry lips. "Is Gavin the father, Lynette?"

"Yes . . . of course. We've been engaged for a long time. Everyone knows that." Her voice faltered and then she sobbed, "What shall I do?"

The melancholy cry of a sea gull was a bitter echo to the sobs caught in my throat. Gavin had tried to break his engagement, but the joy this knowledge brought was shredded by Lynette's confession.

"What shall I do?" she sobbed again, her eyes pleading with me for an answer.

"There's only one thing to be done," I heard myself say in a firm, far away voice. "Gavin must marry you."

Chapter Fourteen

When I returned to the hotel, I discovered that Gavin had left a note for me saying he would see me after dinner that evening.

"Is something the matter?" Ralph Winters asked as he watched me read the note.

"Could you possibly come back and relieve me for a little while this evening?" I asked, crumbling the note in my hand.

"Yes, I don't have anything else to do. What time?"

"About seven."

"Fine," Ralph said. I threw the crumpled note in the waste basket.

He arrived right on time that evening, and I handed him a sealed note to give to Gavin. I had written, "I have talked to Lynette. Now I understand your full obligation to her. I do not wish to see you again."

"Please give this to Dr. Rodene when he comes," I said in what I hoped was a casual tone. Then I threw a light shawl over my shoulders and quickly left the suite.

I rang for the elevator and was surprised to see Ira Deitz on duty so late. Before he could direct me to the stairs with that imperious manner of his, I brushed passed him into the elevator. "Down, please." My voice betrayed my inner distress.

He looked at my distraught expression and asked, "Liz Chantilly didn't come back, did she?"

I blinked, not comprehending the question for a moment. "Liz Chantilly? Oh, the woman who used to live in the tower suite? No, of course not," I snapped.

"Those rooms getting to you, huh?" he said in satisfaction. "I knew they would. Liz doesn't want anyone else living there."

"What nonsense!" I was in no mood to listen to Ira Deitz's gloomy pronouncements. "Please take me to the main floor." I had to get away before Gavin returned to the hotel and came to get me as if nothing had happened. *As if nothing had happened!* I felt hysterical laughter bubbling up in my throat.

I must have made some audible sound for Ira Deitz peered at me from under his bushy gray eyebrows. "You shouldn't stay in Liz's rooms . . . she doesn't want you there." He shook his head. "When she went mad, her family had to drag her out of there. You should have heard the threats she made. I think she put a curse on those rooms."

At some other time I might have been amused by his dour warnings, but right now my thoughts were filled with anguish that blotted out everything else. When the elevator reached the lobby, I gave a furtive glance in both directions and left the hotel by the rear door. I did not want to take a chance on running into Jack Harvey so I went under the arched passage which led to the gardens on the opposite side of the artists' quarters. I desperately needed some place to be alone, to assuage the bitter heartache that Lynette's admission had brought.

I walked down the same garden path I had taken

the night I fled back to the hotel to rescue Cassie from the balcony railing. It seemed an eternity ago. I felt no uneasy apprehension tonight, just bitter, painful heartache. My thoughts were too heavy for me be aware of my surroundings. Lights from the carriage driveway did not penetrate through the grove of orange and magnolia trees as I walked with my head down, wanting to cry aloud from the hurt in my chest.

The faint sound of a fountain's spraying waters beckoned and an occasional garden lamp sent a ray of light upon the walk. Dark shadows still claimed most of the garden and the bustle of the hotel grounds was muted. It was the kind of soothing, quiet sanctuary that I needed. Like a wounded animal seeking the dark isolation of a protective burrow, I hurried forward into the depths of the landscaped grounds.

When I reached a bench placed off the path in the dark circle of some thick junipers, I wearily sat down upon it. There, hidden in the shadowy arbor, I let the shawl fall off my shoulders and covered my face with my hands. The tears that I had kept in abeyance came spilling out, and sobs choked in my throat.

Gavin and Lynette were lovers! When he came back from Europe she had given herself to him, expecting that they would soon be married. I could understand how it had happened . . . the joyful reunion . . . Lynette's clinging adoration . . . her loving nature. At that time, Gavin had intended to make Lynette his wife. Then Helen Matley had summoned him to St. Augustine and he had left Lynette in New York. Maybe he had been having second thoughts about marrying her, I thought, but by then it was too late. If he had hoped to put some distance between them he had failed; Lynette had followed him here. Now I understood why. Undoubtedly his fiancée intended to press for a wedding here in St. Augustine, as Amelia Dorcas had hinted. Lynette must have been devastated when she discovered that Gavin was even more hesitant about setting a date than he had been before. Maybe she had been using Vance Danzel to make Gavin jealous, but her strategy had not worked. Not knowing that Lynette was pregnant, Gavin had told her he wanted to end the engagement. But it was too late. Now Gavin would do the honorable thing. He would marry Lynette, he had no choice. She was carrying his child.

A rustle in the canopy of trees startled me. I stiffened. My head swung in that direction, peering into the thick grove. The low hoot of a night owl reassured me. I knew then how raw my nerves were.

I took a deep breath. I had to get my life back in order, forget about Gavin Rodene and what might have been. My chin came up. A cool evening breeze bathed my hot cheeks. The sound of the distant fountains and the soft rustling of birds in the trees was reassuring and comforting. I drew in the pungent garden smells and sweet floral incense. An inner strength flowed through me and with it, new determination. I had always been able to do what must be done. When my father became ill, I had taken courage and handled each day's challenge. That was the kind of resilience I must draw upon now. Self-pity had never been part of my makeup. I gave one last swipe of my hankie across my eyes, swallowed hard, and then stood up. No, it was not my nature to cower and hide. With a determined step I headed toward the servants' dining room for a late cup of tea.

"What a nice surprise!" Jack unfolded his long legs and held out a chair for me. "I was just thinking that I needed some good company to salvage a very bleak day."

"My sentiments exactly," I answered, smiling wryly.

His thick red eyebrows matted in a straight line as he studied me. "What's happening? Cassie all right?"

I nodded.

"It's Dr. Rodene, isn't it? You can't mention his name without a sudden light going on in your eyes."

"It's that obvious?" No wonder Amelia Dorcas had no trouble reading the signs, I thought in consternation.

"You try to hide your emotions, Brianna, but I'm afraid that lovely mouth and tragic eyes give you away. Well, I meant it when I said you have a friend if ever you need one." He poured me a cup of tea from a steaming clay pot. "Want to talk about it?"

"No. It's all over."

"I wouldn't bet on it," said Jack, frowning as he looked past me to the dining room doorway.

My heart lurched. I spilled the hot liquid as I hastily set down my cup. I dared not turn around and look.

"Your Dr. Rodene is heading this way and I would guess from his expression that he's got something on his mind. Want me to get rid of him?"

"Yes," I croaked. My sense of control had instantly dissipated. I didn't want to see Gavin, not now. I couldn't take any more. Talking with him would tear me apart. Besides, there was nothing to be said. Lynette had said it all that afternoon.

"There you are, Bri!" Gavin greeted me in an exasperated tone. "I've been searching the grounds for you." His ruffled countenance was at odds with his immaculate appearance: dark maroon frock coat, crisp white shirt with a soft, striped cravat tied at this throat.

"Didn't you get my note?" I stammered.

"Yes." He pulled the piece of paper from a pocket in his dark gray trousers. "Would you mind telling me what this means?" His eyes flashed a wintry gray. "I don't like to play guessing games."

"The lady doesn't want to talk about it," said Jack pugnaciously, rising to his feet.

Gavin gave him a withering look and turned back to me. "Let's go some place where we can talk."

"No." I couldn't bear to be alone with him. The ache was too great. Nothing he said would change the facts. "Please leave me alone. There's nothing to talk about."

"You heard the lady!" Jack clenched his huge fists and crowded Gavin so that he had to take a step backward.

I knew that in a minute Jack would try to physically remove Gavin. My red-headed knight was about to do battle for me, but Gavin wasn't going to be pushed around by anyone. The cords in his neck were rigid, and I knew he was having a difficult time restraining his temper.

He didn't know! Lynette hadn't told him! I was on my feet. "Wait!" I stepped between them. "Please go, Gavin. Talk to Lynette. She has some news for you. After you hear it, you'll know why I don't want to see or talk with you . . . ever again!"

His penetrating gray eyes searched my face. "I see. Well, far be it from me to impose my company where it isn't wanted." His scathing gaze went from me to Jack.

He thought I was rebuffing him because of Jack. He looked hurt and betrayed. I wanted to explain, but it was not my place to give him Lynette's news.

He spun on his heels and left the table with an angry stride. His graceful, aristocratic bearing brought new pain into my chest. I knew that body. I had felt it tremble in ecstasy against mine, I had touched and molded every rippling muscle with my own hands. I watched him cross the dining room and fought an impulse to run after him.

Jack sat back down and took my hand. "I don't know what the bastard's done but I wish I'd flattened my fist on his nose when I had the chance."

I half-expected Gavin to try and talk with me again, but he didn't. Apparently Lynette had given him her news. I was grateful that he had spared me another painful scene. I should have known that Amelia Dorcas would be the one to open the wound with her malicious gossiping.

I was in the reception room, waiting for Cassie to finish her treatments, when the awful woman came in and spied me sitting in the corner. With her nostrils flaring excitedly, Amelia walked over and pulled a chair so close to mine that our heads almost touched. The sickly sweet jasmine perfume that she wore poured over me, filling my nose and mouth with its cloying scent.

"Have you heard the news?" she cackled. "Lynette's *enceinte.*"

There was no need to ask how Amelia knew.

Nothing escaped her notice. She took to gossip like a dog to a bone, delighting in the delicious taste of scandal. She might have overheard a conversation . . . or perhaps Lynette had been foolish enough to tell her. Lynette had been so distraught that Amelia could have readily offered a shoulder to cry on, I thought. Getting the whole story from Lynette would have been easy.

"Yes, I've heard," I answered as evenly as possible, firming my chin. "However, I can't imagine why any of her *friends* would want to spread such news about."

The rebuke was lost on Amelia. She was like a race horse in a starting gate; there was no way to stop her. "The poor darling's simply beside herself. You would have thought Lynette would know better. Her reluctant fiancé is making the situation almost intolerable." She leaned closer and in a conspirator's tone hissed, "Can you imagine? The respectable Dr. Rodene caught with this trousers down like that?"

My temper flared. Despite her jewels and silken attire the woman was coarse as a guttersnipe. "I don't think anyone wants to listen to your vicious gossip, Miss Dorcas!"

"Especially you, Miss Anderson?" Amelia's moist smile broadened. "Could it be that Dr. Rodene's reluctance to do the honorable thing has something to do with you?" She licked her lips as if tasting something juicy.

I couldn't answer. I knew anything I said would be twisted and shaped to suit the woman's malicious tongue, but my anguished expression seemed to be enough for Amelia.

She gave a throaty laugh. "Did you know that Vance and Dr. Rodene came to blows this morning in the fourth-floor corridor?" She nodded, reading the flicker of concern in my eyes. "I opened my door just in time to hear Vance tell Rodene that he'd marry Lynette himself if the circumstances were different. The poor boy's gone through his inheritance . . . he needs a rich wife, we all know that. Gallantry is something Vance can't afford, but he put Dr. Rodene to shame all right. Can you imagine how embarrassing it is for Lynette? Dr. Rodene dragging his feet when every one knows they rang the bell before they went to church. There'll be a wedding at the Ponce very soon." Her beady eyes fixed me with a viperous gleam. "I wonder if you'll be invited . . . circumstances being what they are."

I rose to my feet and walked away with a rudeness that only delighted Amelia.

In the days that followed, Ralph and I began taking Cassie for short walks each afternoon. It was exciting to see her begin to break out of her dark shell. She even spoke a few intelligible words now.

"Cassie's starting to respond," said Ralph on one such afternoon. "She's on her way back."

"Do you think the treatments are doing it?" I asked skeptically. I knew that I was biased against Dr. Vonfeldt and his electro-treatments.

"No. You're the one that's doing it."

"Me?" I said in surprise. "What have I done?"

"You've made it safe for her to reach out to you and accept you as being real, not a part of the confused dark regions of her mind. I've seen it happen before. The mentally ill person can seem utterly lost and then, for some inexplicable reason, try to break through to someone. If they are not rejected, they begin to move out of the darkness little by little."

"No, it's you," I protested. "You knew how to handle her, Ralph. Giving her the doll and all."

"Thank you, but Cassie wouldn't have accepted the doll if you hadn't brought her this far." He laughed and his narrow face took on a boyish charm. "You got the door open—I'm just sticking my foot in it."

Cassie's improvement was the only bright spot in my dreary days and nights. I spent my free time with Jack, watching him paint, or just walking and talking. He seemed to understand that my wounds needed time to heal, and he did not talk about Gavin or ask for any explanation of the scene he had witnessed in the dining room.

One afternoon he suggested that we make up a foursome with Cassie and Ralph, and take a walk through the narrow streets of St. Augustine. Although the sky was overcast, the day was warm and quite pleasant. I exerted myself to be a pleasant companion, though deep in my heart I wondered if the world would ever be bright and lovely again.

"You haven't seen the fort, Brianna," Jack said as the four of us strolled down San Marcos Avenue, where the huge fortification rose on the south side of the street.

"Neither have I," offered Ralph. "I haven't had much time for sightseeing since I got here."

I did not especially want to visit the gray fortress but Jack and Ralph looked at me hopefully. "Shall we take a tour?" Jack asked.

The men obviously wanted to go and I felt guilty because Ralph had been spending so many of his off-hours with Cassie. I didn't know what I would have done without his help and companionship. "All right," I said, for his sake forcing some interest to my leaden voice.

As we approached the gray fortress made of coquina blocks and situated on the highest point of elevation, my eyes followed the ramparts and towers that stretched along the water. It looks like a sleeping beast, I thought. I had always been sensitive to the past because my father was a professor of history. I tried to ignore the oppressive feeling that the fortress engendered, but I was unable to stifle a shudder as we passed over a drawbridge into a gloomy inner court framed by thick, high walls and parapets. A Spanish coat of arms hung over the main gate, inscribed with the date 1756, the year the fortress was completed and named Castillo de San Marcos.

I was grateful for my dark blue morino dress with long tight sleeves. Its cape-like collar kept me from shivering in the shadowy, dank corridors of the fort. Cassie seemed comfortable in her white shirtwaist and brown walking skirt and she followed Ralph's guidance as he kept a light hand on her arm.

A young soldier with corporal chevrons on his sleeve stepped forward to be our guide. His forage hat was decorated with an eagle insignia, and he wore the garrison uniform, a dark blue wool jacket with five brass buttons as polished as the belt buckle embossed with the U.S. initials. His sky blue trousers were trimmed with a narrow white stripe down the outside seam. Apparently visitors were welcome at the fort, for he immediately took charge. "This way, please."

"All right?" whispered Jack, noticing my reluctance.

"Fine."

Jack stayed close to my side as we began our tour of the windowless chambers which had been used to confine prisoners. I wasn't about to faint. My father had trained me too well for that on similar excursions to battlefields. It helped to pretend that I was listening to the guide's lecture for him. He would have loved seeing this fortress. I experienced a poignant sense of loss just thinking about my father, and my expression must have shown it, for Jack slipped my arm through his. I smiled at him gratefully.

Ralph took Cassie's hand and the four of us followed our guide through the dank, sunless corridors.

The corporal gave a running commentary as he showed us the gloomy facilities. "When the fortress was in the possession of the British, Charleston patriots were confined in these chambers." He indicated an enclosure large enough to hold a dozen men. The ugly gray walls were stark and so high that they tripled a man's height to the slanted roof. Their thickness kept out any warmth or glimpse of the sun, and they seemed to glisten with a cold patina. The stone floors were rough and bare. According to the corporal, Indians with iron bound chains on their feet had been confined for years in these bleak quarters. "They were taught English by gracious women of the town who helped the savages become civilized," he assured us.

Then our guide took us underground to show us the hidden dungeons. These had been walled up at some time, but were discovered when the Castillo de San Marcos came into the possession of the United States, in 1821. "Skeletons and chains and a gold ring were found among the rubbish, as well as instruments of torture like the iron cage," our guide intoned.

I had read tales of the horrors of the Spanish Inquisition, and it seemed to me that the cries of pain and moans of dying men lingered within these walls. I was sensitive to the ghostly atmosphere and I felt as if a legion of tormented spirits surrounded me.

Jack and Ralph seemed oblivious to the heavy miasma. They kept the guide busy answering questions about the fort's tumultuous history, and Cassie seemed comfortable and content in the almost-black chambers. The absence of light reassured her.

As we passed through the dark chambers, the heavy doors and iron bars reminded one of a time when Spain's hold upon the new world depended upon such thick walls, and the courage of those who manned them. "There's a tale of young lovers sealed into one of these tombs by a vengeful father," the guide said quite pleasantly.

I felt a cold prickling up my spine. I knew that the story was probably just a gothic fabrication, but it added to my dislike of the place. I was glad when the guide took us back to the enclosed courtyard, where a bustle of men in uniform carried out their duties. The fresh air eased away the shivers that had crept into my body during the tour of the dungeons.

We climbed shallow steps to the high parapets raised above the ramparts. The young corporal pointed out openings which allowed a view of the harbor and battery. These spaces had been designed for cannons and firing soldiers, he said, and demonstrated a gunner's ladle for us. It was a copper scoop affixed to a pole, used for measuring powder and loading it into a cannon.

Cassie stood quietly, with the gaze of someone turned inward, looking quite serene in this setting of war and human suffering.

I stepped back from the huge gun and let Jack and Ralph ask some questions about the cannon. As I looked out at the sloped ground around the fort, I tried to blot out the vision of men approaching the walls and being blown apart as the cannon and rifle fire fell upon them.

I turned away abruptly. "I think we've seen enough." I started down the steps with Jack at my heels. We were about half-way down when I turned around to see if Ralph and Cassie were coming.

I froze.

Cassie was leaning out over one of the openings in the parapet. Suddenly she gave a piercing cry and lurched backwards, tottering at the top of the rock steps. Later I could not decide whether Ralph had tried to catch her with an outstretched arm—or if his hand had pushed her back! Cassie wavered like a wobbly top, ready to pitch forward down those treacherous stone steps.

As I screamed, Jack leaped forward. Taking three steps at a time with his long legs, he reached Cassie as she fell and scooped her up in his arms.

I raised horrified eyes to Ralph Winters. "What happened?"

He seemed to have trouble speaking. "She looked over the parapet . . . the height must have triggered a memory. She jerked away from me. I'm sorry . . . she could have had a bad fall down the steps."

His expression was unreadable. Surprise, fright—or disappointment?

I tried to shake off the sinister overtones of the

incident. No one was to blame; I was letting my imagination run away with me. It must have been the atmosphere, I reasoned. All the talk about dungeons and death had put morbid overtones on a simple loss of balance. Of course Ralph had been trying to catch Cassie when she lurched away from the parapet, I reassured myself. *But why was Cassie leaning through that aperture in the first place?* She had shown no interest in anything during the tour of the fort. Ralph must have led her over to the opening, I conjectured. Cassie had been several feet away from it when I'd started down the steps.

Had he been pointing out the view to her? No, Cassie had not been looking across the water, but had been looking down. It seemed to me that Ralph had been forcing her to look below when she had screamed and pulled away. Obviously the height had frightened her.

All the way back to the hotel, Cassie sobbed and whimpered. Ralph seemed duly contrite, and Jack dismissed the whole thing as a lucky escape from what might have been a serious accident. Ralph offered to come back in the evening but I told him that Cassie and I would retire early.

Cassie refused to eat anything at dinner time. All the progress we had made with her seemed to have been wiped out in one careless moment. I was furious with myself for having agreed to the tour in the first place. A nebulous uneasiness had been there, but I had ignored it.

After I tucked Cassie in for the night, I went over everything again in my mind. The nagging suspicion that Cassie's fall had not been an accident would not leave me. But why would Ralph Winters push her down those treacherous steps? The answer that came to mind was like the sharp stab of cold metal. *To silence her.* Had the young attendant been hired to precipitate such an accident? Was Cassie making too much progress for someone's peace of mind?

I paced the sitting room and the horrible cabbage rose wallpaper caught my shadow as I went back and forth. Like someone piecing together a giant puzzle I kept rearranging the clues in my mind. I had been convinced after the scissors incident that someone was setting a treacherous plan into place. Was Ralph Winters a part of it? Had he worked his way into my good graces and Cassie's acceptance to be in position for some diabolical checkmate?

I'm becoming hysterical, I worried. All the good work Ralph had done with Cassie had been wiped out by one eerie incident. But why would he try to help Cassie regain her mental health only to push her down the steps that could have broken her neck? It didn't add up—unless Cassie was about to remember the thing that someone wanted to remain hidden in her tormented mind! Had Ralph been hired to make certain Cassie was disposed of if she made too much progress?

I sat down on the parlor chair and covered my face with my hands. It was this horrid suite, I thought. Its isolation from all the gaiety in the luxury hotel made me feel vulnerable and cast aside. I needed Gavin. If only he could be here now, with his protective arms, his strong shoulder, his ability to shut everything else out.

Almost as if in answer to a prayer, a knock at the door jerked my head up. I held my breath as I opened the door.

A small gray-haired woman with wild eyes stood there, garishly dressed in a floral gown with Victorian collar and cuffs, a fringed striped shawl, and a hat that looked like a flower pot.

I gasped for I instantly knew who she was.

Liz Chantilly had come home.

Chapter Fifteen

The disheveled, gaudily dressed woman stared at me. Liz Chantilly's face was wrinkled and motley with age spots. Several of her teeth were missing but there was nothing shabby about the woman. Her clothes were of good material and the loops of pearls she wore were probably real. Several rings glittered on her blue-veined hands.

Before I could say anything, the spry little woman pushed past me into the sitting room. Her eyes lost their wild look and a childlike smile curved her lips. She slowly turned around in the middle of the floor as if drinking in the beloved furnishings: the awful green vine print on the settee, bright raspberry parlor chairs, gaudy swag drapes, and busy carpet.

"I came home," she said in a vigorous voice that belied her fragile look. She clutched a faded portmanteau that didn't look very full. She had not brought much with her.

My mind scurried to find the right approach to handle the situation. I was not frightened. My experience at Gray Oaks had prepared me for handling Liz Chantilly. I tried to remember everything Ira Deitz had said about her. *Gone mad . . . screamed when they took her away.* I wished now I had asked him more questions. I would have to alert someone. The woman had obviously made her way here by herself. The authorities would probably be looking for her. "You're Liz Chantilly," I said to confirm the woman's identity.

She didn't answer me or look in my direction. My strange visitor did not seem to be aware that anyone was in the room except herself. She marched right by me and headed down the short hall, turning into Cassie's room with a proprietary air.

"Miss Chantilly!" I said rather sharply, hurriedly following her. What was the woman going to do?

The gnarled old lady stopped abruptly when she reached the bed. She looked down at Cassie sleeping peacefully there. The girl's face was clearly visible, her hair tucked neatly into the new lace nightcap I had bought for her. Because Cassie had been restless after the incident at the fort, I had given her a spoonful of laudanum to help her sleep. She stirred, and for a moment I was fearful that she would awaken to find this odd woman bending over her. I held my breath, not wanting to make a scene by trying to remove the intruder.

Just as suddenly as she had entered, Liz Chantilly left Cassie's room and went across the hall to the bedroom that I was occupying. She took off her hat, opened the portmanteau, and took out a few night garments. I thought she was going to undress but she didn't.

With a sigh, the woman stretched out on the bed as if exhausted from her journey. In less than a minute, her heavy breathing told me she was sound asleep. A satisfied curve to her lips softened her wrinkled face and, with her eyes closed, she looked at peace.

I went back to the sitting room, trying to decide

how to handle the situation. My heart had been touched by the woman's need to return to the rooms where she had lived. "I came home," were the words she had spoken.

I knew that I would have to reveal her presence here to someone. Ira Deitz had not told me where her family had taken Liz, but it must have been somewhere in the St. Augustine area. The determined runaway did not look as if she had come far.

I started to ring for a hotel attendant to report my unexpected guest and then I hesitated. I hated to have some impersonal employee drag Liz Chantilly away in the night. It would be better if I could contact some of the family and let them come for her. Ira Deitz would know whom I should notify, but he would be gone by this hour.

Since she had lived at the Ponce since the hotel opened, surely the hotel manager would have the name of her relatives. It seemed to me that Liz Chantilly must have had some pull with Henry Flagler to move in and decorate her suite the way she wanted. I decided to tell the manager about my surprise visitor and let him notify the family.

I checked on Cassie. She was still sound asleep and would not wake from the laudanum until morning. I shut her door. Liz Chantilly was snoring lightly. She seemed settled for the night, too. I laid a light cover over her sleeping figure.

Then I smoothed the coil of brown hair at the nape of my neck and adjusted the white ruffled cuffs of my modest navy blue day dress. Very quietly, I left the suite and took the elevator downstairs.

Even though it was late, the hotel was bustling with people coming and going from the main lounge, dining room, and game tables. My simple daytime attire looked out of place in the swirl of taffeta, velvet brocade, and satin gowns worn by ladies who graced the arms of gentlemen in evening dress. I slipped as unobtrusively as I could through the crowded lobby to the main desk, and asked to see the manager. The same pinch-nosed desk clerk was on duty as the night I had requested that he ring Gavin's room. He recognized me with the same haughty glare.

"The manager?" his icy stare slid over me. "I'm afraid he is *not* available." He turned away, giving his ingratiating smile to an elderly gentleman who had come to the desk and asked for his key.

"Then I will speak with the person next in authority," I said in a voice loud enough to bring an angry flush to his long neck. "Who is your immediate superior?" Before he could answer, I sensed someone behind me. A familiar touch on my arm drove all strength from my legs.

"What is it, Bri? Has something happened?"

I knew that if I turned to look into those gray-green eyes, I would forget that I must keep up my defenses. I kept my gaze straight ahead. "Just a little problem."

"Is Cassie—?" He moved in front of me.

"She's fine," I said, managing to avoid his face. "I need to get some information from the manager."

"His office is just off the arcade," he said. "Come, I'll show you. It's late, but I saw him in the lobby a few minutes ago."

The desk clerk was still ignoring me. I hesitated and then shrugged. There was nothing I could do but suffer Gavin's nearness as he put a firm hand on my elbow and guided me across the marble floor.

I gambled on a quick glance at his profile. The familiar hard thrust of his cheekbones was darkened by shadows. It seemed years instead of days since I had traced them with a lover's touch and threaded my fingers lovingly through his dark hair. A deep ache overtook me and I turned my eyes away.

"Here we are." He opened a glass door for me and followed me in. No one was in the oak outer room. I could see a private office through an open door.

"Mr. Markham?" Gavin raised his voice and it echoed through the quiet rooms. He led me into a richly paneled office, furnished with Spanish Renaissance furniture similar to the rest of the hotel's decor. "He doesn't seem to be here at the moment."

"Maybe there's someone else I could talk with . . ." my voice trailed off. I tried to smile and lighten the mood. "I need information. I have an unexpected visitor, Liz Chantilly."

Gavin looked blank.

"I guess I didn't tell you about her. She's the elderly lady who had lived in the tower suite since the hotel first opened."

"Oh, yes. The one responsible for that atrocious decor."

"That's right. She looks exactly like the furnishings, horrible clothes, bright and gaudy, and pearls dripping all over her." I smiled. "She's harmless enough, though. The elevator man said she really put up a fuss when her family took her away from the hotel."

Gavin frowned. "Her family probably decided she was too senile to live alone. I remember Vance said something about the hotel not having time to refurbish the rooms after she moved out."

I nodded. "Well, she came back tonight. I opened the door and there she was!"

"What on earth—?"

"I think she was homesick. I don't know where she came from, but right now she's asleep in my bed. I'm sure someone must be searching for her. I wanted to find out the name of a relative, rather than turn her over to some impersonal hotel steward."

"She has to go back," Gavin said firmly.

"I know that," I flared. "But it's obvious that she thinks of the tower rooms as home. No telling what she's gone through to get back here. She . . . she reminds me of my father. The same other-worldly look in her eyes . . . so vulnerable." My voice caught. "I feel so sorry for her . . . so helpless." My eyes filled with unexpected tears.

"Darling, you can't save the world." His reprimand was gentle, his eyes warm.

"I know." My lips trembled. He called me darling. For a moment my eyes caught his and the world danced away. "Don't," I whispered huskily as he reached out to touch me. I turned away and sat down in a heavy chair with velvet cushions. "I'll wait until the manager comes back and find out who we need to contact. Thank you for your help," I said, in a tone of dismissal.

He sighed and ignored the distance I tried to put between us. "We need to talk, Bri, but this isn't the best place . . . or the best time."

"There's nothing to be said."

"You know I love you—"

"That doesn't matter any more. Not the way things are now."

"For God's sake, Bri, I've been trying to get this mess straightened out. I don't want to involve you if I can avoid it."

I gave a bitter laugh. "It's a little late for that, isn't it?"

"You don't know the circumstances."

I firmed my chin. "Lynette explained to me exactly what the circumstances are. I don't condemn you for what happened. I understand." I proudly kept my head high and my tears at bay. "When you returned from Europe, Lynette had every reason to believe that you were going to marry her. And when you left her again, to come here, she followed you." I couldn't keep the edge of censure out of my voice.

"I see. You have it all explained and neatly rationalized." He sat down in a nearby chair, pressed his hands together, and stared at the floor as if searching for words. The weighted silence in the room was oppressive. Then he gave a deep sigh and raised gray agate eyes to mine. "The baby isn't mine."

I stared at him as though he had suddenly begun to speak in a foreign tongue. "Not yours!" What kind of fool did he think I was? How could he deny his responsibility? "No, of course not," I said sarcastically. "It's obvious that Lynette is mistaken." Disappointment in him sparked my anger. I had never expected him to lie to me; I had thought him man enough to accept the consequences of his actions.

"You don't believe me?"

"No. I asked her if the child was yours. She said it was."

An angry flush mounted in his cheeks. His gaze burned with the smoldering heat of rage. "Why do you believe her and not me? I had hoped for more trust from the woman I intend to marry!"

"Gavin . . . I . . ." I stammered, suddenly aware that I had not considered that he might be innocent, that Lynette might have lied. I had asked her who the father was, and Lynette had left no room for doubt in my mind. "Lynette said . . ."

"You could at least have suspended judgment until you'd heard the truth. And now those dagger eyes of yours condemn me as a liar!"

"But Lynette . . ."

"I tell you! I have never touched Lynette in that way." He pulled me to my feet and held me tightly against him. "Look me in the face and tell me I am lying! Tell me!" He shook me angrily and then kissed me, choking off the words he demanded to hear. His kisses bruised my mouth and his anger spent itself in the fury of mounting passion.

I clung to him, my senses reeling. I wanted to believe him, The black world of loneliness was shattered by his embrace, anguish and heartache fell away from me. My passion-laden eyes searched for reassurance as he raised his lips from mine.

"It's true, Bri. I swear it," he said huskily.

I could not organize my thoughts, or still the sudden joy that thrilled through me.

"It's been hell staying away from you." he said as he held me close. "But it won't be long, I promise you."

"But . . . Lynette . . . I don't understand. Who—?"

"I can't betray her confidence. You understand, don't you, darling? I must continue to protect her. She needs me now more than ever."

The words brought their own chill. Protect Lynette? What did that mean? Did he intend for the world to go on thinking the child was his? Already people like Amelia were condemning him for not doing the honorable thing by her. Who would believe that the child was not his? It was common knowledge that Lynette had been paired with Gavin Rodene since they were children.

"But if the child isn't yours?" Even now, I could not believe that Lynette had become infatuated with someone else while he was gone. She had said she was about three months pregnant . . . the timing was right for Gavin's return from Europe!

"I'll work it out, I promise you."

The moment of ecstasy was over. He would do what he must for Lynette. I wanted to lash out at him, "What about me?" But I kept my silence. My pride would not beg him to abandon his fiancée. I knew the strength of his character. His honor was a formidable adversary.

"I'm doing everything I can to resolve the situation in the best possible way for every one." He would have kissed me again but I moved away. His agate eyes narrowed. "You don't believe me!"

"That you are going to protect Lynette?" I answered in a choked voice. "Of course, I believe you. As for everything else . . ." My tortured eyes traveled over his face.

"What would you have me do?"

"That's not fair," I snapped, and was saved from saying anything more by the arrival of Mr. Markham, a portly gentleman who looked surprised to find us in his private office.

He made profuse apologies for not being there to receive us. He seemed to know Gavin, but the manager's practiced smile did not erase the harassed expression that remained in his eyes.

"I'm sorry to bother you at such a time," I apologized. I told him as succinctly as I could about Liz Chantilly's return to the hotel. "Her family needs to be notified, and I was hoping you had the information as to where they could be reached."

He visibly relaxed. Obviously he had been prepared for some complaint. "Yes, of course. I'm sure we have that information in the files. Please allow me to take care of the matter. Miss Chantilly was quite difficult the last few months that she was here, quite an embarrassment to everyone. She should have never been allowed to lease that suite . . . some influence with the Flaglers, I believe. In any case, I am truly sorry that she has inconvenienced you."

"Not at all. I know that someone will be looking for her. She's perfectly welcome to stay the night if they can't pick her up until morning. She's asleep in my bed."

"May I offer you and Miss Danzel different accommodations until she is removed?" he offered quickly.

I was about to refuse when Gavin intervened. "A sensible suggestion," he said. "Miss Anderson doesn't need to lose a night's sleep over the matter."

"No, of course not. We have some nice adjoining rooms."

"On th fourth floor?" asked Gavin, without changing his expression.

I knew that Gavin, as well as the Danzels, Lynette, and Amelia Dorcas, had rooms on that floor, and for a moment, I was ready to protest. I didn't want to be set down in a nest of vipers . . . or to be that close to Gavin. Only the embarrassment of calling attention to the matter kept me silent. I was afraid the manager was already speculating about Dr. Rodene's personal interest in the matter. He might have noticed our earnest expressions when he came to the office.

We thanked him and left him making the proper arrangements.

"You look like a war frigate ready to launch a volley of cannonballs," chided Gavin as we walked across the lobby to the elevator.

"Your interference is insufferable! How dare you take charge like that!"

"It isn't easy when you're so prickly about accepting help."

"I don't need your help. I could have managed very nicely tonight without all this upheaval of changing rooms. The fourth floor! I would have chosen a room in the opposite wing."

"I know. That's why I suggested a room close to mine." His mouth curved in that rare smile which softened his eyes to jade green. "Not for the reason my heart desires but for professional reasons."

"Professional!"

"As your physician." I sputtered but he went on. "I'm determined that you're not going to lose more sleep than you have to. How are things with Cassie?" he asked, as we entered the wrought iron cage and the operator moved the controls to lift it upwards.

Gavin's question brought back the incident at the fort. Under different circumstances I would gratefully have told him about Ralph Winters. The disturbing uncertainty of what had happened refused to be put to rest. Had Ralph made Cassie look over the parapet? Had his hand on her back been in restraint or force? Was he really good for Cassie, or was he a part of the same treacherous evil as the incident in Jack's studio? These questions rose to the surface with Gavin's question, but my emotions were too tangled to confide in him. I didn't know what to think about anyone, especially Gavin Rodene. He had kissed me, pleaded with me to believe that he had never made love to Lynette, only to take control in that infuriating, dominating way of his. "There's no need for you to accompany me back to the suite," I said haughtily.

"I'm curious to meet your Miss Chantilly. Besides you'll need help changing rooms with Cassie."

"I can manage by myself," I said rather childishly.

"I'm sure you can, but there's no need to, is there?"

His calm professional manner was a contrast to my prickly attitude. He didn't seem to notice. When we reached the tower, he guided me down the short hall. "Did you lock the door?"

My heart took a sudden leap. "No, I didn't." *What if Cassie had got out?* I pushed open the door to be greeted with relief and surprise. Cassie had left her bed but she sat in the parlor chair with her back to the door, still wearing her ruffled lace nightcap and white nightdress.

"What are you doing out of bed?" I scolded, going around to the front of the chair and looking at the still figure. Then I screamed!

It wasn't Cassie sitting there, but Liz Chantilly! She must have awakened, put on her night gown and cap, and then come out to the sitting room and sat down in the chair. She wasn't asleep.

She had been strangled with a woman's white silk hose tied viciously around her throat!

Chapter Sixteen

I don't know what I would have done if Gavin hadn't been there. He took charge. Reacting quickly to the appalling situation, he whisked me and Cassie down to the fourth floor and into the rooms which Mr. Markham had assigned us. Like someone functioning automatically in a state of shock, I put Cassie to bed again. The young girl was cooperative and readily fell back asleep in the strange room.

Gavin put a firm arm around my trembling shoulders and led me into the adjoining bedroom. "You stay here. I'll be back as soon as I can. I'll have to alert the authorities."

"Why would somebody do such an awful thing?" I sobbed, looking up at him. "That poor woman never did anybody harm. It doesn't make sense."

"No, it doesn't, unless . . ." he paused. "Unless someone mistook her for Cassie."

"But they don't look anything alike."

"From the back, sitting there in that chair, they do. You even called her, Cassie, remember?"

My eyes widened. "That's right. I didn't know it was Liz Chantilly when we first came in. I remember now, Liz took out a white nightgown and cap from her portmanteau. They were so much like Cassie's—"

"That someone slipping into the room could have made the same mistake. I've been convinced from the very beginning that both you and Cassie were in danger. This verifies it!"

"Someone wanted to murder Cassie—just like before!"

"Only this time the killer wasn't leaving anything to chance."

I closed my eyes against the horrible sight that would live with me forever. Gavin sat down beside me on the bed, pulled me close, and held my trembling body against his. "Thank God, you were downstairs with me when it happened."

Yes, thank God. And then I felt guilty. Maybe if I'd been there, it wouldn't have happened. Or maybe there had been more than one silk stocking, ready and waiting, an inner voice cautioned.

Hysteria threatened to engulf me. I wanted to plead with Gavin not to leave. It was all I could do to keep from clinging to him and giving way to sobs.

He tipped up my chin and his steady, smoky green eyes bore into mine. "I'll be back in a little while, darling. Now, lie on the bed and try to relax. I'll take care of everything."

Tenderly he covered me up, tucking the blanket up to my chin, though I was fully dressed. Shock had made my body like ice. He kissed my cold lips and then quickly left the room, taking the key and locking the door from outside as if he did not trust me to stay. Any other time I would have been furious with him, but I now felt only gratitude that I did not have to handle the abhorrent situation.

As I lay there, my body chilled and rigid, my mind refused to contemplate the horror of what had happened. For a long time I was unable to force any rational sequence into the blur of images that taunted me. But as warmth eased back into my body, my thoughts stirred and questions plagued me.

I wanted to cling to the belief that the horror had nothing to do with me or Cassie, that it was just a bizarre coincidence that Liz Chantilly had been strangled with a woman's stocking in the isolated tower sitting room. But I knew I was only fooling myself. It was unlikely that anyone had deliberately followed the harmless, senile old woman to the Ponce to murder her. I had to agree with Gavin. Someone had meant to strangle Cassie. The same old questions pricked at me . . . and I still had no rational answers.

As if the trauma had happened to someone else, I began to consider the sequence of events. When I had left the suite Liz Chantilly was stretched out on the bed, fully clothed. She must have awakened and decided to put on her nightdress and ruffled cap. Then she had wandered back into the sitting room and sat down with her back to the door.

It was true, I had mistaken her for Cassie as she sat there—and so had the murderer. Both Liz and Cassie were of slight build, and their hair was out of sight when tucked inside the nightcap. I tried to visualize the scene as it must have occurred. Someone opened the door, eased in quietly, stood behind the chair, and then garroted poor Liz without ever seeing her face. *Maybe the murderer didn't even know he or she had strangled the wrong person!*

I threw back the covers, unable to lie there any longer. Suspicions that would not shape themselves into conviction taunted me. New fears filled my body with heat and dispelled the remaining chill. Cassie was still in danger! The murderer had failed . . . and might return.

I went into the adjoining bedroom and looked down at Cassie's sleeping face. As usual, I was startled by the relaxed sweetness that sleep always brought to the girl. I sat down on the edge of the bed and took Cassie's hand in mine. It was reassuring to feel her warmth in my own cold hands. Once more my protective urges came to the fore. "It's all right, Cassie. I'm here. I'm here . . ."

I leaned over and kissed her cheek. Cassie's breathing was even and deep, and the doll was cosseted in her arm. Thank heaven she had no comprehension of the reasons she had been taken from one bed and settled in another, I thought.

I went back to my own room. I felt a rising urgency to do something, but what? Gavin had told me to stay here, that he would be back soon. How would he handle the situation? I could imagine Mr. Markham's consternation that a murder could happen in his luxurious hotel. And what about Liz's family? I wouldn't like to be the one to tell them what had happened.

At that moment a piercing cry drove all thought from my mind. I rushed back into Cassie's bedroom and found her sitting up in bed. Her eyes were wide open, and she was holding out the doll with stiff arms, staring at it and screaming.

"Cassie! It's all right." I took the doll out of her hands.

Without warning, the girl lunged at me, her nails scratching my arm. "No, let him go! Don't push Teddy . . . don't push Teddy!" The cries tumbled out in a frenzied fashion, more words than she had spoken in all the weeks I had known her. Something had been released inside Cassie's head. She snatched the doll back, cradling it in her arms as she sobbed.

Was she reliving her little brother's fall from the window? I put my arms around those trembling shoulders. "What is happening, Cassie? Tell me."

The distraught girl's words were unintelligible, choked with sobs. If only she would tell me, I thought as I comforted her. It was obvious that Cassie was remembering and pouring out her anguish. Little by little, her sobs began to subside. I leaned her back upon the pillows, expecting that she would close her eyes and fall back asleep, but her eyes remained wide and rounded.

"Why didn't you come when I called?" she asked me in a normal, even tone which was more disconcerting than her screaming or garbled talk.

"But I did, Cassie. I came right away."

"No. You were in the next room. I was hiding and heard giggling."

With skin tightening on my neck, I realized that even though Cassie was looking straight at me, she was talking to somebody else.

"You heard giggling?" I repeated. If only she would go on talking!

"Yes, and I needed you. Why didn't you come?" Her tone was pathetic, pleading, and bewildered.

"I don't know," I answered.

"You lied."

"Why, Cassie?" I prodded, almost afraid to breathe. "Why did I lie?"

"Because you wanted them to think it was my fault. But I didn't do it. I tried to save Teddy."

"Who did it, Cassie?"

"You pretended that you didn't know."

"Please tell me. Who did it?" I held my breath, waiting. "Please, Cassie. Please tell me. Who pushed Teddy?"

Cassie's eyes began to close. "You ran away," she said in a faraway tone. She was slipping back into that dark region, untouched by reality. "You ran away and left me."

"Cassie! Who ran away? Tell me!" I resisted the impulse to grab her thin shoulders and shake them.

No answer. Her dark eyes were closed completely now, her facial muscles relaxed. Her breathing took on a heavy rhythm. Cassie was asleep again.

I went back into my room and sat on the edge of the bed, drained. My heart was racing. The enormity of what had happened overtook me with a paralyzing rush. *Cassie was beginning to remember the traumatic scene which had sent her into the protective darkness of insanity!* The true story of what had happened to Teddy Danzel was going to come out. *Was that what someone was afraid of?* It had to be, I thought.

Who was it that Cassie had accused of lying? Who hadn't come when she called for help? Apparently, she had heard giggling in the next room. A woman then? Lady Edwina? Or was it Vance who had not come? Lady Edwina and Vance had to be at the center of the conspiracy to keep Cassie quiet. How many others were involved? Gavin had been there that day—was he a part of it, too? How many others? Dr. Vonfeldt? Ralph Winters? At one time, I might even have included Jack Harvey in the list. There wasn't anyone I really trusted, not even the man I loved so passionately. He had tried everything he could to get me away from Cassie.

Where was Gavin? Why didn't he come back?

I lay back on the bed, trying to understand. The twists and turns and unanswered questions marched in legion, confusing me until, at last, they drove me into an exhausted, fitful sleep.

My eyelids raised slowly and, for a moment, I forgot everything except that Gavin was there, sitting on the edge of the bed, drawing me into his arms and kissing me. Then I remembered.

When a myriad of questions leaped to my lips, he silenced them. "Later," he whispered. "Later. It's three o'clock in the morning. I wanted you to know that everything's been taken care of. There will be questions, but we don't have to think about that now. Tomorrow is soon enough." He stroked the thick tresses of hair that fell around my face. "I shouldn't have awakened you, but I wanted to make certain you were all right. My room is at the end of the hall if you need me."

For a moment I almost pleaded with him to stay, but I choked back the impulse. There were too many unanswered questions between us.

"I love you, Bri," he said softly, stroking my forehead and letting his dextrous fingers trace the gentle curve of my face.

I wanted to tell him what Cassie had said but something held me back. Even when he bent his head and kissed me, flaming my desire, I held myself rigid against him and pushed him away with my hands.

The muscle in his cheek flickered "You still don't trust me, do you?"

"Gavin—" I stammered. I longed to lose myself in his embrace, shut out the world and all its ugliness, but I couldn't. There were too many unanswered questions between us.

"All right. Have it your own way." He sighed and stood up. "I brought you some clothes," he said in that controlled, professional tone of his. He nodded to a satchel. "I thought you and Cassie would need something to wear. I don't suppose it would do any good to tell you to stay in your room until I say otherwise? There are going to be a lot of questions coming your way. I'll be five doors down the hall if you need me. Keep the door locked." With that he left the room, shutting the hall door firmly behind him.

It was bewildering how he could dominate my mind and body, making everything else insignificant. Was I a fool not to trust him completely? He had been with me when someone killed Liz Chantilly instead of Cassie. But Dr. Gavin Rodene could have been the one Cassie was talking to when she said, "I needed you. Why didn't you come?"

I turned my face into the pillow and let the tears trickle down my cheeks to dampen the pillow. When I awoke three hours later, the hotel was quiet, and Cassie remained sound asleep.

I took off my wrinkled clothes, freshened my tired body in the elegant bathroom, and changed into the clean clothes Gavin had brought in the satchel. My face burned as I slipped into the dainty undergarments which Gavin had touched. He had thought of everything from the skin out, and had chosen a floral pink dimity dress that I'd considered much too frilly for daily wear. I had worn it only once, and that was to a summer wedding.

I slipped it over my head and smoothed the tight bodice over my waist and hips, deciding it was an appropriate attire for my present surroundings. As I looked in a gilded mirror, my reflection blended with the carved and gilt Chippendale furniture, which included a huge bed with magnificent headboard, ornately decorated chests, and several chairs with tapestry covers. The walls were a French blue and the soft Aubusson carpets had a pastel floral design. In different circumstances I would have enjoyed the luxurious accommodations, but I couldn't forget the reason that had brought me here.

After I finished dressing, I opened the hall door and looked both ways down a spacious corridor painted oyster white and carpeted in a lovely burgundy pattern. Rows of closed doors greeted my eyes. Somehow the knowledge that all these rooms were filled with people was reassuring. I was about to step back into my room, when a movement at the end of the corridor caught my eye.

I stared fixedly at a woman easing out of a doorway five doors away—Gavin's room! A chiffon peignoir floated like a pink cloud around her rounded body. I recognized Lynette as she furtively hurried to a room across the hall and quietly closed the door.

I blinked as if the figure had been an illusion. Then I shut my own door and leaned against it. Why would Lynette be coming out of his room in her nightclothes? No woman would appear in front of a man in such attire unless there had been something intimate between them.

I walked over to the window, staring outside as the hotel gardens lost their shadows to the bright sunrise. The wondrous splashes of color made no imprint upon me. A horrible sickening feeling plummeted to the pit of my stomach. Dr. Gavin Rodene was an accomplished lover, artful and persuasive, and I knew beyond a doubt that many women had trembled under his touch. He had put his spell upon me that first day on the train, and I had never since been free of him. Trust me, he had said. He had sworn that he and Lynette had not been lovers. I wanted to believe him. Desperately, with every hope I could cling to, I wanted to believe him, but the evidence against him could not be denied.

I didn't know what to do except carry on with the regular morning routine. When Cassie woke up, I managed to keep up my usual monologue, treating her like a child who was not ready to speak, even though I hoped she would start talking again. If Cassie remembered last night's incident, she gave no sign of it. As usual she gave a lot of attention to the doll, covering it up and then hugging it protectively.

I was tempted to try and pry information from her but I resisted. I didn't want to disturb the delicate balance that might be leading Cassie out of her mental disorder. Little by little Cassie might tenuously find her way back to normalcy—if someone let her live that long!

I stiffened when there was a brisk knock at the door. Trying to still a nervous flutter, I opened it, expecting it to be Gavin. It was Vance Danzel.

He brushed by me, his manner agitated and short. "The manager told me you were here. Is Cassie all right?" He looked at his sister sitting placidly with her doll in her arms.

"Yes."

"What are you doing on this floor, Brianna? Why did you change rooms?"

"Didn't the manager tell you?"

"No, something's all hush-hush. From his manner I thought . . . I thought something had happened to Cassie."

Was he surprised that she wasn't the one with the strangle cord around her neck? If Vance had thought Cassie was sitting in that chair, he might very well be alarmed when the manager told him that his sister had been moved to this room. If that were the case, his bewilderment could be quite genuine.

"What is it, Brianna? You're staring at me like you don't even recognize me."

I couldn't help but scrutinize his handsome face. Strain showed around the edges of his light brown eyes. His charming smile was absent and the corners of his mouth turned downward. It was as if I were really seeing him for the first time. *Cassie could have been referring to her brother last night. "You lied," she had said. "You wanted them to think it was me."* I gave myself a mental shake, trying to get my thoughts under control. I mustn't let Vance and his sister know that Cassie had begun to talk. "I'm sorry," I said quickly, lowering my gaze. "I don't know how to tell you this. A woman was strangled last night in the tower sitting room."

"What?" His reaction was real enough.

"Yes. Liz Chantilly, who used to have that suite. She came back. And . . . and while I was downstairs reporting her presence to the manager, someone strangled her with a woman's white stocking." Listening to myself describe the incident, I was amazed at how void of emotion my voice was. I could have been explaining some inconsequential happening. How little time it took, for the human mind to gain control of the horrible, I thought on some detached plane.

"My God! Where was Cassie when all this took place?"

"In bed."

"Thank God for that. She might have been hurt

by the lunatic. You should have never left her alone!" He quickly vented his feelings in anger, lashing out at me for going downstairs and leaving both Cassie and the old woman alone in the suite. He didn't seem to consider that I might have been another victim if I'd remained. "Why didn't you send down word that the woman was there? Why go down to the manager's office yourself?"

"Because I wanted Liz Chantilly's family to come and take charge, not some impersonal hotel staff member."

"Your first responsibility was to my sister, not to some stranger! I'm afraid that everyone else has been right about you, Miss Anderson." The use of my formal name was ominous. "You have not performed your duties as I had expected. Perhaps I did feel sorry for you and let my sympathy influence my judgment. I did not want to believe Dr. Vonfeldt's assessment of the situation. He warned me that your father's mental derangement might be hereditary. Your mental health does seem to be in question."

I blinked as if to clear a whirlwind suddenly roaring in my ears.

He smiled then, gently, with a hint of apology. "I hate to say this, but it's only your word, Brianna, that someone *else* strangled that woman."

Chapter Seventeen

I made him take a step backward as I thrust my face into his. My ready temper leaped out of bounds. "How dare you say such a thing to me!" I would have slapped him if he had not put out a restraining hand, holding me away.

"I didn't say such a possibility was true," Vance said hastily. "No, of course not."

"That's exactly what you said. I demand an apology."

"Yes, yes, of course. I apologize. Forgive me. It's just that . . . well, everyone has been riding me for keeping you on . . . filling my ears with all kinds of—"

"Lies!" I finished for him. "I'm fed up with being used as a pawn in some diabolical scheme that you and your sister have cooked up."

He looked genuinely shocked. "What! What are you talking about?"

I wished I could have brought the words back. I hadn't intended to confront him with my suspicions but my righteous indignation overrode my caution. "Someone wants Cassie brought to harm! The incident on the balcony . . . and now this!"

"But it was that other woman who was killed."

"By mistake! She was sitting with her back to the door, wearing a nightcap and gown similar to

Cassie's. I think someone came up behind her and strangled her without knowing she was the wrong person."

There was a moment of weighted silence. I searched Vance's face for some flicker of guilt. I was startled by a smooth, oily voice behind me.

"A very interesting speculation," said Dr. Vonfeldt coming through the open hall door. He closed it behind him and I felt a stab of fear. I did not want to be in a closed room with these two men. Instinctively I backed away from them. If I screamed would someone hear me?

"I'm glad you came so quickly, Doctor," said Vance. He sent a furtive look at me. "Brianna's been saying some strange things."

"Yes, I overheard. You really shouldn't give in to hysterics, Miss Anderson," he said in a tone I had heard used so often with the mental patients at Gray Oaks. Its false, soothing timbre only threaded my taut nerves. "I knew that you should have been removed from your responsibilities. I warned Vance and Lady Edwina that you were much too emotional for such a position. Now it seems I was right," he held out his white hands in a helpless gesture. "If only you had come to me for help, allowed me to treat you . . ."

His vanity had been injured! I wanted to laugh at his pompous, conceited air. If I had fallen all over him like the other women guests did, he might not have been such a formidable enemy. He had picked up on my aversion, and now he would make me pay for it.

"Of course it's not too late," he said smoothly. His white-toothed smile caressed me. "I'm certain we can stem these hysterical tendencies if you put yourself in my care. Otherwise—" he shrugged.

Blackmail! If I agreed to his treatments, he would give me his support. "And if I don't?" I asked aloud.

"Then it is my professional opinion that Mr. Danzel should dismiss you."

I was cornered, checkmated! If I refused to put myself in Dr. Vonfeldt's care, I would be dismissed. Any protection I could offer Cassie would be gone. Vance stood there waiting, not meeting my eyes. He would do whatever Vonfeldt suggested; the doctor was in charge. The impact of Vance Danzel's weakness shook me. At that moment, I was positive that Cassie had been talking about her brother when she said, "You lied. You wanted them to think it was me."

I pulled my eyes away from Vance, fearful that he might read my thoughts. It was only a matter of time until Cassie revealed exactly what had happened the day her little brother fell to his death. Once I knew who was responsible for that horrible deed, I would know who wanted Cassie dead. How could I desert Cassie now? More than ever, I felt the need to protect her. A vicious murderer had made a mistake. I was positive he or she would try again.

I swallowed back my anger, my accusations, and gave Vonfeldt a cold, hard stare. "All right."

"You'll put yourself in my care?" His black eyes traveled from my face down over my breasts and hips. "A very sensible decision." He smiled a wet smile. "Especially now, since there will certainly be some inquiries into your emotional stability."

A soft-footed chill went up my spine. *Would the police believe the vicious gossip that my father's mental deterioration had been visited upon me?* I realized with sudden horror that, as Dr. Vonfeldt's patient, he could give out any kind of a diagnosis concerning my mental health and it would be believed! There was only one escape: to leave this minute. If I stayed—?

"We want to protect you," said Vance, his charming smile back in place. "You'll need friends now, Brianna."

"And both of you are my dear friends," I said sarcastically.

"But of course." Dr. Vonfeldt reached out and touched my arm. "Tomorrow we will begin some very beneficial baths to ease away the tension I feel in your body." He stroked my forearm, his dark eyes glittering.

I almost ran from the room as an urge toward self-preservation overwhelmed my need to protect Cassie. The impulse was heightened as Gavin opened the door, and I rushed to his side, forgetting everything but the need to reach out for his strength.

"What's going on here?" Gavin's glower was a sharpened scythe cutting across the two men.

"I've been conferring with my patient," said Vonfeldt smoothly. "Miss Anderson has put herself in my care. She has agreed to start some beneficial health treatments tomorrow."

Gavin felt my arm tremble under his hand. "Is that true?" He searched my colorless face.

I nodded. How could I explain? If only he understood that I had been forced into it. "But not until tomorrow." My pleading eyes met his.

Gavin took the cue. "It's Miss Anderson's right to choose whatever medical treatment she desires. If she wants to consult you tomorrow that is her prerogative, but there's no need to change her plans for some rest and relaxation with me today, on a non-professional basis, of course. If that's all right with you, Bri?"

"Yes." I grabbed the chance to escape like someone clutching at a life preserver.

"I'm sure you can arrange for someone else to care for your sister today, Vance." Gavin's glacial expression challenged Vance to object.

"Of course, of course. Brianna needs a day off after what has happened," Vance said smoothly, his smile back in place.

"Are you sure Cassie will be all right?" I asked anxiously, the question leveled at Gavin alone.

"There's a very competent nurse at the school who would be most willing to fill in for you today. If it's all right with you, Vance, I'll ask Miss Tewsberry to attend Cassie."

Vance took a deep breath as if to gain his composure. "That will be fine. We'll leave Cassie here on the fourth floor. I'll keep an eye on her myself."

Alarm leaped into my eyes and Gavin laid a reassuring hand on my arm. "I'm sure that the police will be asking a lot of questions of everyone. Cassie will be getting a lot of attention," he said pointedly, his eyes sending me a message. "She'll be quite safe. And Miss Tewsberry is a pleasant, motherly type. Cassie will be in good hands," he reassured me.

"Where are we going?" I huddled close to him in the hansom cab as the driver sent a sharp-looking bay horse trotting at a fast pace down Sevilla Street. I had forgotten about seeing Lynette coming out of his room that morning. Nothing seemed important except that I was here with him. I knew I had become an emotional beggar, willing to accept the crumbs of being with him whenever I could.

"To the school. Helen has a guest room where you can rest." His tone was gentle, concerned. "I'm taking charge now, my darling, whether you like it or not. You're out of that situation—and you're going to stay out!"

"I can't."

He swore under his breath and I saw the cords in his neck tighten.

"I really shouldn't have come with you today. I should have stayed with Cassie."

"I would like to be able to understand your behavior and your complete lack of concern for your own safety, but I can't. I cannot believe you put yourself in that German bastard's hands."

"I had no choice. Vance was going to dismiss me if I didn't."

"That's the best news I've heard. Vance gave you the perfect opportunity to leave! And you turned it down?" His look was incredulous.

I nodded, my anguished eyes begging him to understand. "Don't you see that Cassie needs me more than ever? She's beginning to remember. She was talking, really talking! Not to me . . . but to someone else."

I felt Gavin stiffen but I firmed my chin, plunged ahead, and told him about Cassie's nightmare. "I know she was reliving that moment when Teddy was sent to his death."

I watched Gavin's face. The flicker of his eyes and the set of his jaw betrayed him. A sense of satisfaction overtook me. I was about to force Gavin to tell me what he knew.

"You were there, weren't you?"

He sighed deeply. "Yes. We all were. Edwina had

arranged a garden party for Sir Wilfred. There were all kinds of things going on—tennis, croquet, swimming—and tables loaded with food and drink."

"Vance said he wasn't there."

"He was for a while, I saw him. But after the accident, he said he'd left the party to run some kind of errand. If Cassie saw Vance push Teddy out the window, why didn't Vance silence her?"

"You said she was found hiding in the attic when your father arrived at the house?"

Gavin nodded. "Cassie had crawled way back under in a tiny space under the stairs. They couldn't reach her and spent hours trying to coax her out. They even contemplated taking up the attic stairs to remove her."

"Then she could have escaped from Vance to where he couldn't get to her!"

"It could have happened that way, but maybe it didn't. Someone else could have been to blame."

"Who?"

The silence was broken only by the steady clopping of the horse's hooves. Then Gavin said in a strained tone, "Lynette."

"Lynette?" I breathed in dismay.

Gavin nodded. "I saw her playing with Teddy just before he disappeared. I think she might have taken him up to the attic herself. Not to harm him, but to create a stir so everyone would come looking for the two of them. Sometimes I didn't pay her as much attention as she thought I should, and when that happened she had ways of putting me on the rack. One of her favorite tricks was to disappear and put everyone in a frenzy thinking she was lost or drowned. Lynette was fond of creating scenes like that. Harmless, childish. But something could have gone wrong. Maybe she didn't watch Teddy closely enough . . . and he fell out the window. Cassie could have seen the accident."

"The horror of it was too much for her," I said.

Gavin nodded. "I didn't want the whole thing stirred up again. If it happened that way, no good will come of it. Lynette was a long time getting over the events of that day. Even though she never admitted to any culpability in the tragedy, I can't be sure she wasn't responsible for the little boy's accident."

"And you were afraid that Cassie would remember Lynette was the one who let him fall out of the window."

"Yes. Until now I've kept my suspicions to myself. All these years I've feared that Lynette's childish carelessness might have cost Teddy his life, even though my father was convinced Cassie had done it. The girl certainly seems the most likely one. But it *could* have been Lynette—or someone else! And that's why I wanted you out of the picture. If Cassie remembered and told you anything that would point a guilty finger at someone, then you would be in as much danger as she. The minute she began to regain her memory, both of you would be at risk. And now, my worst fears have been justified. It could have been you or Cassie, instead of Liz Chantilly, strangled in that chair!"

"Why would Vance and Lady Edwina bring Cassie here, leaving Gray Oaks?"

"If the doctors there said Cassie was on the way to recovery, they could have decided to bring her to St. Augustine, knowing Dr. Vonfeldt to be the charlatan that he is." Gavin gave me a wry smile. "But they didn't plan on you being so good with her. Cassie hasn't slipped back at all."

"No, she's getting better, and that means . . ."

"That Cassie's a real threat to someone."

"I think it's Vance."

"It was a woman's stocking that was tied around Liz Chantilly's neck," Gavin reminded me. "I don't think we should rule out Lady Edwina. She wasn't fat and clumsy when little Teddy fell to his death. In fact, when she and Sir Wilfred were married she was quite trim. They hadn't been married very many years when the tragedy happened." Gavin's forehead furrowed. "It was rumored that old man Danzel was putting all his hopes on the young Teddy because his two older children had been such a disappointment. It was said he planned to leave the bulk of his inheritance to Teddy. No, we can't rule out Lady Edwina. Maybe she saw the biggest share of the inheritance going to the youngest male and decided to do something about it."

"She was against Vance hiring me," I said thoughtfully.

"Maybe Lady Edwina saw traits in you that her brother missed. Dogged determination, loyalty, and intelligence, to name a few. Add to that exasperating stubbornness." He gave me a wry smile. "She might have known you weren't the namby-pamby companion she wanted. If she's worried about Cassie remembering too much, and if she can't get around to doing her own dirty work, she had to hire it done."

"Ralph Winters!" An image of his hand upon Cassie's back, at the head of the stone stairs, came before my mind's eye. I told Gavin about the incident. "I'm sure he led Cassie over to the parapet and made her look down. She screamed and lurched away from him. He reached out—I don't know if he was trying to catch her or push her. But if it hadn't been for Jack's long legs and quick action, Cassie would have fallen."

Gavin was thoughtful. "Maybe Ralph was just trying to jog Cassie's memory by making her look down from that height. That's an accepted technique, you know, trying to duplicate the circumstances that brought on an emotional trauma. When Cassie looked down, she reacted. Her scream proved that. Maybe in her mind she saw her little brother sprawled on the rocks below. This reaction might have caused her to behave the way she did last night."

"Do you think so?" I had difficulty thinking about the incident at the fort in a positive way. Once I made up my mind about something or somebody, I had a hard time changing it. My father had cautioned me more than once about jumping to conclusions. I could have misinterpreted everything. Gavin looked at me quizzically. "What was that heavy sigh for?"

"I want to trust Ralph. I hope it's true he was just trying to overcome her trauma. If we're right that Teddy's fall was not an accident, and that Cassie took the blame for it, the person who has tried two times to kill her will try again."

"That's exactly why someone else can risk this situation, not you! You have this absurd sense of honor and loyalty—"

"Like someone else I know," I challenged, with a twist in my stomach. Both of us were caught in different kinds of commitments, his to Lynette, and mine to Cassie.

"I'm sorry, Bri. It's you I love but I . . ."

I put my fingertips against his mouth. I didn't want to hear any more about his responsibility to Lynette. For the moment I wanted him to be mine.

"Kiss me," I ordered brazenly.

"Yes, ma'am." He grinned and did as he was ordered.

Helen Matley fussed over me like the mother I'd never had. In her spare bedroom, she helped me undress and slip between lavender-scented sheets. "I'm not tired," I kept saying.

"You're going on nervous energy. Now take a pleasant nap for the rest of the morning. We'll have a nice lunch and you can tell me everything then. Gavin has a full schedule with the children today so we'll be on our own." She leaned over and kissed my cheek. "Then we'll talk. Gavin has told me everything . . . Lynette's pregnancy . . . and her claim that he's the father. It's not true. He loves you."

"But I saw her coming out of his room this morning in her nightclothes. No woman does that unless—"

"Unless she's trying to make a case against someone." Helen's clear blue eyes did not waver. "Gavin has been seriously involved with several women, but if he says he is not responsible for Lynette's being *enceinte,* then she is lying. I know Gavin. You can believe him."

My smile was one of relief.

"He's going to marry you, not Lynette," said Helen in a matter-of-fact tone. "Now you get some rest. You look all tuckered out. Just let go." She patted my arm. "Think about the wonderful things that lie ahead." She gave a merry laugh. "If I were thirty years younger, I'd be after Gavin myself. He's a wonderful, caring, sensitive man. And you're a very lucky girl." She smoothed the covers around me, smiling serenely.

"You make everything sound so simple."

"It is simple. Don't you doubt it for a minute. No one's going to come between you and happiness."

Because I desperately needed Helen's optimism, I believed her, and drifted off to sleep a few moments later. I didn't wake up until nearly one o'clock. The high-pitched twitter of laughing children outside my window put everything right with the world. A deep, refreshing sleep had made the shocking horror of last night lose some of its emotional overtones.

When I had dressed and brushed my hair into its usual thick coil upon my neck, I opened the door and crossed the hall into the pleasant sitting room. I was surprised to see Helen sitting on a sofa talking with an Italian-looking gentleman who occupied a parlor chair close by.

"Oh, come in, dear. You look refreshed. This is Mr. Oliveros. He's been waiting to see you, Brianna. He's from the police."

Chapter Eighteen

There was nothing in the man's appearance to bring fright up into my throat like bitter bile. The detective resembled many of the Minorcan inhabitants of St. Augustine. His walrus mustache accented a rather square, tanned face set on a solid frame. He nodded politely, instantly rising to his feet at my entrance. "I'm sorry to intrude, Miss Anderson," he said with a slight bow. His coarse brown nankeen pants and jacket bagged comfortably at the knees and elbows as though they had seen several seasons' wear.

Oliveros? Why did the name seem familiar? I didn't understand why I sensed a hovering menace lurking just out of sight.

"Please sit here, dear," said Helen, patting a place beside her on the cushioned sofa. Her clear blue eyes had reassuring smile lines around them as if she were trying to ease my sudden fright. "Mr. Oliveros needs to chat with you about what happened." The word "chat" was a misnomer and I knew it. The man was here to interrogate me.

I sat down, my spine rigid enough to snap. I folded my hands in a tight clasp upon my lap and firmed my chin as I returned the man's steady look. I had known that there would be questions, I silently assured myself, and I had nothing to hide.

Nothing at all. It was Vance's malicious suggestion that I could have been the one to tie the strangling stocking which made me feel I must be prepared to refute such accusations.

"Very unfortunate. Quite disturbing," Mr. Oliveros granted with a clearing of his throat. His thick figure filled up the easy chair. "I know that you are a companion to Cassie Danzel. I am somewhat familiar with the situation because of my sister, Domincea." He did not smile and I realized why his name had triggered an unpleasant reaction. He was *Domincea's brother!* I had never really liked Domincea and had sensed that the stoic woman felt the same way about me. No telling what kind of prejudice she had created in her brother.

"I was sorry to hear that Domincea had been dismissed," I offered. "It didn't seem fair under the circumstances." I was being honest. Even though both Cassie and I had benefited from Ralph Winters, her replacement, I felt that Dr. Vonfeldt had used Domincea as a scapegoat to absolve himself from blame over the unfortunate suicide.

"It was very unfair," he agreed in a flat tone, his eyes alive, sharp, and—angry? "My sister is a dependable, hard worker. Didn't you find that to be so, Miss Anderson?" Implicit in the question was the same reserved, almost abrasive, unfriendliness as his sister's. Maybe the Oliveros family was indicative of St. Augustine natives who resented wealthy hotel guests taking over the town they had created though great hardship and tenacity.

"Yes, Domincea was very dependable." That much was true. Was it antagonism that coated his question? Had Domincea felt that I was somehow responsible for dismissing her. If there were hard feelings, her brother certainly was not impartial in any interrogation involving me or the Danzels. The realization was like a stone weight sinking in my nervous stomach.

"Would you be kind enough, Miss Anderson, to tell me why Miss Chantilly returned to her former accommodations in the hotel?"

"I don't know why for certain. I think she was simply homesick," I said evenly. "The only words she spoke to me were 'I came home.' " Then, as succinctly as I could, I related everything about the woman's arrival and the horrible scene that had awaited me and Gavin on our return to the suite.

"Miss Chantilly was asleep on your bed when you left to go downstairs and report her?"

I nodded. "Yes."

"She was fully dressed?"

I nodded again.

"Then how do you account for the fact that she was later found sitting in a chair, wearing a night-cap and nightdress?"

"She must have awakened while I was gone and—"

"How long was that, Miss Anderson?"

"I . . . I don't know." I knew that my cheeks had suddenly begun to burn. The intimate scene between me and Gavin in the manager's office came back. "A half an hour, perhaps."

"That long? Are you certain?"

"I'm certain I was gone long enough for her to put on her night clothes and come out into the sitting room," I countered.

"I see. What took you so long?"

"The manager was not in his office. Dr. Rodene and I waited for him. Surely you have already talked with Mr. Markham."

Oliveros's dark eyes were not readable, but one black eyebrow twitched as if his bland exterior were at odds with his busy mind. "I've been talking with several people. I was told that you met the Danzels when your father was a patient at Gray Oaks, a Philadelphia sanitarium, I believe."

Here it comes. I must have winced for Helen patted my arm reassuringly. My stomach lurched as I tried to moisten my suddenly parched lips. "Yes. Vance Danzel liked the way I behaved with my father and some of the other patients. He thought I would be good with his sister."

"I see. I am surprised that, after the draining experience of your father's illness and death, you would accept such a position."

"I had no other means of support at the time. But I fail to see how my financial situation is really anyone's concern but my own. Any rumors about my emotional instability are just that—rumors!" I wanted to tell him about my conviction that Dr. Vonfeldt had deliberately spread the vicious innuendoes, but I didn't dare. He might accept such an attack on a doctor as evidence of my delusions. "I hope that you will get to the bottom of this matter very quickly, Mr. Oliveros. I am willing to help you in any way I can. We must find this murderer!"

"Do you know why anyone would want to kill Miss Liz Chantilly?"

"No." I kept my gaze steady.

He frowned. "I've talked with Mr. Vance Danzel. He said that you'd suggested that his sister was the intended victim. Can you explain why?"

"I mistook Miss Chantilly for Cassie myself when I first came in. She was wearing the same kind of ruffled nightcap and white, high-necked nightdress . . . and was sitting with her back to the door."

"I see. Do you know why someone might want to strangle Cassie Danzel?"

"Yes." I took a deep breath and told him about the tragic fall of Teddy Danzel. "It might not have been an accident."

"I see. Are you ready to accuse someone of responsibility in that death?"

"No, of course not. I don't have any proof . . . yet. But if Cassie continues to improve, she may be able to give us an account of what really happened. That provides a motive, doesn't it?"

"You think someone doesn't want that to happen?"

"That's *exactly* what I think." I had forgotten about my initial negative reaction to Domincea's brother. This man was listening to me, really listening. Behind that flat expression was an active, searching mind. It was a relief to pour out the growing apprehensions I had endured since that first incident, when I had found Cassie on the balcony. Oliveros let me tell the story in my own way, his expression impassive but his black eyes alert and honed, as if trained to detect the truth from any bank of lies.

"And don't forget that strange incident with the painting," prompted Helen, obviously pleased that I had lost my nervousness. She had been listening to everything I said, nodding her head, her face as expressive as the policeman's was controlled.

When I had finished, Oliveros didn't say anything. He sat there in his slightly rumpled clothes as though waiting for me to think of something else.

"That's . . . that's everything," I assured him. "You believe me, don't you?"

"You seem sincere, Miss Anderson, but it's been suggested that you've been under a great deal of strain for a long time. I understand you are to begin treatments with Dr. Vonfeldt tomorrow?"

"Only because I was pressured by my employer to do so!" I flared.

"Not because the doctor believes that you need help? It has been suggested that you might have been the one to strangle Miss Chantilly."

The cold, chilling menace had taken form. It invaded the room like a malevolent reptile, numbing me with its presence. I didn't know how to protect myself against its venom.

"Why, Mr. Oliveros," Helen said in her usual pleasant, lilting voice, "such ridiculous accusations aren't worth your time. Brianna has told you what the real situation is. Now you go out and find this demented person before something else horrible happens."

"Yes, of course." There was a hint of patient amusement in his tone. "I thank you ladies for your time." He rose and bid us good day.

I put my head in my hands. How had all this happened?

"I think you need some exercise, my dear," said Helen brightly. "And some fresh air. Put on your bonnet. We'll take a tour of the grounds."

I was drained by the events of last night and today. I let Helen coax me to my feet, grateful to have someone take charge and direct my thoughts away from the apprehensiveness that was like a penetrating, bone-deep chill.

As we strolled the grounds, everyone we met greeted Helen fondly. The children were as noisy and friendly as any group of active youngsters. The lamentable fact that they could neither see nor hear did not seem to inhibit them from having fun.

I tried to make the correct responses to Helen's chatter but I felt detached from reality, suspended, waiting. I was glad when we returned to Helen's quarters and I was able to excuse myself to take another rest before dinner.

I sat in a chair by the window and let my unseeing gaze fix on the developing shadows outside. My thoughts kept returning to the interrogation Oliveros had leveled at me. Maybe I had talked too freely. I worried that I had been foolish to pour out all my suspicions to the detective. Such honesty could be dangerous. In Oliveros's mind, they could have only cemented a conviction that the rumors about my emotional instability were correct. I knew he could easily attribute the murderous incidents to me. I could have put Cassie on the balcony; I could have plunged the scissors into the painting; I could have strangled Liz Chantilly before going downstairs for help.

I put my hand over my eyes and tried to ease the growing pain there. I had headaches so rarely that the growing discomfort at the base of my neck took me unaware. My neck muscles were taut, a hard bulge, as if they had been tied in a knot.

The bedroom door opened. "What are you doing sitting in the dark?" asked Gavin as he came in.

"Oh, I didn't know you'd come back. I . . . I have a headache." I touched my hand to the back of my neck.

"Here, let me see." He stood behind my chair and let his long, dextrous fingers massage the cords of my neck.

I winced. "Ouch."

"Try to relax." For several minutes, he gently kneaded my tense neck muscles. "Don't stiffen.

Pretend your body is a mass of wet spaghetti. All soft and stringy."

I chuckled. "Not very appealing . . ."

"That's where you're wrong." He came around to the front of the chair and, before I could protest, he lifted me up, then set me on his lap as he took my place in the chair.

I curled up against him like a child, but it was a woman's feeling that spread through my body as he tipped up my chin and laid a long lingering kiss upon my lips. My heart raced as his hand molded the curve of my waist and then moved to cup a breast.

"I love you, love you . . ." His kisses deepened and his tongue tasted my lips before gently parting them. A wild sensation jolted me as his questing tongue echoed a caressing touch upon the hardening nipple of the breast he was fondling. Delightful sensations raced from my mouth into soft hidden crevices of my body.

I felt his virility respond to my own rising need and lost myself in passion-laced insensibility. I was startled when he abruptly withdrew his lips and hands from my body, and laid his head back on the chair rest. "You enchantress," he breathed heavily, looking at me with half-closed, desire-filled eyes. "You had best remove yourself to the footstool and put some safe distance between us."

"No."

"You are a wanton woman."

"Yes." I did not stir.

Firmly he loosened my arms from around his neck and then set me on the stool. Then he bent over and kissed the top of my head. "That's better. Helen will be calling us any moment for dinner. She's very understanding, but she also has a rigid sense of propriety. I'm afraid she's going to insist upon helping with our wedding plans. There's a lovely chapel on the grounds . . . just right for a small wedding."

"Wedding?"

"Yours and mine," he said, as if there had never been any question about it.

"What about Lynette?"

"I'll have to force Vance to marry her."

"Vance!" I searched his greenish gray eyes to see if he was being serious. They were steady and quite solemn.

"Yes, Vance. He is her lover. While I was in Europe Vance began seeing Lynette. I guess he had deep feelings about her even when we were children. But Lynette was always linked to me, and Vance stayed his distance. They met accidentally while I was gone and she was swept off her feet by his attention. I think Vance loves her, as much as he's capable of loving anyone, but Lynette doesn't have any money. He's gone through his inheritance. I think Edwina is footing most of his bills, and she's made some bad investments. She isn't about to support Vance in a penniless marriage. I tried to force him to admit his responsibility—"

"This morning I saw Lynette in the hall . . ."

"Yes, she was pleading with me to find a way to save her honor."

"Amelia Dorcas told me about a fight she had overheard between you and Vance. She said Vance was trying to shame you into marrying Lynette."

"Perhaps he might have been successful, if you hadn't been in the picture. I've been taking care of Lynette for years, but now I've fallen in love, for the first time in my life. And I need you, Brianna, darling . . ." His voice thickened. "I can't bear to think that you might not always be with me. I can't worry about Lynette and Vance. They have made their own commitments; now they'll have to live up to them. It's you I want in my life. Lovely, stubborn, brave, exciting Brianna. I love you, hopelessly, completely. You will marry me?"

I had a hard time finding my voice. "Yes . . . yes," I squeaked. Laughing, I raised my lips for a sealing kiss but a movement at the door made me draw back.

Helen peered into the shadowy room as she gave a light rap on the open door. "Dinner is on, if you two are ready to come out of the dark and join me."

Gavin chuckled as he stood up and pulled me to my feet. "I was helping Bri get over a headache."

"Is that what it was?" Helen said dryly.

"Headache?" I echoed, suddenly remembering. You *are* a miraculous doctor," I teased. "It's completely disappeared."

Laughing, he slipped his arm around my waist as we went to dinner. Helen had prepared a simple potpie with chunks of chicken and vegetables simmering in thick white gravy, a green salad with mushroom dressing, and an angel food cake for dessert. Helen was a gracious hostess, and kept the conversation light and varied during the meal.

With Gavin sitting beside me, brazenly touching my leg under the table, I put all the unpleasantness of Oliveros's visit out of my mind. We exchanged sly lovers' glances and thoroughly enjoyed the home-cooked meal. Helen was not fooled. She smiled knowingly and pretended not to notice how lost we were in each other.

"I think I've convinced Brianna that I would like her to be here with you each day when I finish work," said Gavin. "If you'll let her use the guest room, Helen?"

My hand froze with a piece of cake halfway to my mouth. I set the fork down quickly.

Gavin covered my hand and squeezed it. "You can't go back to the hotel, darling. Helen told me about Oliveros's visit and all the vicious rumors going around about you. You're not going to do yourself or Cassie any good in such a situation. You've told the authorities what you suspect. Let Oliveros take it from here."

"What if he didn't believe me?"

"I think he did," said Helen. "And I agree with Gavin. It would be better if you put some distance between you and whatever is going on. Stay here until Mr. Oliveros does some investigating."

"But what about Cassie?"

"She'll be safe enough," said Gavin. "Nobody's going to harm her with Oliveros poking around. And you don't want to put yourself in Dr. Vonfeldt's clutches, do you?"

I shivered. "No. I don't think I could stand it if he touched me."

"Good. It's settled then. We'll go to the hotel, pick up your things, and I'll bring you back here to stay. Then I'll get everything out in the open with Lynette. I told you everything was going to work out."

"But—"

"Darling. You have to let go sometime. It's our future we're talking about." He lifted my hand and pressed it against his lips. "I want to take care of you."

I let myself give in to the love that flowed through me and put aside my unspoken objections. He was right. It was time to let go.

When we returned to the hotel, we discovered that Cassie had been moved back up to the tower suite. I slipped my arm tightly through Gavin's arm in the elevator. It had been about this time last night, I thought, when we went up to the fifth floor and found Liz Chantilly's still-warm body.

"All right?" Gavin asked quietly.

I bit my lower lip and nodded. I thought the memory of finding Liz Chantilly would rush back when we opened the door, but it didn't. The chair was gone and Ralph Winters was sitting alone on the couch.

"Where's Miss Tewsberry?" asked Gavin.

"She's in the bedroom with Cassie. She's been hard to handle all day. We've tried everything to get her settled down. Maybe you can do something, Brianna."

I threw off my bonnet and hurried into Cassie's bedroom. Plump Miss Tewsberry sat on the edge of a chair placed near the bed. She was openly relieved to see me and Dr. Rodene. "I've done my best," she said quickly, "but I'm afraid this is out of my experience. I really don't know what to do with her. I'm glad you're back."

Gavin thanked her, and she left.

Cassie was sitting straight up in bed. Her hair was tangled and her expression pinched. A moaning came from her throat, and her closed eyes were only slits. My heart fell when I saw her. At that moment, I realized how far Cassie had come since our arrival in St. Augustine. She hadn't been like this for a long time.

"What's the matter, honey?" I put a false brightness in my tone. "My goodness, it's past your bedtime. And look at your hair. It needs a good brushing." I sat down on the bed and put my arm around Cassie's thin shoulders. Then I took a hairbrush and began to stroke the thick dark strands in a slow even rhythm. The hair brushing and my easy chatter was a nightly ritual, and as I continued talking in a calm, normal tone, the girl slowly relaxed.

"Yes, I'm back. Everything's all right." I braided Cassie's hair and tucked it up under her night cap. Cassie's thin hand came up to touch my face. As she moved her hands over my mouth, nose and cheeks, Cassie's heavy eyelids raised. Her gaze was steady as she looked at me. The moaning stopped. There seemed to be recognition in those intense eyes.

"Cassie, honey, I'm back." Tears beaded at the corner of my eyes. I eased her back onto the pillow, tucking trailing wisps of hair away from her forehead. Gently, I bent over and kissed her wan cheek and eyelids. "It's all right, Cassie," I murmured. "I'm here. Go to sleep now. I'm not going to leave you. I'll be right here if you need me."

Then I lifted my head and looked at Gavin. His mouth was tight and a muscle flickered in his jaw. I didn't say anything. He just looked at me, and I saw the defeated slump in his shoulders. My anguished eyes begged him to understand.

Chapter Nineteen

The next morning began like any other. The daily routine of dressing, eating, and getting Cassie ready for her treatments kept me from thinking about the wisdom of my refusing to go back to Helen's. I knew that Gavin was disappointed, angry, and apprehensive.

He had told me that he was going to go to the policeman, Oliveros, and insist on some protection for me. I promised to have dinner with him at the hotel that night; by then I hoped to have my thoughts in order. Maybe I was being overly sentimental about Cassie's need for me, but Ralph Winters didn't think so. He had argued with Gavin that Cassie had almost slipped away from us when I had deserted her for even the day.

"It's Brianna's welfare I'm concerned about," Gavin had told him in clipped tones. "I don't want her here. I'll do everything in my power to convince her to turn Cassie over to someone else!"

I wished I could. If only I could just walk away! I didn't understand myself why Cassie had taken such a hold on me. Maybe it was because I could see hope for her recovery. My father had been beyond help, but this young woman was fighting her way back. It was a slow, hard journey, and Cassie had a chance to make it. How could I turn my back on her and perhaps jeopardize that tenuous recovery? No, I wouldn't! Cassie needed me, apparently trusted me, and I was committed to giving her all the help I could.

When the hour approached for Cassie's morning treatments, I left the suite with trepidation. I didn't want to go to the Casino. My thoughts had been centered upon Cassie, and now I remembered that Vonfeldt would be expecting me this morning too—the price I had to pay to keep Vance from dismissing me. I would have to submit to the indignities of his treatments and suffer those white hands crawling all over me. I felt sick to my stomach.

As we came out of the hotel entrance and started across the street, I saw that Vance was also heading for the Alcazar. Dressed in fawn-colored morning coat and trousers, his tawny hair caught the sunlight as he walked with a sensual grace that caused several young girls to simper and giggle when he tipped his hat to them.

I slowed my pace. I did not want to meet Vance Danzel. His charm had tarnished. I did not trust him, and I knew I would have difficulty being polite to him. He was the one who was forcing me to accept Vonfeldt's treatments. I crossed on the opposite side of the Alcazar's courtyard to avoid seeing him.

Cassie and I climbed the curved stairway to the main door, and when we entered the Casino's reception room, my stomach was a tremulous mass in my middle. I knew that there was no way to avoid Dr. Vonfeldt. I was an unwilling pigeon caught in a trap.

Sir Wilfred was in the reception room, waiting. He tipped his hat in a gracious manner. "Good morning, ladies. Busy place this morning, isn't it?

Lady Edwina came early. Could hardly wait to have a cold plunge bath." He shook his gray head. "I had a very bad night." He peered at Cassie. "Do you think those electrical treatments are doing her any good?"

"Of course they are!" Vonfeldt's oily voice flowed into the moment of silence. "Aren't they, Cassie?" his white smile flashed. In an avuncular manner, he patted her arm. "Just look at her. Better every day. I've told Lady Edwina that she should try some electro-therapy too."

He turned his smile on me and I felt myself recoiling from its lascivious wetness. "Miss Anderson has agreed to follow my advice. She's going to put herself in my hands, aren't you, my dear? You need to relax . . . loosen up your muscles . . . give your body a chance to be soft . . . and supple." His eyes lingered on my neck and bodice, and then he cleared his throat. "Well, now come this way, ladies. Ralph is waiting for Cassie in the electro-therapy room. After she is properly robed, Miss Anderson, please come into my office and we'll decide on a morning routine for you." His smile was slick as oil.

I helped Cassie into the usual white robe, and then Ralph took charge of her. The young man peered at me through his thick lens, and I thought he was trying to send me some message. There was no chance to find out what it was. Vonfeldt possessively took my arm and guided me out of the electro-therapy room into his office.

"Now then," he said with grating softness. Closing the door, he stood so close to me that my nostrils quivered with his unpleasant bay rum shaving tonic. "I am delighted you have decided to avail yourself of our facilities."

"I had no choice."

He ignored my antagonistic tone. "You will find our health program quite pleasant. A soothing warm bath, a brief stay in the steam room, and then, when you are all warm and relaxed, the attendant will bring you to me." His dark eyes glazed with anticipation. "My hands will be like a soft, pulsating surf rippling over the muscles of your body. People who suffer from neurasthenia—"

"I don't suffer from anything!" With an angry flounce, I moved away from him and sat down in a high-backed chair. "I am perfectly healthy, Dr. Vonfeldt. Sound of body and mind. I'm here because Vance Danzel made it a condition for keeping my job. You have successfully started vicious speculation about my mental health."

"Now, now, there was nothing malicious in my concern over your welfare, my dear." The endearment was as comforting as a snake shedding his skin.

"You used your position to spread lies about me!" I fought to keep my anger under control, and failed.

"I simply suggested that your father's illness might have affected your own stability. Surely you can appreciate my desire to help you handle the pressures of your present position?"

"Is that what you're trying to do? I don't think so. I think you know a great deal about who is trying to kill Cassie Danzel!"

His eyes instantly lost their sensuous gleam. "You are more disturbed than I thought, Miss Anderson. I wouldn't stand for such an accusation if I were not aware of the extent of your emotional instability. I think we had better discontinue this conversation."

"Why? A demented mind *is* at work here—but it isn't mine!" I couldn't keep my voice from rising.

By contrast, his words were quite unemotional and clipped as he ordered me to retire to the dressing room. "When you are ready, one of our attendants will to conduct you to the ladies' bath." His white smile was back but it didn't reach his eyes. "We will help you get control of your emotions, Miss Anderson."

I knew that I had played right into his hands. My behavior had only alerted him to my suspicions. If Cassie hadn't been in the next room, I would have walked out. The ordeal ahead of me was almost more than I could stand, even for Cassie's sake. I tried to still a rising surge of panic. There's nothing to be afraid of, I schooled myself. Set your teeth and bear it. Play a waiting game . . . see what happens.

I had just started to undress when I heard a commotion out in the hall. Loud voices. Scurrying feet. What was wrong? A stab of panic was instantaneous as I heard the unusual clamor.

Quickly, I opened the hall door a crack, listening.

"It's Lady Edwina!" I heard somebody say. "Heart attack."

"Dr. Vonfeldt is trying to revive her."

My first reaction was a selfish, detached relief that Dr. Vonfeldt was going to be too busy to pay any attention to me. My fingers trembled as I quickly refastened my dress and went down the hall to see if I could be of help.

There was a crowd clustered around a small, recessed marble pool. Lady Edwina must have been sitting on an immersed bench when she tipped forward, I decided. Her hair was soaked and her face glistened with water as she lay stretched out on the marble floor. Dr. Vonfeldt was bending over her, and two female attendents in white uniforms were trying to help revive her. Women bathers, who must have been sitting in the same pool, were sobbing. Nearby Sir Wilfred leaned on his cane heavily, watching with an expression of utter bewilderment as they tried to revive his wife.

"Get all these people out of here," roared Dr. Vonfeldt to one of the attendants. "You, too, Sir Wilfred."

He looked so befuddled that I gently took his arm. "There's nothing you can do, Sir Wilfred."

"She's not going to die, is she?" he croaked in an anguished tone. "She can't die. She can't die."

"The doctor's doing everything he can," I said soothingly. "Come with me. You'd better wait somewhere else."

He gave another tortured look at his wife's prone body and then allowed me to lead him from the room. As we started down the hall, the door to the electro-therapy room opened.

"What is it?" asked Ralph. "I thought I heard a commotion."

"It's Lady Edwina. Apparently she's had a heart attack." I answered. Ralph sent a look back at Cassie. "I was just getting her out of the cabinet. Will you finish for me? I'll see if I can be of help."

I nodded.

Sir Wilfred followed me into the room like someone who didn't know where else to go.

"We'll just be a minute," I said as I opened the electric light cabinet. He stood quietly nearby, leaning heavily on his cane as I began to undo the straps of the cabinet. I saw that his eyes were fixed on Cassie, his shallow breathing muted.

Suddenly a soft prickling drew the skin tight on my neck. Perhaps it was his quiet breathing that had triggered the memory, for suddenly it was there, clear and undeniable. It was as certain as anything I'd ever known. The faint scent of scotch reached my nostrils and I identified it as *the same smell* that had been in the sitting room the night I returned to find Cassie on the balcony.

My fingers were suddenly thick and unwieldy as I worked to unloosen the straps around Cassie. The truth was like an iron vice twisting my stomach. *Sir Wilfred!* I couldn't stifle an audible gasp. I was nearly paralyzed by the sudden knowledge that the murderer was here, standing a few feet away! I had to get Cassie out of there as fast as possible. If Sir Wilfred suspected that I knew—! Terror screamed loudly in my head.

"Come on, Cassie . . . that's it. Treatment over for today." My voice sounded strained and hollow, and laced with fear. Nervously I opened the latches, eased back the roof. Cassie was so vulnerable lying there. She moved in that maddeningly slow way of hers. "Hurry, Cassie." I could not keep from sending a frantic glance back at Sir Wilfred.

It was a mistake! It signaled my inner terror. Frantically I eased Cassie out of the cabinet and removed her blindfold.

Sir Wilfred moved toward us. "Cassie has to die before Edwina," he said, in a conversational tone, as if he had been a silent partner in my thoughts. "Otherwise I won't get the money. I've got to have it . . . to save my family estate."

I stared at him. This clear-eyed man was a stranger, menacing, capable, and ruthless. Sir Wilfred had completely lost his fumbling, doddering look. Hard determination glinted in clear eyes that met mine. "You have not cooperated, Miss Anderson. You've made it very difficult, when it should have been so easy. I talked Vance and Edwina into bringing Cassie here . . ."

"It was you," I gasped involuntarily. "You killed Teddy."

He smiled and touched his precise gray mustache. "So easy . . . and I would have had Cassie out that window too, if she hadn't crawled into the stairwell where I couldn't get her. That would have kept those two young ones from inheriting, and the estate would have been split between Vance and Edwina. I married out of necessity to save my family's property in England, and Edwina's share has not been enough. The bulk of the Danzel wealth went to Cassie! Unfair. Unfair! She has to die! But you first, Miss Anderson."

I was able to throw my hand up, but not soon enough to completely deflect the blow of his cane. The hard gold knob came crashing down on the side of my head. My knees buckled. Colored shafts of light exploded behind my eyes. I lashed out blindly, my fingers curved like claws, trying to make contact with cloth and flesh as I tried to get away from him. "Run, Cassie!" I cried, as I struggled to knock the cane from his hand.

With blurred vision, I saw Cassie standing like a statue, her eyes fixed upon Sir Wilfred as he fought my flaying hands.

His grip was strong, too strong! Before I could prevent it, Sir Wilfred had grabbed one of the straps. He had it around my neck! I gasped and writhed. He tightened the strap, shutting off air to my lungs.

I was going down, down, when I heard him cry out. The vicious garrote around my neck loosened.

Then he slumped over and sprawled on the floor beside me.

"Cassie!" I choked.

I saw then what had happened. The girl had bludgeoned Sir Wilfred with his cane. She had saved my life. Cassie dropped the cane and slumped to the ground, covering her face with her hands. I gathered her into my arms. Blood from the cut on my head ran down my face, smearing her cheek.

"Where is she? Where's Brianna?" I heard Gavin's loud voice in the corridor. The next instant the door flung open. The person I most wanted to see was beside me.

"It's over," I said, with a watery smile. "Cassie's safe now."

Chapter Twenty

Detective Oliveros agreed that Cassie had emerged from her trauma in time to save my life. As Sir Wilfred struggled with me, her memory must been triggered, causing her to relive the traumatic attic scene when Sir Wilfred had pushed Teddy out the window. He had scratched her face as she struggled with him, and then she had escaped into the cubby hole that saved her life.

After his attack on me, Cassie began weeping and talking about the incident that had blanketed her young mind in darkness. In a matter of days she had secured her hold on reality. Like a voyager who had been on a long journey, Cassie was making her way back to a safe port.

All the questions I had been asking were answered by the time Lady Edwina and Sir Wilfred were laid, side by side, in a palm-shaded cemetery on the outskirts of St. Augustine.

Gavin and I, Vance, and Lynette returned to the hotel after the funeral and sat together in the luxurious parlor. Vance admitted contritely that he had lied—he had been in the house at the time of his brother's tragic fall. He refused to meet anyone's eyes as he admitted that, in fact, he'd been in a nearby attic room with a parlor maid.

"So that's where you were?" chided Lynette. "I

had looked all over for you, but I wasn't about to admit I'd been hunting for you at the time of the accident. I wanted Gavin to think I'd been with you to make him jealous. Then that horrible thing happened, and he wouldn't believe that I hadn't been in the house. He was afraid that I was somehow responsible for the poor child's death."

Gavin looked grim and didn't respond to her fluttering smile.

"Little Teddy probably saw me and the girl slip up the attic steps to our rendezvous, and decided to follow," Vance said.

"As the two-year-old tottered up the steps, Sir Wilfred must have seen him," speculated Gavin. "Of course, he didn't know that Vance was dallying with a young maid in a nearby room. Sir Wilfred coaxed Teddy over to the window."

"Cassie must have arrived on the scene just then—she always supervised the youngster," added Vance. "She tried to save Teddy, and then fled for her own life when Sir Wilfred attacked her." Vance confessed that he had been too involved with the maid to hear anything until nearly a half hour later, when the little boy's body was discovered on the terrace floor. "Cassie must have heard the girl giggling when she was hiding under the stairs."

"She said 'I called you and you didn't come'," I murmured remembering Cassie's words.

Vance looked miserably contrite. "When Teddy was found, I didn't want to confess that I'd been with a servant girl at the time. I chose to slip away from the house and pretend that I had been gone at the time of the tragedy. I really thought Cassie had done it. It never crossed my mind that someone else was responsible. Sir Wilfred! I still can't believe it."

"He was the one who put Cassie on the balcony but I came back before he had finished his evil deed," I said, blessing the sixth sense that had made me return to the hotel.

"But why the mutilated portrait?"

"We'll never know for sure," said Gavin, "but I think he was trying to set the scene by throwing suspicion upon Bri. He even set her up to take the blame for strangling Cassie."

"Only he strangled the wrong woman," said Lynette, her baby blue eyes wide with horror.

Gavin nodded. "His wife's inheritance was dwindling and he feared that his sacrifice in marrying her was going to be for naught. Lady Edwina would not be able to support his family's bankrupt estate in England unless she inherited some more money. He had married her to save the family property. He wasn't about to let creditors have it."

"But he seemed such a harmless old man," I said.

"Which made him all the more dangerous," offered Gavin.

"I could have been next," said Vance. "Eventually he might have killed me to get my share of the money." He sighed. "I really thought that Sir Wilfred's suggestion to bring Cassie to St. Augustine was a good one. I didn't know that I was placing Cassie in jeopardy. Nor you either, Brianna."

"We know now that he was the one who was filling Dr. Vonfeldt's ear with suggestions that Brianna's mental health was questionable," said Gavin. "Sir Wilfred wanted to set her up to take the blame when he succeeded in eliminating Cassie. Your sister's heart attack forced him to improvise." Gavin tightened the protective arm around my shoulders as he felt me shudder.

"Just about the time I recognized the telltale smell of scotch," I said, "he told me quite matter-of-factly that Cassie had to die before Edwina. I knew then that she was in dire danger. But I didn't have time even to cry for help before he struck me."

"It's over now, darling." Gavin tipped my chin and smiled reassuringly into my haunted eyes. "Cassie has avenged her brother's death, and she's making great strides in her recovery."

"She saved my life."

"Yes. Thank God!" breathed Gavin.

"And she's going to be all right now?"

"Thanks to you, Brianna," said Vance. "I know there's no excuse for the way I behaved but my own problems made me insensitive to what was really happening. I didn't make it easy for you."

"No, you didn't," I agreed, rather tartly. I'd never quite forgive him for forcing me to accept treatments from the odious Vonfeldt.

He must have read my thoughts. "I'm glad that Dr. Vonfeldt got his walking papers." Vance said. "I shouldn't have let him influence me the way he did. But all of that is over now." Vance gave everyone that bright, charming smile of his. "Now that I'm responsible for Lynette, I'm determined not to run through the inheritance Edwina left me, the way I did my father's money. I want to take good care of her . . . and my child."

"You'd better," said Gavin in a warning tone.

Lynette gave her light, trilling laugh. There was no doubt that she was happy. Her sky blue eyes filled with love as she looked at her handsome Vance. "Thanks to Gavin, you're going to make an honest woman of me after all."

"Pauper that I was, I really thought you and the baby would be better off with Gavin. That's why I told you to swear the child was his." His handsome face colored with embarrassment as he looked at me and Gavin. "I . . . I didn't know how it was with you two. I've been a fool all around, haven't I?"

"Yes." Gavin's blunt answer was only slightly softened by a greenish tinge in his gray eyes. "Now if you two will excuse us, Bri and I have to prepare for our engagement party tonight."

"Oh, isn't it exciting?" gushed Lynette. "Amelia Dorcas is almost ill trying to keep up with all the activity."

I knew a fairy princess could not feel any differently than I did at my engagement party. Romantic strains from hidden violins floated like soft petals upon the exquisitely dressed guests in the luxurious dining room. Silver, crystal, and white linen graced a table loaded with aromatic dishes of Consomme à l'anglaise, Fricandeau of Veal à la Jardinière, orange fritters with brandy sauce, and flaming cherries jubilee. The glitter and opulence were unreal.

I wore a new off-the-shoulder gown of peacock blue satin, with a tracery of silver threads in the bouffant sleeves. The evening gown was fashioned with soft tucks and gathers on the close-fitting bodice, and a full chiffon skirt like a swirl of blue clouds. My deep brown hair was swept up in shiny rich curls held by silver combs. A diamond pendant, a gift of my intended bridegroom, nestled in the cleft of my breasts, a spot which had recently felt the warmth of his kiss.

Helen Matley raised a fluted champagne goblet

in a toast. "To the beautiful bride-to-be and her handsome groom."

Jack nodded. "And a very lucky fellow he is," he said wistfully. Jack's red hair was still slightly unruly, but the artist was looking quite presentable in borrowed evening attire.

As we drank the toast, I looked over the rim of my glass and met Gavin's caressing eyes. A surge of desire spread shamelessly through me. I wanted to be alone with him. We had already made our commitment to each other in the sweetest way possible. I wanted to slip out of all this finery and feel the length of his demanding body upon mine.

His teasing smile told me that he had read my thoughts, and the warm promise in his eyes was all a woman in love could desire.

WHAT AM I DOING HERE?

I was ill at ease in the gathering. How long would it be before the interfering Dr. Gavin Rodene brought up his concern about my lack of professional training?

In the middle of the social chitchat, Amelia Dorcas leaned forward and fixed her preying eyes on Gavin's face. "I was never quite sure exactly what happened that day, when little Teddy Danzel fell out of that fourth-story window to his death. Your father said he might have been pushed, as I recall."

There was a suspended moment of dead silence.

A muscle bulged in Gavin Rodene's neck and a flush of anger crept up into his cheeks. "My father was called to the house when the youngest Danzel plunged to his death from that attic window. There was no way to prove it wasn't an accident. The screen could have been loose. The two-year-old could have climbed out on his own. It could have happened that way."

"Are you saying it didn't?" I asked, feeling my face go hot.

"I'm saying that my father suspected that the child was already dead when he went out the window. There was evidence that there had been a struggle before he fell. Cassie was found in the attic, huddled up in a tiny space under the stairs." He turned to me and looked straight into my eyes. "I do not like the idea of an untrained young woman living here with a possible killer."